MISSING JUSTICE

JUSTICE TEAM SERIES

MISTY EVANS

ADRIENNE GIORDANO

ALG PUBLISHING

MISSING JUSTICE

A rising star at the FBI, Taylor Sinclair has a perfect close rate on cold cases. When the bones of a senator's murdered wife turn up seven years after her kidnapping, the case lands on Taylor's desk, putting her in the crosshairs of the media—and the killer. Success will solidify her career at the Bureau, but a provocative one-night stand with cocky PI Matt "Mad Dog" Stephens could ruin it.

Matt's on the hunt for the killer as well, along with the senator's still-missing child, and believes joining forces with Taylor will get them both the answers they need. He's determined to get the sexy agent to work with him—in and out of the bedroom—but Taylor is convinced the senator is a murderer. Matt is just as certain he's innocent.

With a child's life on the line, Matt and Taylor must plunge into the world of undercover ops as they battle a dangerous attraction that could prove fatal to them both.

To those who work tirelessly to bring closure to the families of missing persons.

1

_C_old case investigators really should stay away from karaoke machines and alcohol. The combo was criminal.

Especially when fellow investigators from the FBI, AISOCC, and dozens of experts from cold case units around the country were gathered together in the same bar listening.

Taylor Sinclair scanned the room as she swished the two fingers of scotch around in her glass. The country's top minds in forensics, law, behavioral science, and medicine had gathered together this weekend in DC to share the latest in solving cold cases, and yet, a handful of them were now killing off brain cells and possible career advancement opportunities while belting out Prince songs in the wrong key.

The woman on stage singing _I Wanna Be Your Lover_ with a bright orange drink in one hand and the microphone in the other hit a high note—flat, of course—and Taylor flinched.

Her bar buddy didn't seem to notice as he jabbered on beside her, nursing a light beer. A journalist who'd applied to the American Investigative Society of Cold Cases but had been rejected, Tom—or was it Ted?—explained his lifelong obsession with missing persons. She understood the passion; it was hers too.

But she also knew why AISOCC had turned him down for their Academia Committee. They only accepted people with the credentials and motives to fulfill their mission of assisting law enforcement professionals with solving cold cases. Tom/Ted might have the passion, but he didn't have the experience, even though he was boasting about his professional skills in the hopes of wooing her to his room upstairs.

He was sort of handsome in that academic way—wire-rimmed glasses, bow tie, and a large vocabulary—but she'd sworn off sex, and alcohol, for the weekend.

At least she hadn't failed on both counts. The scotch had been a prop to help overcome her social awkwardness. To make her seem friendly and normal. Approachable.

Like that's ever going to happen. Who was she kidding? Put her to work on a case and she was a rock star, but in a social situation where she had to make small talk and pretend interest in drunk people's lives? Failure with a capital F.

It was enough to make her drink.

Which she was, thank you very much.

Sex, though, no way. Out of the question. The last thing she needed was to hook up with some random conference attendee and risk the fallout from that. Being the best of the best required keeping her nose clean in public—Meredith's orders. Her boss ran a tight ship and had no patience for agents who let their personal affairs interfere with their careers.

No problem there. Taylor had no personal life.

Even if she did need alcohol to numb herself to the stares and advice from all the experts dying to 'help' her find Isabel.

Like Leo.

Cutting her eyes to the huddle of three men at the bar on her right, she could practically feel the power oozing off Leo

Wellington. The FBI profiler was six feet of confidence, nerve, and a close record that made Taylor green with envy. Only last month, he'd helped her and her cold case team nail the Coffin serial killer, a man who had victims he'd buried alive stretching back thirty years. She had to admit, working with Leo had been no hardship. The man profiled killers and other high-profile criminals with the ease and accuracy Taylor's one-time mentor had until he'd gotten himself fired from the FBI.

She missed Grey. A lot. She'd learned so much from him in the few short months they'd worked together. Before he'd shredded his career.

Now she had Leo. Amazingly proficient and incredibly sexy. Listening to him on the Offender Profiles and Crime Scene Assessment panel at the conference that afternoon, Taylor had toyed with the idea of making Leo Wellington her next *unoffi-cial* case. One that involved one-on-one, in-depth investigation...and a lot fewer clothes.

He was her perfect match—smart, driven, successful. Sex with Leo and a bottle of scotch—the perfect cocktail to kill the anxiety humming under her skin over this conference.

Leo had his back to her, casually leaning on the bar and close enough for her to touch. He smelled like a warm day at the beach all sun and water. He smelled like power.

Taylor looked away, shaking her head to rid it of the thoughts tumbling around in her brain. She wasn't about to shred her career like Grey, and Leo, *the shark*, wasn't about to play nice. He'd use her, like he did everyone else, and take her team away from her if she wasn't careful.

No way in hell. No one was worth that.

Her cold case team had gained national media attention with their success rate. Nothing played on the nightly news as sweetly as missing kids being found alive and reunited with their families. Taylor and her team had returned three this year alone. *Three kids still alive*, and by God, she intended to find more.

The statistics were daunting, but she wouldn't stop until she found every kid who'd disappeared, dead or alive, and gave their families closure.

She owed it to Isabel. If only Isabel were still alive.

Maybe she is. Maybe she's still out there, waiting for me to find her.

Taylor knocked back the last of the liquid in her glass along with the familiar twinge of guilt over Isabel.

"Agent Sinclair." Leo turned, suddenly at her elbow. "Nice to see you. My friends and I were just discussing your case."

Agent Sinclair? She'd thought they were on a first-name basis after working so closely together only last month. "Enjoyed your panel today, Leo. Your insights on the Yvonne Coleman case were fascinating." Leo's friends eyed her with equal parts eagerness and smugness. She recognized both of them from the same panel. "Exactly which case of mine were you reviewing?"

He looked bemused. "Why, your sister's case, of course. Today is the anniversary of—"

Another screech echoed through the bar, courtesy of the Prince wanna-be, and Taylor set her glass on the bar a little too hard. Everybody was a flippin' expert. Everybody had heard about poor Taylor Sinclair and the hunt for her missing sister. Everyone had a goddamn theory and a profile on the abductor.

As if the Bureau's lead cold case investigator hadn't gone over every possible aspect of the case a million times already, eviscerating her heart each and every time.

"Of course. Silly me." Taylor pasted on a fake smile and used her equally fake cheery voice. "Why don't you grab those two agents from Vermont? They're over there at that table. You all can have fun discussing your meaningless theories while I go gag myself."

Tom/Ted raised his brows as Leo sputtered something she didn't hear.

Unfortunately, the Bureau hadn't sprung for any of her teammates to accompany her to the conference. She needed a wingman—or another drink—but there was no one else in the vicinity she was remotely interested in talking to, and even liquor couldn't dull the ice in her chest. She should just call it a night. Try to sleep.

As if.

"I used to like that song," a deep male voice said from behind her.

One distraction coming up.

"Me, too," she said, hoping the man matched the voice as she pivoted to take a peek.

And, *ho-boy*, he was as sexy as that deep voice, but dammit, why did it have to be *him*?

Even in her heels, she had to look up. There she saw blue eyes so vivid in the subpar lighting they nearly blinded her. The smile wasn't bad either. A little crooked, with a couple days worth of beard growth on the jawline, but it matched the messy hair and made his eyes crinkle good-naturedly in the corners.

"Matt Stephens," she said. "What a surprise." *Not.*

Matt "Mad Dog" Stephens looked pleased that she remembered his name. Hard not to when he'd stolen a case out from under her a year ago. Hard not to remember those intense, sky-blue eyes and that crooked smile that irritated the crap out of her.

"Special Agent Taylor Sinclair." The way he rolled her name off his tongue made it sound like he was sucking on a piece of sweet candy. "I didn't take you for a Prince fan."

The karaoke had mercifully stopped and someone hit the jukebox, a Rhianna song kicking in.

Taylor was about to blow Matt off even though he was cute and kind of charming, because no way was she cavorting with the enemy. But then, from the corner of her eye, she noticed Leo and his friends staring at her with *that* look. The one people used for *poor Taylor Sinclair*, sister of an abducted girl and from a broken family.

Show them you're fine. Better than fine.

She gave Matt a flirty smile and playfully punched his arm like they were buddies. *Hello, new wingman.* "Why wouldn't I be a Prince fan? That's practically sacrilegious or unpatriotic, or something, isn't it?"

"I've been trying to talk to you all day," he said, flashing that infectious, quirky smile again.

She fought to keep her lips from mirroring his. "Why?"

"Duh. You're the brainiest chick here. Your close rate makes me a huge fanboy. Plus, I'm not one to ignore beautiful women. Why wouldn't I want to talk to you?"

Damn, he was cute. A liar, but a cute one. "Yeah, so you can steal my cases."

His eyes grew serious. "Look, I know you think I stole the Riley Miller case, but the FBI was limited in what it could do. I have more..."—he shrugged—"resources."

Illegal ones. "So you're feeling guilty. That's good. You can buy me a fresh drink."

He grinned and took her hand, stroking his thumb over her palm. "How about a dance instead?"

She should pull her hand back. "Oh, hell, no. I don't dance with the enemy."

He grabbed her hand again, tickled the palm. "But you'd drink with him?"

Her turn to grin, the ice in her chest melting a smidgen. "Depends on whether he provides top-shelf sustenance."

They stared at each other for a long moment and something changed between them. Something hot and sexy that warmed Taylor's blood even more than the scotch she'd consumed listening to Tom/Ted.

What was she doing flirting with Mad Dog Stephens?

Down girl. She glanced away, toward the bar.

Leo and friends were still watching, still talking. She could tell by the way they kept sizing her up that they were discussing Isabel.

God! Enough. Like she wasn't already struggling to not let pain control every moment of her life without everyone always trying to fix her. If she believed that any or all of the experts here tonight could actually find Isabel, she would have been the first one to huddle up with them and explore their theories. But she'd heard them all, tried all the angles, got her hopes up with every new expert who came along and wanted to analyze the case. She would never give up looking for her sister, that was a given. If only hoping for something made it real.

Mad Dog Stephens tugged on her hand. "Taylor?"

She sighed, giving him her attention again and saw a touch of concern behind his smoldering eyes. Men like Stephens— unpredictable and mouthy—were generally a handful, but she liked a challenge on occasion, and it had been one hell of a dry spell. Plus, he wasn't FBI. He couldn't screw up her career or take her team away from her.

Your odds are looking up, wingman. At least he was an alternative to the scotch for now.

She withdrew her hand from his gentle grip and took a step closer to him, invading his personal space. Would he run when she moved in for the kill or stand his ground?

"Why are you here at the conference, Matt?" She ran a hand over his tie. "Are you looking to steal another of my cases? Why did you leave the police department? Who are you working for now, or did you go out on your own?"

"Jeez, Sinclair." He frowned, but didn't back away. Undaunted by her provocation, he moved closer, his chest grazing her nipples. His eyes searched hers and his voice lowered a notch. "What is this, an interrogation? If so, why don't we take it somewhere more...private?"

Hot damn. He wasn't running. She stood her ground, not letting him intimidate her. She liked—no, *loved*—his cockiness. "I don't trust you, Mad Dog."

"Dance with me and I'll answer all of your questions." He ran a finger over his left chest area. "Cross my heart."

A negotiator. Even better. She could get what she wanted and leave him happy too.

Challenge danced in those blue peepers and she sighed. Men came onto her all the time, but few gave her pause.

Funny, this one did.

Her phone buzzed, the ringtone she knew all too well and avoided skillfully.

"Do you need to take that?" Matt asked.

"Nah, it's nothing." *Just my mother.* And wasn't that exactly what she needed on top of everything else tonight? Her mother calling to sob about Isabel. Perfect.

Pain pinched her heart. *Sorry, Mom. I just can't tonight.* She had enough demons for both of them.

I may need that bottle of scotch after all.

But then she looked into Matt's eyes. He might be the only numbing agent she needed tonight in order to forget about the significance of today.

With all the old shit the conference had brought up, the one thing she didn't want was to be alone with the memories of Isabel. No way she could face that cold, sterile hotel room tonight.

She tapped her foot for a moment. "One dance," she agreed.

The challenge in Matt's eyes morphed into self-assured confidence. If possible, his smile grew even wider. "You won't be sorry."

"*You* will be," she said, as she let him lead her to the floor. "I have two left feet."

The song was pop with a fast tempo and Taylor had no rhythm on a good day. Luckily, her new wingman was a skilled dancer and she had enough alcohol in her system to make her limbs loose. Matt twirled her out, brought her in close, guided her through a sexy bump and grind. She grew dizzy trying to keep up with him, but the light graze of his fingers on her shoulders, hips, and lower back, kept her moving in time with the beat and loving it. At one point, she laughed just because it felt so damn good.

Meanwhile, Leo watched, a subtle tick under his left eye.

Eat your heart out, Wellington. I am not discussing Isabel's case with you.

Not tonight. Not ever.

As Matt spun her across the floor again, a bubbling sensation rose up from her chest into her throat.

My God, I'm having fun.

Fun wasn't in her vocabulary. Not since *that* night.

Damn. She needed a good weekend fling. To burn off the stress of her day job. To refocus her energies on her caseload. *Might not be a bad idea to make sure all the parts down there still work after this latest dry spell.*

But mostly, she needed to forget for a few minutes about the ice in her chest.

Because tonight was the anniversary of her little sister's kidnapping.

She'd hoped the conference could make her forget, but that was stupid. She'd known better, and yet had hoped she could drown herself in work. Now...

The song ended, and out of breath, Taylor clung to Matt. Another song started—this one slow and sexy—and he raised a single brow.

An invitation to stay on the dance floor.

In the middle of the other couples now gluing their bodies

to each other, Taylor held his gaze. "Who are you working for, Matt?"

"Schock Investigations," he said, and then pulled her close and started rocking her body to the slow tune.

"Private investigations, huh?" She liked the way he felt against her. Solid, strong. Competent. "I've heard of them. They work a lot of cold cases, don't they?"

"It's our specialty."

"That's why you're here."

His eyes danced with humor. "You were worried I was only here to stalk you?"

He wanted information on some missing persons case, no doubt, but she gave him credit for trying to seduce her first. "Anyone who stalks me is going to get more than he bargained for."

She believed in giving fair warning.

"Sounds like fun." One of his hands went to her lower back and rubbed a thumb through her silk blouse over the sensitive flesh there. Leaning forward, he sang softly in her ear, "*I wanna be your stalker,*" to the Prince tune.

And damn, if he didn't hit the notes perfectly.

A man who could sing and dance.

My lucky night.

Three dances later, Leo and the other experts in the room were a distant memory as Matt pressed her up against the door of her hotel room while she tried to get the keycard into the lock. His lips nibbled at her earlobe as his hands cupped her ass.

"Will you stop for a second and let me unlock the door?" Taylor chided, but she was laughing. She didn't really want him to stop, but letting him molest her in the very public hallway wasn't professional.

"Here, let me do it." He snatched the card from her hand.

In. Out. Boom. The stupid button went green, Matt hit the door handle, and they practically fell into the room.

"I'm not used to sleeping with the enemy," she told him, flipping on a light as he went to work stripping off her white, button-down shirt.

"I returned Riley Miller to her mother but I'm a bad guy in your book?" He unzipped her pencil skirt, not looking the least bit chastised. "Something about that seems wrong, Agent Sinclair."

The image of the eleven-year-old girl reuniting with her mom after six years of being held captive by her estranged, drug-dealing father filled Taylor's memory. It had been her first case with the FBI's missing persons unit and they'd never been able to solve it. Six years later, Taylor had had the file in her desk drawer, one of the cases she'd still been trying to close when Matt Stephens had come along and done it for her.

He was a hero and the press loved his boy-next-door looks and cavalier attitude. She could only imagine the number of women who had thrown themselves at him after that.

But those women weren't here and she was. *Good for me!*

Having a weekend fling with him wasn't the best idea, but it wasn't the worst either. He was a playboy and playboys didn't want commitment—that worked for her. Her job was everything.

"I think you owe me some mind-blowing sex in order to make it up to me," Taylor said, kicking off her shoes.

Matt let her skirt drop and then he shoved her unbuttoned shirt off her shoulders. For a moment, he stood still, his eyes raking over her from head to toe.

Taylor sucked in a breath, pulling in her abdomen at the same time. Total vanity, but she couldn't help the reaction. She wanted the man in front of her to continue thinking she was the brainiest, sexiest woman in the place.

He reached out and touched the satin of her bra, brushing

his knuckles against her tight nipples and whistling softly. "You are stunning, Agent Sinclair."

Taylor sat on the bed and reached for the zipper of his slacks. "Bring it on, Mad Dog."

Ringing phone.

Matt opened his eyes to a ray of light slipping through the curtains. He stared at the back of a very attractive blonde head, but focused on the sound of a ringing cell phone.

Not his.

Good. Because his extremely engorged dick had plans that didn't include phones.

He might do some talking, but it wouldn't be on the phone.

He locked one leg over Taylor and tightened his arm around her waist. Jesus. They'd slept like this? All wrapped up? When it came to getting a solid night's rest, being a decent sized guy, he needed space. A lot of it. Particularly in crappy hotel beds.

Taylor's arm shot out, her hand blindly searching for the still-ringing phone on the bedside table. The glare of the digital clock announced the time to be 6:43.

"Ignore it," he croaked.

"Can't. Boss's ringtone."

"Then I'd definitely ignore it."

He bit the back of her shoulder, nudged closer, bringing that badass erection flush against the curve of her ass, leaving no doubt what he—and it—had on their minds.

"That's a healthy beast you're sporting there, Mad Dog. Now shut up while I talk to my boss."

At that, he laughed. This woman. From the first day he'd met her, back when he'd supposedly *stolen* her case, he'd had a thing for her. An undefinable yearning that left him wanting to...possess. And that was also unusual. Women weren't objects to own. He'd lectured his buddies on this fact for years, but at thirty-three, he'd suddenly found a woman who challenged, cajoled, and rattled him enough that he'd fantasized about pinning her to a mattress and bringing a smile to her face.

Which he'd done three times last night. *Here's hoping for a fourth.*

She cleared her throat and poked at the phone. "Good morning, Mer."

Matt busied himself by pulling her closer and nibbling on the back of her shoulder blade. Was he being an idiot? Sure. But Taylor getting a call before seven a.m. meant something was cooking and being the dedicated civil servant she was, she'd look to hightail it from this bed before he had the chance to put that fourth smile on her face.

The nibbling? Hopefully she'd see it as the prelude to what could be a fantastic morning.

"Yes," she said. "I understand. I'll be there."

Matt stopped nibbling. Dammit.

She tossed the phone on the nightstand. "I have to go."

"Okay."

But he didn't loosen his hold. He did abandon his nibbling campaign, opting for a full attack of licking.

She let out a soft moan and his hard-on became painful. How many times had she moaned like that last night? When he was so deep inside her and still wanted more.

"Matt, I can't. I have to—"

"Shh," he said, sliding his hand up and cupping her breast. "We should start the day off right."

She arched her back, pressing her nipple into his palm. "You are so evil."

"I know. If you want, we can make this a quick one. Or," he swirled his tongue over her shoulder again. "We can go slow. Really slow. Your call, Sinclair."

All he knew was he wanted her. Again. Wanted her under

him, with the morning sun cracking through that curtain so he could see her hair fanning across the pillow, see her eyes go wild when he made her moan.

"I...can't," she said. "I caught a case."

A case. A shot of envy whipped him. The woman was a machine when it came to solving cold cases, especially those involving missing children, and lately her team had been racking up some serious close rates. What drove her, he couldn't be completely sure, but suspected. Make no mistake, you didn't get that good at your job without some serious motivation. He understood that on an emotional level most couldn't.

And he wanted to know what this case was. He'd find out. After last night, he intended on seeing a whole lot more of Taylor.

All he had to do was get her to agree.

Starting right now. He nudged even closer, this time licking that spot on her neck he'd accidentally discovered during round two.

"I want you," he said.

She reached back, wrapped her hand around his dick and squeezed, making his eyes nearly explode from his head. "I know," she said.

Closing his eyes, he dropped his head back and his body started to hum. The motion of her hand made his limbs go slack and oh, boy, she was gonna get it.

The mattress shifted. Hopefully she was getting onto her back where he'd do incredible things to her. His mind roared and just as he opened his eyes, ready to pounce, she let go, ripped the sheet off and jumped from the bed.

What the fuck?

She bit her lip, hiding a smug smile and—damn—he should have seen that coming. The scheming witch. She'd duped him. Made him think they'd have some nice, hot, goodbye-sex so he'd loosen his hold on her. And then she slipped away.

She stood beside the bed, staring down at his chest—she liked it. She'd told him so a hundred times last night.

"Taylor," he said, "that wasn't nice." He held one hand out. "Come back to bed. Let me make you scream."

Her eyes flashed, but she shook her head. "No, but I'll take a raincheck."

Freaking career girls. A raincheck. He wanted more than one, no doubt about it. "Seriously? You're going to leave me like this? I'm hard as a brick."

She laughed as she tied her hair into a messy knot on top of her head. The movement made her tits bounce and his eyes followed the motion of those perfect breasts he'd damn near devoured all night. She leaned over him, kissed him quick and leapt back before he could pull her on top of him.

"This is an important case, Mad Dog. Otherwise I'd happily fuck you all morning and maybe into the afternoon."

Damn, that mouth. She'd been talking filth all night. He didn't care one way or the other. Some women used it as a tool to amp up the sex. He never minded, but he also didn't need it. Her? All that hot nastiness coming from a pulled-together woman who wore traditional suits and a pair of diamond earrings that probably cost more than his entire college career? Total turn-on.

"Now you're just making it worse," he said. "How about I hop in the shower with you?"

She gathered up a bra and what looked like a red thong —*Jesus, help me*—from her suitcase and set it on the bed.

"No," she said. "You're too much of a distraction."

"That's good."

"Not when I have a case to work." She went to the closet, pulled one of her FBI-wear pantsuits out. "I'd love to do this again with you, but we'll have to set some boundaries. Mainly you not stealing my cases."

And here we go. "Once again, I did *not* steal your case. I beat you to solving it. That's all."

Because that's what good investigators did. They solved cases. No matter who it supposedly belonged to. And he didn't allow himself to be lured from the PD homicide squad into the private sector to not solve them.

"Right," she said. "Whatever. But if you want a replay of last night, we need to come to an agreement. No sharing information about cases. No crossing lines. No work talk, period."

"Boy," he said, "you sure know how to kill a mood."

She met his gaze, then let it slide down his body. "You are a tempting man, Matt, but my job is my life. This?" She waggled a finger between them. "This could have serious complications."

As if he wanted to screw up his own career? Plus, he didn't like what she was implying about his work ethic. "Complications. Sure. Got it."

He sat up, put his feet on the floor and snagged his boxers from the lampshade. The lampshade? Whatever.

She cocked her head as he jammed his legs into his shorts. "Oh, so now you're mad?"

"Mad? No. I'm absorbing the rules you've set. Taking it all in." He pulled on his pants, shrugged into his shirt, walked to her, and kissed her hard with plenty of tongue. "Thanks for clarifying, Special Agent Sinclair. Call me when you need to get *fucked* again."

Was he being pissy? Damned straight. They'd had a great night and suddenly she was accusing him of...what? Some kind of investigator espionage? Like he'd deliberately try to steal her cases.

Well, fuck that.

"Matt, come on."

He held up a hand. "It's all good. You've outlined the parameters of what you feel our relationship should be. Got it. Maybe you could have consulted with me first, but hey, why should we have to talk, right? I'll just come on by, toss you on the bed and bang away. Works for me."

"That's not what I meant."

Her phone rang again. Same ringtone. Matt shook his head. "Get your phone, Taylor. It's your boss again. If you want a replay, you know where to find me."

2

"*T*ell me you didn't."

Meredith Sardana unlocked her car doors with a blip of her key fob and motioned at Taylor to get in.

The Special Agent in Charge of the East Coast Missing Persons Unit was a legend in the FBI. A legend who'd done a lot for Taylor's career and appeared to be priming her for even greater things.

"Didn't what exactly?" Taylor dared ask, cringing at the multitude of things Mer might be referring to as she slipped into the passenger seat of the woman's white Taurus.

Blowing off Leo? *Check.*

Sleeping with Matt? *Check.*

Missing that morning's last panel of the conference on Human Remains Detection and DNA Laws? *Check.*

That last one could be lumped in with sleeping with Mad Dog Stephens. They'd stayed up most of the night exploring each other's bodies and Taylor hadn't gotten more than a few hours of sleep. She'd managed to call her mom during a brief intermission when Matt had fallen asleep, but she'd forgotten to set her alarm, which for her, never happened.

Never.

She never missed work, never came in late. She racked up sixty-hour workweeks on a regular basis, especially when she was deep in a case.

And she was always deep in a case. Mer loved her for it.

If you want a replay, Matt had said, you know where to find me.

Boy did she want a replay, but that might be a really bad idea.

Meredith started the car and didn't wait for Taylor to click her seatbelt in before she took off. Sunlight bounced off the US flag pin on the lapel of her jacket and Taylor couldn't help but notice her dark red lips were tight and unforgiving. "A little bird told me you reached out to Justice Greystone this morning."

Ah, *that*. "He and his partner, Mitch Monroe, were lead on this case when it went down eight years ago. I thought it would be beneficial to have Grey's input on whether or not he believed the senator might be guilty of killing his wife."

"Oh, please. You want Greystone involved because you know the Jarvis case was one of the few he never solved. You're pandering to him."

"I am not!" she lied. Time to change the subject. "Who is this little bird, by the way?"

"I have eyes and ears everywhere, Taylor." Mer waved her off and shot out of the parking lot and into traffic. "I don't give a rat's ass what Greystone believes, and do not even mention the name Mitch Monroe to me. He Who Shall Not Be Named is nothing but a smartass boat anchor and you know better than to tie him around your ankle. If they'd done their job and analyzed the kidnapper correctly when Felicity Jarvis disappeared, the team of agents working her case might have caught the guy and we wouldn't be here, on our way to break the news to Senator Jarvis that his wife's remains have been found in a scrapyard six miles outside of the city."

"*May* have been found." Taylor knew better than to correct

Meredith, but she couldn't help it. "All we have are a few articles of evidence suggesting it's her. Until we get DNA—"

"Do not school me on procedure and evidence, Agent Sinclair. They found her engagement and wedding rings with the bones. Rings that have Felicity and Senator Jarvis's initials inscribed on them and the date of their wedding."

"Those rings might have been stolen. If she ran away, she may have sold them herself. Grey thinks—"

Mer's look stopped her cold. Yep, she was pushing it, but one thing Taylor had learned in her time working cold cases was that proof wasn't proof until she had a definite match between remains and the victim. DNA, dental records, facial reconstruction...something more than a couple of rings.

Which her boss had drummed into her head a million times. So why was Meredith insisting the bones found at the Drummond scrapyard had to belong to Felicity Jarvis?

Meredith's lips tweaked with a patient smile. "You're right. It's just..."

"Just what?"

Meredith had been with the FBI for twenty years and had mentored Taylor for the past five since being assigned as SAC of Missing Persons. Women and minorities within the Bureau weren't rare anymore, but they weren't common either. There was still a good-ol'-boy system in place. Meredith ticked off some important boxes—female and a minority. A third generation Hispanic American, her ethnicity had played a role in her getting a job with the Bureau in the first place, according to the man who'd hired her. Her boss at that time had made it clear to her he didn't want her. Didn't want women, period. But she'd had the ambition and tenacity to work for him anyway, and work her ass off besides, as evidenced by the fact Meredith was still at the FBI, while her original boss was long gone.

Mer's knuckles were white from gripping the wheel as she took a turn. "There's already a lot of heat on this, Taylor. Mrs.

Jarvis, the baby, the media spin when it happened. Cunningham is all over my backside about it. It's all going to come back around, and if we don't solve it and put this case to bed for good, the Bureau is going to end up with another black eye over it."

Assistant Director Cunningham would never stand for that. "I understand."

Taylor had still been finishing her degree in criminal justice when Felicity Jarvis had disappeared. Her husband claimed she'd been kidnapped, that she'd noticed a man in a truck following her for several days before it all went down, and had actually called him from a store to say the man in the truck was outside in the parking lot. The senator had told her to stay inside and he would come get her, but by the time he'd arrived, she was missing.

She'd been eight months pregnant with their first child, and the case of the beautiful, young, pregnant wife of a freshman senator had made national news.

The case had played well for Walt Jarvis, his popularity rising exponentially as he repeated his story over and over again in the press. His grief from not telling his wife to call 911; his remorse in not assigning her a bodyguard in the first place. His plea to her supposed kidnapper to let her and the baby go.

The million-dollar reward he'd posted for her safe return hadn't hurt either.

But there were plenty of things about the disappearance that hadn't added up. No one at the store had seen Felicity exit the place or any man in a truck who might have been following her. There was nothing on the security video from the store, whose parking lot camera was conveniently on the blink. Other things about the senator's story bothered Taylor too. One of the reasons she'd used her car's Bluetooth to call Justice Greystone that morning on her way into the office.

Had Grey told Meredith she'd called? Didn't seem like him. Was Taylor's car or her phone bugged?

God, she was getting paranoid, but really, there was no other way her boss could know about that phone call unless the woman had ESP.

Which was possible.

"This will be a feather in my cap if we solve this," Meredith said. "Yours too."

Taylor nodded. Meredith was one of the candidates next in line for the assistant director's job. The director had already tapped her, and Cunningham was less than six months from retiring. "I won't let you down," she said. "I will solve this case."

Meredith smiled. "I know you will, *mi hija*."

Mi hija. Only when it was just the two of them did Meredith call her 'my daughter'. Since Taylor's own mother rarely called her anything, it was nice to be thought of by her mentor in such a way. Hers spent her time with friends, reliving the awful night Isabel had been taken. At least she had friends to share her grief with.

Fifteen minutes later, Meredith pulled into the senator's curved drive, the two-story colonial rising above them. By the matching Beamers out front, Taylor guessed the senator and the new Mrs. Jarvis were both home. After Felicity had been gone seven years, Walt could legally file to have her declared dead and he had. He and Ann had tied the knot a year ago. "You didn't tell them we were coming, did you?" Taylor asked.

Meredith parked near the front door. "No, why?"

Hmm.

"I'd like to take lead on questioning the senator, if that's okay," Taylor said as she got out of the car. "I have a list of things I'd like to ask him about that don't add up."

Meredith got out as well and shut her door, giving Taylor a nod over the hood. "You're in charge of cold cases, Taylor, so this is your baby, but watch your step. Besides, you probably know more about the details of the case than I do after consulting with Greystone."

Another dig about her going to him. Just a little rivalry between old friends or was it more? "Did you have a thing for him back in the day?" she teased.

"Justice Greystone?" Meredith rolled her eyes, then smirked as she diverted her gaze to the sidewalk. "Maybe a little," she admitted, "but so did half the women in the department."

"Grey is easy on the eyes, and definitely the best profiler I've worked with."

"Until he screwed up his career and got fired." Meredith's voice held a hint of warning. "You have Leo now. He's easily as good as Grey."

That was debatable, but whatever. The sidewalk wound around to the front door, elaborate topiaries edging the steps and ferns hanging from pots on the porch. Flower boxes hung under every window and looked as if they were straight out of a Martha Stewart magazine. "I'm not going to screw up my career, Mer."

"Good. I haven't put all of this work into you for you to blow it on something stupid."

Something stupid could translate to a dozen different things. No matter how many cases Taylor closed, there was always another. Some of them, like this one, were potential land mines because of the people involved.

"Guilty or innocent?" Taylor asked as she punched the doorbell and dug out her badge. It was a game they liked to play right before questioning a suspect.

Meredith had her credentials out as well. "Innocent," she said, then quirked an eyebrow at Taylor.

Taylor had reread the file on Felicity Jarvis for the dozenth time while waiting for Meredith to get out of her morning briefing. She had no doubt. "Guilty as hell."

The eyebrow went higher. "Based on what?"

"Gut feeling."

Another eyeroll. Meredith didn't believe in gut feelings.

Taylor grinned and reached over to ring the bell again but the door swung open before she could do so.

An older, petite woman in a maid's uniform barely glanced at their IDs before stepping back. "Señor and Mrs. Jarvis are expecting you in the library."

"I knew it." Taylor shot Meredith a look. "Someone tipped them off we were coming."

As she stepped across the threshold, the SAC murmured, "The senator has friends inside the Bureau. Tread lightly."

Taylor called bullshit. That little tip-off had cost her the element of surprise. "I'm going to the director about this."

Meredith gave her a knowing look that said the director wasn't going to care. The maid closed the door. "Follow me, please."

The house's interior matched the exterior. Wood floors, elaborate staircase, pretty antique chandelier in the entryway.

As they followed the maid to the library, Taylor tugged on Meredith's sleeve. "If you have a chance to get the wife away from Walt," she said under her breath, "I'd like to question him alone."

Mer nodded at the divide and conquer request.

Innocent until proven guilty, Taylor reminded herself as they continued down a long hall. Regardless of what her gut said, she had to believe in the system and do her job. She was about to tell a man that his first wife and unborn child were most likely killed and left to rot in a scrapyard. Even as callous as she'd become over the years from having to deal with kidnappers, rapists, and murderers, the horrible reality made her sick to her stomach. Telling a family member news like this was the worst part of her job, even when it brought closure.

The maid stopped in front of double French doors and

opened them, ushering Meredith and Taylor inside. "The FBI are here," was the only introduction.

Cozy, with the typical dark woods, plush carpeting, and heavy drapes that stuffy rich people in DC liked. A man at one of the far windows turned and a willowy blonde thanked the maid from a couch near the fireplace, dismissing her.

The second Mrs. Jarvis uncrossed her legs and made her way across the room to shake Meredith's, then Taylor's hand. "Ann," she said. She motioned toward the senator making his way over. "And I'm sure you're familiar with my husband, Walt."

Senator Jarvis came up beside his wife and shook their hands as Meredith introduced them. "Meredith Sardana, Director of Missing Persons, and this is my lead investigator of cold cases, Taylor Sinclair."

Walt's shake was firm and he gave Taylor a brief, sad smile. He was older than Ann, handsome. "I understand you have news."

"Shall we sit?" Taylor said, motioning them to the couch.

Walt and Ann sat side by side, Ann taking one of the senator's hands and holding it between both of hers.

"Is it Felicity?" he asked. "Did you find her?"

"Senator," a familiar voice said. "I'd be very careful what you say without a lawyer present."

Taylor whirled and her stomach dropped.

You've got to be kidding.

What the hell was *he* doing here?

Matt stood in the doorway staring at the woman he'd only hours before stripped naked and licked parts of her his mother would slap him for. At least when his mother was sober.

He'd take that slap and a dozen others if it meant another spin—or twenty—with Taylor Sinclair.

Even if she was a federal agent. And a damned good one to boot.

Something Matt had never achieved. The failure to be accepted into Quantico still stung, but he wasn't one to wallow in the nastiness. Still, he couldn't deny the shot of envy over Taylor's success.

Or the irritation he still felt over her earlier boundary-setting lecture.

"Hello, Agent Sinclair," he said. "Interesting coincidence seeing you here."

Not one to be intimidated—*atta, girl*—she lifted her chin.

"Yes," she said. "Imagine that."

The brunette beside her wearing a near matching pantsuit to Taylor's gave him a cursory glance. A pair of bookends these two.

"Taylor, who is this?" the woman said.

Recovering nicely, Taylor extended one hand. "Meredith Sardana, meet Matt Stephens. He's a private investigator. Matt, this is my boss, SAC Sardana."

"Excellent," the woman said. "Just what we need. A PI. Wait...Stephens? You're the one who solved the Miller case, aren't you?"

A mighty federal agent and all her self-righteous bullshit. It wasn't the first time he'd been on the receiving end of that sort of attitude. Wasn't this the thing that ate at him from the inside out? "I did. I left the PD soon after. Now I work for Schock Investigations."

Senator Jarvis waved Matt into the room. "Matt, glad you could make it on such short notice. Come in."

"Thank you, sir." He strode into the room, but kept his distance, moving to the chair by the window rather than inserting himself into the conversation.

All players knew he was there, but if he stayed back, maybe

they'd disregard him, get a little careless and allow him to pick up a fresh lead or two.

Not likely, knowing Taylor and her bulldog instincts, but maybe the fact that he'd rocked her world a few hours ago might throw her off her game.

To that end, he offered her a slow smile and a wink. Couldn't hurt. And it sure was fun to rattle this woman.

"Senator," Taylor said, "we really should speak privately."

The senator shook his head. "It's fine, Agent Sinclair. Before I filed Felicity's death form, I hired Matt and the Schock sisters to help with the investigation. He signed a confidentiality agreement. Whatever is said in this meeting won't be shared."

All of that was true. When the present Mrs. Jarvis came on scene and started putting the pressure on about a wedding, the senator had been forced into action regarding his first wife's disappearance. For seven years, he'd hung on, hoping, praying to whatever god would listen, for the return of his wife and child.

Like a lot of things in life, those hopes and prayers sunk like the Titanic and Senator Jarvis hired Schock Investigations to either find his wife or give him a reason to not declare her legally dead.

When Matt and the sisters had been unable to locate Mrs. Jarvis, the senator, understanding the odds of finding her after so long were slim, took the legal steps necessary to make way for Mrs. Jarvis *numero dos.*

In response to the senator's refusal to bust Matt from the room, Taylor met his gaze for a few long seconds. She didn't like it. Him being here. He couldn't blame her. Not three hours ago she'd given him her rules of engagement. No sharing cases, no crossing lines, no work talk. That's what she'd said.

At the time, neither one of them could have known they'd be sitting here together.

"Agent Sinclair," the senator said, clutching his wife's hand. "Please. Tell me why you're here."

Again, she eyed Matt and he cocked an eyebrow. Whatever her intention upon walking in here, Senator Jarvis blew that away by requesting that Matt stay. But Taylor hadn't become an ace FBI agent by not being fast on her feet. She'd rebound.

She took the seat across from the Jarvises, Meredith dropping beside her. Both women sat erect, shoulders back and Meredith nudged her chin, silently giving Taylor the go ahead. Interesting.

"Senator, we've had a development in your wife's"—she glanced at Mrs. Jarvis—"Felicity's case. Human remains have been found in a scrapyard not far from where Felicity went missing. Rings were found with the body."

The air in the room went still and a painful silence ensued. Matt cut his gaze to the senator who'd dipped his head, his shoulders slumping as if his spine has been hacked out of him.

Matt sat still, refusing to move or draw attention. But he watched. Moments like these, the brutality of them, often gave unlikely clues. The senator was his client but husbands got a hard look when it came to their wives suddenly vanishing.

Everyone remained quiet, even Mrs. Jarvis number two, while the senator absorbed Taylor's words. After a long minute, Mrs. Jarvis stroked her husband's back and whispered something Matt couldn't make out. Whatever she'd said, the senator responded by lifting his chin and circling one hand, urging Taylor on.

She gave them the normal song and dance about how they needed DNA or dental records for confirmation, and then she pulled out her phone, poking at the screen before turning it so the senator could see the screen.

"Do you recognize these?"

Matt was too far back to get a good look, but it was definitely a photo.

The senator sucked in a breath and jerked back as if someone had slapped him. "Oh, dear God."

Ann rubbed his back again and peered at the pictures as well. "Those are rings, aren't they? Felicity's?"

The senator's Adam's apple bobbed. He squeezed his eyes shut for a second, then nodded. "I had them custom made... The hearts engraved on the side of the wedding band..." He swallowed, nodded. "They're hers."

Taylor put the phone away. "While the bones were found several miles from the abduction site, I have to warn you, it is possible those bones are *not* Felicity's. We'd like her dental records to confirm identity."

"Of course, of course," the man said, tears welling in his eyes. "Anything we can do to help. Ann can call Dr. Lock."

"Not necessary," Matt said. "I have them. And unlike *some* investigators, I'm happy to share."

Taylor gave him a look that should have incinerated him. *Yeah, sweetcheeks, I went there.*

He held her stare, waiting for her to speak. To make a move. To *challenge* him.

But, surprise, surprise, the corner of her mouth quirked and she licked her bottom lip, a small, knowing movement that brought him back a few hours to that last time he'd buried himself inside her.

Damn the woman. She'd done that on purpose.

She turned her attention to Jarvis. "Senator, I'm sorry to ask this at such a delicate time, but as long as we're here, I wonder if I could go over a few details about the case with you?"

Ann patted his knee. "I'll get you a drink." She hopped up and started for the door. "May I get you all something? Coffee, tea, water?"

Matt's gut fired at Ann's sudden need to leave, but maybe the woman simply didn't like discussing Mrs. Jarvis *numero uno.*

The FBI twins shook their heads in unison and Matt smiled at Ann. "Water would be nice. Thank you."

Ann waved a hand, her large diamond sparkling in the soft overhead light. "No problem."

"Senator," Matt said, "as a former homicide detective, I would urge you not to say anything else until you contact a lawyer."

Walt held his hands wide. "I have nothing to hide. You know that."

That's what they all said. Right before the cuffs got slapped on. "I know, sir, but trust me on this one. You need a lawyer."

Walt's mouth dipped into an uncharacteristic frown. As a popular senator that the Republican Party had earmarked for a presidential run, Walt squeezed every ounce of benefit from his good looks and flashing smile. The man, above all else, knew how to work a news cycle.

After considering Matt's suggestion, he nodded. "All right. Agent Sinclair, Agent Sardana, I'll be happy to speak with you after I consult with my attorney. Can I call you later today?"

"Sir," Taylor said, "if I could just confirm a couple of things from your original statement, it would help tremendously in bringing a swift close to this case."

Time to get rid of the Feds.

Matt finally stood, motioning to the door. "Agent Sinclair, Senator Jarvis has requested his attorney's presence. Given the news you've just shared, you should respect his wishes."

3

ou go on ahead," Taylor said to Meredith on the steps of the senator's house. "I'll catch up with you later."

"Later?" Mer's voice was full of warning. "Taylor, what are you up to?"

"Mr. Stephens said he would share Felicity's dental records. I need to catch up with him and give him my email, that's all. I'll grab a cab back to the office."

Her boss didn't believe it for a minute. "Is there something going on between you and the PI I should know about? Besides the fact he closed one of your cases for you?"

Ouch.

"No," Taylor lied. Seemed like she was doing a lot of that today. Guilt sat like a tart apple in her stomach. "We met at the conference and chatted. I didn't realize he'd been hired by Senator Jarvis, but as long as he can provide the dental records, I might as well use him."

And maybe he has other information I can use too.

Mer made her way down the steps and to her car, shaking

her head. "Keep me posted," she said over the hood, then climbed in and drove away.

A vintage Mustang was parked kitty corner of the matching Beamers. Taylor pulled out her phone and walked over to the car, setting a hip against the passenger door as she scrolled through her phone contacts. She needed Matt's number so she could text him to get his fine ass out here, but she didn't have it. No doubt Janiece, her cold case team's computer guru, could get it for her faster than Siri.

She'd just hit Janiece's number when a voice cut through the mental riot act going on in her head. Too bad because she'd planned on laying that baby on Matt.

"Are you stalking *me* now, sweetheart?"

Taylor ended the call to Janiece before it connected and did a slow pivot to find the man himself standing on the front steps with that shit-ass, cocky grin on his face. "I'm too tired to be your stalker."

"That's what happens after a night with me and no coffee to recharge your batteries. We should go get some. Or maybe you're ready for another orgasm to recharge yourself? I'm happy to oblige."

Could he say that a little louder?

Taylor flicked her gaze over his shoulder and prayed no one inside was listening. The door was closed, the windows empty of eavesdroppers, thank God. A sigh of relief escaped her lips. "You are so goddamn arrogant."

He smiled big, but kept standing on the steps several feet away as if she had cooties. "Hey, what can I say? Mad Dog loves to pleasure a beautiful woman. Now come over here, stalker, and tell me what you really want."

Gah! He was infuriating. Taylor stomped toward him but since he was still on the steps, he towered over her. Not the best strategy for reading him the riot act.

So she climbed the steps to get face-to-face with those pretty baby blues.

Good thing her heels gave her four inches, because she still came up short and had to tip her face up to meet his gaze.

"You're damn right you owe me coffee," she said, lowering her voice, "and I'm not totally ruling out a midday quickie, but I want those dental records ASAP. Give me your phone."

She held out her hand. He hesitated a moment, his wide smile turning wolfish as he handed her his cell. "Bossy. I like it."

Reining in the urge to stomp the top of his foot with one of her heels, she pulled up his contacts and punched in her phone number and email. "Why don't you have your phone password protected?" she chastised while she typed.

"I have nothing to hide."

Right. His tone suggested he found her scolding humorous. Another urge to stomp on his foot rose and she squelched it. "Here's my cell number and email. I expect those records by lunchtime."

"What about not sharing our cases, Agent Sinclair? That's a no-no according to your rules. You wouldn't be offering me another roll in the sack just to bribe me, would you?"

She looked him square in the eyes, giving him one of his own grins back. She was tired, but she wasn't going to bite. "You don't follow rules, do you, Matt?"

He slid close, brushing his chest against hers and copping a feel of her ass. "Breaking them is so much more fun," he teased as he leaned down and nuzzled her ear.

No longer able to hold back, she cuffed him on the bicep. A nice, firm one she'd had the pleasure of squeezing most of the night. "Stop being an idiot. You know what I meant this morning and this is a whole other ball of wax. We're on the same case. It only makes sense for us to work together."

He gave her space again as he took his phone back and slipped it into his jacket pocket. "Not sure I see it that way.

Seems to me, we're looking at the same case in very different ways. If I didn't know better, I'd think you suspect my client is guilty of murdering his first wife."

"Is he?"

Matt's expression darkened. The smile fell off his face. "You are really something, Taylor."

"I'll take that as a compliment."

Another step back. "Maybe you should request a copy of Felicity's dental records from her dentist. I'll send you the phone number and you can contact him yourself. Should only take a day or two."

She tapped her foot, reeling in her exasperation. He was all flippant, flirty, and downright annoying until she poked at the heart of the matter. "Matt, come on. We both want to wrap up this case quickly and give everyone involved closure, especially your client."

"Nice play, Agent, but this teamwork speech is going nowhere." He scooted around her and headed down the steps, ignoring her plea for him to stop.

"How's your plan about not sharing cases working out now, slick?" he called over his shoulder as he crossed the drive to his car.

Steaming, Taylor let him get in the Mustang and nearly drive away before she swallowed her ego and flagged him down. If he'd investigated Felicity's disappearance, he might have fresh insight for her. She needed to get in his good graces.

She wanted to get back in his bed.

Stupid, stupid, stupid.

But sometimes a girl needed an orgasm of epic proportions and Mad Dog Stephens could deliver on that front, many, many times a night.

Passing that up would be a real crime.

She hustled down the steps and walked over to his car as he

rolled down the passenger window. "Ready to play nice, sweetheart?"

Did she have a choice? "I need a ride."

The look on his face told her he knew that and liked having her at his mercy. "So you need a ride, coffee, *and* Felicity's dental records. What do I get in exchange?"

Another wolfish grin. God help her.

She opened the door and slid into the passenger seat. "I put my contact information in your phone, Mr. PI. If you really think the only reason I did that was to get those dental records, then you better go back to being a beat cop."

With a smug smile on his face, he shifted from park and jetted out of the driveway.

Matt hooked the left off the Senator's street and headed back toward DC. His stomach rumbled leading him to believe it might just be lunchtime. He glanced at his watch as he drove. 12:30 on the nose. Lunchtime. His body ran like clockwork.

He stopped at a traffic light, glanced over at Taylor and found her running her hand along the seam of her seat. He'd just had the leather stitched and if it popped again, someone was gonna get an ass-whooping.

"Did that seam open?"

She looked up at him with those sultry green eyes that he'd spent hours refusing to get enough of and the air in the car evaporated. Just gone. This woman. From the first time he'd seen her, she'd been doing that to him. Kicking him in the chest and stealing his oxygen. Now, after their slamming night together, he wanted her. All of her.

And he'd have her.

Yep, yep, yep.

He just had to convince her.

"I'm hungry," he said. "You? I'll buy lunch."

If Matt's memory served, they were only a few blocks from that great food truck he'd accidentally discovered after getting lost on his way to the senator's that first time.

"Eat later," Taylor said. "I have work to do."

"Listen, sweetcheeks. You need to keep your strength up. You had a long night. Besides, you're gonna love this place. It's grilled cheese on steroids. Every kind you can imagine. Last time, I had the one with bacon and the homemade guac. A-*mazing*."

"What's the name of the place?"

Lured in with grilled cheese. Damn, she was easy. Who didn't love a good grilled cheese?

He swung a U-ey in the middle of the four-lane street, spotted the cop sitting in his squad on the corner—*whoopsie*—and gave him a mea-culpa wave.

Before the cop could light him up, Taylor held her badge to the window, obviously hoping for some law enforcement unity. Maybe they *would* make a great team. In bed and out.

"Look at you," Matt said, "throwing your federal weight around."

"Saving your ass, *slick*," she said, tossing his own word back at him.

Oh, how he loved a woman with a smart mouth.

"Taylor, we will make beautiful babies together."

"Not if I don't enjoy this lunch we won't." She poked her finger in the air. "And it better not take too long. I have things to do. Where is this place?"

A smart mouth *and* she didn't get all pissy about the babies comment. True love. Had to be.

"It's a food truck."

"A food truck! Forget it. Are you trying to kill me? Do you know that 48 million people a year experience a foodborne illness? How do we know this truck is clean?"

Whack-job. But...her outrage ranked a solid ten on the cuteness scale. And there was that true love factor to consider. Plus, he liked her. A lot.

Working on instinct, as in, he had no idea where the truck was, he took a right, hoping it would lead him to the park. Once he found that, he'd be golden. He'd just follow the road until he stumbled upon said food truck with the rampant foodborne illnesses. "With all the awards this truck has won, it has to be clean. Bet on it."

She scoffed and dug into her purse for something. "You are such a liar. I'm looking it up."

"Go ahead. Peggy's Food Truck. I guarantee they've won awards. I hope."

He flashed a grin, blew her a kiss and went back to the road ahead. Where the hell was that park?

"Ha!" Taylor said. "I knew you were lying."

Giving up on her research idea, she shoved the bag toward the floor, bumping the buckle against the dash along the way. After stowing the bag at her feet, she licked her thumb then gently rubbed at the telltale spot where her bag had bumped the dashboard. "Sorry I smudged. This is a nice car."

"Thanks."

"What year is it?"

"69 Mustang. Shelby GT500."

Taylor let out a low whistle. Whether or not she actually understood the beauty of muscle cars was a mystery but her reaction hinted at an appreciation.

"Built her myself. Call it therapy."

Therapy he'd started when he was twenty-two and his sister had gone missing tossing him into a rogue wave of anger and grief he was completely unprepared—emotionally speaking—to navigate.

"You built this yourself? Now I'm really impressed."

"Thank you. I even added the air conditioning. That took some figuring out. It was fun though."

Still searching for that park, hell if he'd admit he couldn't find it, Matt made a left. There. At the end of the block, a burst of trees, their green leaves shining in the sun. Hope bloomed inside him because Taylor was a smart woman and in the next five minutes she'd figure out he was lost and break his balls.

Hard.

"This was my third try. I sold the first two then found this baby. I started with a rusted out frame. That was back when I was in homicide. With those hours, the car took me a couple of years."

"You take good care of it."

At the end of the block, he braked for the stop sign and looked over at Taylor, holding her gaze for a long second and his body temperature spiked. *Is it hot in here?* Goddamn, he needed to turn up that self-installed air conditioning. He'd never had sex in this car. Hadn't even considered it. The logistics alone might be tough, but Taylor? She might drive him to try it. "There's something you should know," he said.

"What's that?"

"I take care of everything I love."

The car behind him honked, but he kept his gaze locked on Taylor as he ran one finger down her cheek and that was a mistake. A big one. Between the heat and his hands on her, the little man between his legs stirred. Damn, she made him nuts.

She leaned over, slid her hand over his thigh and smiled. "Mmm, mmm, mmmm. You *are* good."

"Honey, you haven't seen anything yet."

Spotting something over his shoulder, her eyes popped wide just as her hand reached his inner thigh and he knew the excitement lighting her face had zero to do with his expanding dick. She lifted her hand away—his rotten luck—and poked her finger at his window. "There it is!"

Half a block down sat a bright yellow truck with a giant red flower on it. "Yep. That's it."

He cruised the block and parked at the curb. Before he could make some—er—adjustments to compensate for the bulge in his jeans, she'd hopped out, not even giving him a shot at getting the door for her. Always in a hurry, this one.

He checked the door lock and met her at the front of the car. "Next time, I'll get the door for you. Give me that at least."

The corner of her mouth quirked. "Are we on a date now?"

"Do we have to be for me to use manners? Next time, I'll get the door."

He wasn't a caveman. Not by a long shot. In fact, he had no issues listening to women or taking orders from them. Hell, his bosses were both women. Certain things, however, in Matt's opinion, and that of his mother and father, made a man a man. Opening doors for women was one of them. And he refused to engage in a debate about it.

To drive that point home, he slid his arm around her waist and guided her across the street before she could argue.

The lack of cars didn't make for hazardous conditions, but touching her would never be a hardship and as they stepped up on the curb his mind flashed to the night before. An image of her, flat on her back, naked as a jaybird as he ran his hands over her body, his nicked up fingers sliding across her smooth, creamy skin, filled his mind. He looked over at her and took in the perfect curve of her cheek and the fullness of her wicked mouth that drove him insane all night. For many reasons.

"What?" Taylor said, casually wiping her lips. "Lipstick smear? Why are you staring?"

"Other than I think you're beautiful?"

At that, she blinked a couple of times, but stayed quiet. Dumbstruck apparently.

"Matt, I—"

"Hey, y'all," A plump woman—Peggy—said from inside the truck. She eyed him a second. "You're back. It's been awhile, Matt. Nice to see you."

Whatever Taylor was about to say would have to wait. The way it started out, he wasn't sure he wanted to hear it anyway.

"Hi, Peggy," he said. "I was in the area and craving your guac and bacon."

"You got it."

Taylor ordered the Muenster melt. With tomato. And soup. So much for not being hungry and the concern over food contamination.

One of the tables was already occupied by what looked like two moms and a couple of toddlers. The moms stopped talking and watched them make their way to the empty table beside theirs.

"Ladies," he said, nodding at them and offering up a smile.

After settling in, Taylor leaned forward like she had a juicy secret. "The moms think you're hot. They've been staring at you since we walked up."

"How do you know they're not staring at you?"

That shut her up.

"You're funny, Taylor."

Their eyes met and a few seconds of silence lingered between them, but with the zinging happening inside him he didn't need words to know she felt the same way. With Taylor it was all about heat, heat, and more heat.

Jesus, he could do her right here, right now. No problem.

"So, Mad Dog, let's get to know each other."

He cracked a smile. "Gee, I thought we already had."

"Oh, ha, ha. Never mind that. Tell me one thing about you."

Where was this going now? Did she honestly think he didn't get that she was on a fishing expedition. "Like what?"

She shrugged. "I don't know. What are you afraid of."

"Blood."

She laughed. "Blood! You were a homicide investigator. How are you afraid of blood?"

"I was a damned good homicide detective too. But hey,

everyone is creeped out by something. I can look at it, it just gives me the willies."

A tray with two sandwiches, soup, and a couple water bottles appeared in front of them as Peggy swished by on her way to deliver the moms' orders.

For a woman who didn't want to eat, Taylor wasted no time scooping up her sandwich and digging in. He watched her mouth work as she chewed. When her eyes fluttered closed, he knew the explosion of flavor had hit her. He'd had the same reaction the first time. *Knew it.* She dropped her shoulders and moaned and, oh, jeez. That moaning—and her mouth, that fricking mouth—might put him on his knees, begging for another crack at paradise Taylor-style.

"Wow," he said.

She swallowed her food then straightened up again, ready for another bite. "It's so good. Excellent choice. Foodborne illnesses and all."

That's it. All over. He set his palms flat on the table, leaned over, half standing and kissed her. Softly. No tongue wars in public. Just enough to take that irreverent mouth, to feel her lips against his and satisfy himself.

And, God bless her, she responded. Kissing him back, even running her hand along his jaw and cupping his cheek and the hard-on that had been brewing waved a white flag. *Toddlers.* Right beside them. Cursing his lack of control, he backed away from the kiss, waited for her to open her eyes where he saw the same flashing heat he'd seen in the bar last night. He dropped his gaze to her lips again, thinking about the words that had spilled out while they pounded away on each other.

"Your mouth is wicked," he said. Sitting back down, he glanced at the eagle-eyed moms who'd made no secret of their eavesdropping. Since they were listening anyway, he might as well acknowledge it. He angled toward them and jerked his thumb at Taylor. "I love her lips."

"Holy moly," one of the moms said. "You two are hot."

Matt smacked the table and went back to his sandwich. "You know it, lady."

"Oh, my God," Taylor muttered. "You're insane."

"So I'm told."

In three bites, he inhaled half his meal while ignoring his brain's reasons he and Taylor should avoid future fuckfests. He'd spent ten years ruminating over his failure to be accepted into the FBI academy. The feds had wounded his ego like no one before and the subsequent self-reflection contributed to his becoming a top-notch detective. As good as he was, that failure still stung and now he had a thing for a woman who not only had his dream job, but she was working cold cases, further sticking that hot knife of envy into his gut.

And here they were, working the same goddamn case after they'd spent the night exploring positions a contortionist would applaud them for.

He hadn't just screwed the pooch on this one. He'd screwed the FBI agent too.

Dropping his sandwich, he dug his phone out of his pocket. With the senator being Matt's client, as well as a potential suspect, this whole thing was a disaster. Matt and Taylor? Opposite sides right now. No way around that.

Still. A woman had been murdered.

Ah, fuck it.

He tapped a few keys on his phone and hit send. "There."

Taylor picked up her water, unscrewed the cap. "What?"

"I just sent you Felicity's dental records."

"You did?"

"I told you I would. I keep my promises, Taylor. Every time."

"Thank you. You saved me some time."

He shrugged. "A woman is dead. We need to find her killer."

No matter how they dealt with each other on a personal level, they needed to get Felicity justice.

4

*T*he Smithsonian was relatively quiet for a Tuesday morning, which Taylor suspected was exactly how Grey preferred it.

She sat on a bench in front of a floor to ceiling sculpture and wondered what Matt was doing.

Who cares? She hadn't heard a peep from him after he'd dropped her at the J. Edgar Building the previous day. Not even an emoji response to her thank-you text for Felicity's dental records.

She'd halfway expected a booty call last night, but no dice. Zip. Her hours had been spent in the bowels of her department with the other three members of her team going over every note, picture, and statement pertaining to the Jarvis case until well after ten, then a frozen dinner and a glass of wine consumed at her laptop at home while she Googled Matt and the firm he worked for.

Schock Investigations consisted of Meg and Charlize—Charlie—Schock, two sisters with a diverse and extremely sought-after team of professionals who specialized in missing persons and cold cases. Their claim to fame was taking on the cases law enforcement had failed to solve.

Meg was an elite forensic sculptor. A Yale fine arts graduate, she taught forensic sculpting for an international forensics organization. Previously, she'd worked with law enforcement agencies worldwide. Charlie had gone to school for psychology and specialized in criminal forensics, evaluating and profiling criminals, and also providing expert testimony in judicial cases. She had field experience, too, having one time been an agent for the FBI for a few short years before she left the Bureau to join her sister in building their own investigative service.

Sometime around midnight, Taylor had finally crawled into bed, setting her phone in its charging station and double-checking her texts and voicemails to make sure she hadn't somehow missed one from him.

Again, zip. She might as well have fallen off the face of the planet.

She was stupid for hoping all those things he'd said to her the previous day had actually meant something to him.

Maybe he caught another case, she told herself for the third time since she'd gotten up that morning. But really, how much time did it take to send a text?

"Well, that's depressing," a male voice said from behind her.

Taylor looked over her left shoulder to find Mitch Monroe eyeing the Nevelson sculpture, hands in his jean pockets as he rocked back and forth lightly on his heels. A red T-shirt under his jean jacket read, "Don't piss me off or I'll stop taking my pills."

The smartass shirt seemed appropriate for the former agent who'd gone to the dark side and had a nasty reputation for taking people down with him.

Please tell me Grey didn't pawn me off on him.

Taylor returned her attention to the sculpture. "Where's your boss?"

"Why did this artist use all black?" Mitch asked, ignoring her question. "Is this some kind of Goth shit or something? It's so...bleak."

A sigh escaped Taylor's lips. "Goth didn't exist when Ms. Nevelson created her art. The program says she liked black paint because it conjures totality, peace, and greatness."

"Greatness, huh? Maybe I should wear more black."

God save her.

Getting away from the land mine behind her would be a smart move. She grabbed her bag and started to stand when Grey slipped onto the bench to her right.

Damn, he moved like a stealth bomber. "Wasn't sure you were going to join the party," she said.

He wore dark sunglasses, a smart suit, and tie. Unlike his partner, who now stared at the sculpture with a new appreciation on his face, Grey was clean-shaven and had his hair slicked back. He might have left the FBI, but he was Bureau to his bones. "Sorry. Had to park the car."

"His new Challenger," Mitch said with a hint of jealousy. "He totaled his last one, and he's particular where he parks the shiny new wheels now."

Grey gave her the tiniest of affirmative smiles. Taylor lowered her purse again, glancing around to make sure they were alone. No one else was in this section of the 4th floor. Maybe it was too early for art connoisseurs or other people didn't like black either.

"Dental recs confirm it's Felicity," she told Grey, settling back into her place on the bench.

He stared straight ahead as if he were enjoying the art, even though they were alone and his sunglasses had to darken the black sculpture even further. "You obtained dental records already? That was fast."

"I sweet talked the PI who's working for Walt—he had a copy. Then I dropped your name with the ME. I told her I had your notes from the case. Dr. Smith fast-tracked the bones with the forensic anthropologist assigned to the case. Thank you for that, by the way. I don't throw your name around often, but it does help with certain people. The forensic gal had a preliminary report on my desk before I got to work. Being as how the whole thing revolved around the senator, it wasn't hard to expedite the process, but I do appreciate using your name as an ace card. Sorry I didn't ask you first."

Grey chuckled. "I would have done the same in your position."

"Who's this PI?" Mitch huffed.

Mitch had always made her nervous, but she supposed since he and Grey had been partners at the FBI, he might have insight into the case. "The senator won't talk to me without his lawyer present. Tried to set up a meeting for yesterday afternoon, but the lawyer was conveniently already engaged."

Grey didn't seem surprised. "Have you told Jarvis you have confirmation of the identity?"

"Not yet. The forensic anthropologist is still working to figure out a cause of death. From her preliminary examination, some of Felicity's bones are still missing, and so are the baby's. When those are found, we'll know more. Walt will have questions regarding both subjects, so I'm giving her a few more hours to work. Hopefully, I'll have some answers."

"Jarvis hired a PI?" Mitch paced up to the large sculpture and examined a section closer. "For what?"

Taylor withheld another sigh. "The senator wanted to remarry last year and needed to have Felicity declared legally dead. He hired Schock Investigations. Matt Stephens looked into the case and couldn't uncover any evidence suggesting she might still be alive. Felicity was declared legally dead, and he married Ann."

Mitch dropped onto the bench on the other side of her and

leaned forward to look around her at Grey. "Matt Stephens. Why does that name sound familiar?"

"He's a friend of Tony's."

Mitch sneered. "Moose doesn't have friends, so whoever this bozo is, he must be a douchebag."

"Moose?" Taylor said.

"Ever seen Tony Gerard?" Mitch made tall and wide motions with his hand. "He's frickin' Bigfoot and he's got the cranky attitude to go with it. Grey loves him."

"Matt helped out with Fallyn Pasche," Grey said, completely unruffled as always. "When Tony was babysitting me."

Mitch snapped his fingers. "And look how well that turned out. DC's top fixer nearly died." He hit Taylor with his steely gaze. "I'd stay away from Stephens, if I were you. If he's as bad at being a PI as he is a bodyguard, you shouldn't trust him."

Taylor swung her attention to Grey. "I heard about that case. You ended up in the hospital after a car accident, didn't you? No wonder you needed a new Challenger."

"Tony saved my life," Grey said. "And Stephens isn't responsible for what happened to Fallyn. He's a good guy and I trust him."

Taylor didn't remember all the details, only that Pasche, a political fixer, had nearly been killed. Matt's involvement was news to her. She should ask him about it if she ever spoke to him again. "I asked him The Question."

Grey's brows lifted. "Are you investigating Matt?"

In a manner of speaking. Taylor gave a noncommittal shrug.

A nod from Grey, his eyes studying her. "And what did he say?"

"Blood."

"What question?" Mitch interrupted. "What are you talking about?"

By studying Grey during the brief time they'd worked

together, Taylor had learned a few tricks from the profiler. One of them being that asking random questions kept your suspect off-track, and their answers to those random questions often told you more about them than straight-forward ones.

Those dark brows of Grey's lowered. "He's scared of blood?"

Taylor nodded. "Weird, right?"

"Keep digging," Grey recommended.

Mitch demanded an explanation again about The Question and what they were talking about. Taylor and Grey both ignored him.

"So what do you think about Felicity's body turning up at the scrapyard?" she asked Grey. "Still believe Jarvis is a prime suspect? I like him for it, but a scrapyard? Seems messy for him."

Grey was quiet. Taylor imagined she could see the finely-tuned cogs turning in the former profiler's brain. "The senator is a puzzle. I never could figure out if he was lying or not. Even gave him a polygraph and the results were all over the board."

Taylor had examined the polygraph results but her instinct said *all over the board* meant guilty.

"Motive?" Mitch asked, leaning around her again. "I never heard of this Ann when we were investigating? Is it possible they were a thing back then?"

She had no idea, nor any proof that Walt and Ann might have been involved romantically, but maybe Matt knew more about that little tryst than she did. "I'll check into that."

"Felicity was the one with the money," Grey mused aloud. "Not Walt. He inherited everything after she was declared legally dead. The money, the house, all of it. Money is always a motivator for murder, but doesn't seem smart to make her disappear and be forced to wait seven years for the courts to declare her dead before you can officially become rich."

"I always believed he didn't want the kid," Mitch added. "Another good reason to get rid of Felicity."

Taylor stared at the black sculpture, not really seeing it. Her skin crawled at the thought of what had happened to Felicity. To her baby. "The CSI team is still working the site, so until they're done, I can't be sure what role the baby may have played. Maybe nothing."

Grey removed his sunglasses and cleaned them with a cloth from his jacket pocket. "Felicity's bones are the best lead at this point."

Taylor jumped up, the warm spurt of adrenalin that always came when she knew she was onto something pumping in her veins. "Did you tell Meredith I called you yesterday?"

"No." His voice sounded slightly perplexed. He set his glasses back on his face. "She knew?"

"Chastised me properly." Taylor fidgeted with her handbag strap, then rounded on Mitch. "I don't suppose you had anything to do with that?"

"Me?" He looked genuinely abashed. "First of all, I didn't catch wind of this whole thing until I walked into the..."—he shot a look at Grey—"*office* this morning."

Grey had a secret hideout for his Justice Team. Taylor felt a certain annoyance that he didn't trust her with the where-abouts, hence why they were meeting at the museum.

"Secondly," Mitch continued, "I hate Sardana. She's a total bitch. It's not like we're pals who shoot the shit on occasion and I threw her some gossip about you. Thirdly, why the hell would I waste time tattling on you? Grey may like cold cases, but I don't. I'm only here because he promised to take me by the gun range for target practice after he was done helping you. Which he shouldn't be doing. If you haven't noticed, the FBI doesn't necessarily like us anymore."

At least with Mitch you knew where you stood. No beating around the bush. No bullshit. "Funny, cuz I heard through the grapevine, you've been doing some independent work for us."

"Yeah, the unsolvable cases you Feds can't be bothered with because you don't want to step on toes."

Grey had told her that his Justice Team specialized in cases involving people who were considered above the law. Foreign diplomats, judges, district attorneys. They also looked into election fraud and other delicate cases.

"Monroe." Grey's tone was borderline scolding. "We're not here to talk about *our* cases. We're here to help Taylor with hers."

Mitch did a childish eye roll. "I know, but I like to rile her up. She's got that whole Caroline demeanor going." He winked at Taylor and she knew he'd been an ass on purpose, just to test her. Kind of like she'd gotten in Matt's face that night at the bar, just to see if he would run. "You know I can't resist sassy women."

Oh, good Lord. No wonder Meredith hated him.

"Well, someone told my boss," Taylor said to both men, "so if it wasn't any of us, I'm guessing either my phone or yours is tapped."

Grey didn't say anything but the look on his face dittoed Mitch's soft curse. "It can't be us," Mitch insisted looking to Grey. "Right? We have the highest security tech software and a genius IT geek who scans for bugs and cameras every day."

That left door number 2. Taylor's stomach sank.

...eyes and ears everywhere. That's what Meredith had said.

"She has spies," Taylor reluctantly confirmed.

"This case could get dangerous for you, Taylor." A muscle in Grey's jaw jumped. "If the senator *is* responsible and you expose him, he could lose everything—the money, the house, his new marriage, his power and fame. Most men will do anything—*anything*—to keep that from happening."

"Yeah," Mitch added. "You're not going to know who's working for him or who you can trust. I sure as hell wouldn't trust Sardana any more than Stephens. She might even have some type of software like Teeg is working on that can track your vehicle better than GPS or Google Maps."

Wasn't that a lovely thought? "Do I want to know about this software?"

Grey shook his head. "It's in beta mode and was developed for the intelligence community. It's basically an eye in the sky. Agents zoom in on addresses in real time and get close enough for facial rec to get accurate intel on the criminals involved in things like drug deals and such. Nothing illegal, I assure you."

Hmm. She really didn't want to know. "Meredith is my mentor. She's been priming me for the past several years to take over the entire Missing Persons unit, not just cold cases. I trust her, even if she is checking up on me."

"She'll throw you under the bus if it serves her purpose or the Bureau's," Grey warned.

Nice. Just what she needed to hear. From an expert on the subject, no less.

Grey and Mitch were jaded, and while they might have gotten the shit end of the stick with the Bureau, they weren't entirely innocent of creating the situation in the first place. Taylor hefted her strap onto her shoulder. "I have to go. Thanks for the input."

She started to walk away, but Grey stood and blocked her path. "I have people who can watch your back, Taylor. Keep you safe."

The guy had a good heart and she appreciated his concern. If anyone found out she was consulting with him—*continuing* to consult with him on an active case—she could lose her job. "I'm a trained agent, Grey. I'll be all right."

His lips firmed and he moved aside.

Her heels clicked on the tile floor as she headed for the elevators to take her downstairs. Mitch's voice called after her. "DNFU, Sinclair. Stay away from Stephens. I'm telling you, he's a douchebag."

Do Not Fuck Up. The irony of a screw-up like Mitch telling her not to fuck up her career, her life, made her want to match his earlier eye roll.

"Takes a douchebag to know one," she called back, giving Mitch a cheeky smile and wave as she climbed into the elevator and hit the down button.

Before the doors closed, she saw him flip her the bird. Yep. Same ol' Mitch and Grey. How the two of them ever stayed friends was beyond her.

Matt parked the Mustang in his normal spot behind the office and sat back for a second, letting the late morning sun warm the car's interior. Rather than deal with the cost of rent in the nation's capitol, the sisters had opted for a first floor unit in Vienna, Virginia, a thirty-minute drive from DC.

Meg's minivan was to his left and on the other side of the minivan sat Charlie's convertible. The sisters couldn't be more different in their choice of vehicle. Being an artist, Meg liked the minivan for its cargo area and the resulting ability to transport big shit all at once. At any given time, Meg might have easels, various types of stands for sculpting, canvases, large bins with art supplies, whatever. And it seemed all of it was in her vehicle.

Her sister, on the other hand, preferred the sleek convertible BMW that Matt barely fit in.

Funny ladies.

A minute later, he pushed through the office's back door into the narrow hallway. "Honey! I'm home!"

Ahead, on the right, were Meg's and Charlie's offices. Directly across from them was Matt's. Meg had offered to switch offices with him and give him the bigger one, but given his schedule and the lack of time he actually spent in said office, he didn't need extra space. All he needed was a desk, a chair, and a computer. Boom.

Besides, Meg's office doubled as a secondary art studio and, like her vehicle, she needed all the room she could get.

"Hey, Matt." Charlie's voice drifted down the hallway, the echo gobbled up by the thick carpeting and array of Meg-created artwork lining the steel-gray walls.

Meg had given him a whole dissertation on the whys and hows of steel gray, but he was a guy. What the hell did he care what color the walls were?

He stopped at the first open door, found Meg, as usual, putting her hands to work. Today's project? A skull reconstruction.

Entering the office, Matt let out a low whistle, drawing his boss's attention. She tugged on her earbuds and swung them over her shoulder for safekeeping.

"Hi," she said. "I didn't hear you."

She rubbed the back of her clay littered hand across her forehead in an attempt to tame the wisps of honey blonde hair that had broken free of her ponytail. He studied her face, took in the slight darkness under her eyes contrasting with her pale face.

"You look tired." He propped his ass on the cherry credenza that weighed more than him and gestured to the sculpture. "How long you been at it?"

"I couldn't sleep last night. She's bugging me."

Meg went back to the sculpture. It appeared to be a woman, but, as yet, she hadn't added hair or any sort of coloring to the face. Basically, what she had here was clay carefully molded over high cheekbones, but without a doubt, the vic was female.

"She's young," Matt said.

"My anthropologist says early twenties."

Her anthropologist. The one she'd met while working a case last year. The two had dated briefly, but the relationship, from what Matt knew, fizzled. Meg, by her own admission, couldn't dedicate herself to a relationship when there was so much to be done on the missing persons front.

"Cause of death?"

Using her thumb, she smoothed more clay around the eye area. Blue eyes. That's what Meg had given her. Whether the young woman actually had blue eyes, Meg couldn't know. If she didn't have proof of the victim's eye and hair color, she went on instinct.

"I'm not sure."

Meg and Charlie had been contacted two weeks ago by the sheriff from a small town in Maryland. Months earlier, he'd read about the sisters in a law enforcement newsletter and had saved the article. After two years of holding on to this skull and trying to solve the case on their own, the sheriff's need to identify the vic prompted him to pick up the phone and ask for help.

The sisters, as they were known, a forensic psychologist turned private eye and a sculptor, liked to dabble in cold cases in their down time. They'd become an unofficial resource for law enforcement officials with stalled cases. Whether they didn't have the manpower, the expertise, or the budget, for whatever reason, these cases sat unsolved. At least until the sisters got involved.

With this particular case, the sheriff had a skull and seventy percent of the victim's bones, which he turned over to the sisters. Meg went to work on the skull and bones while Charlie studied the case file.

Matt gestured to the skull. "Do I need to do anything with this case yet?"

Meg shook her head. "Not yet. Once I finish here, we'll send out bulletins. See if anyone recognizes her. Poor thing."

"Any hits from NaMus?"

NaMus, the National Missing and Unidentified Persons

System was a database developed by the Justice Department to improve the information available on missing persons and human remains.

"Nothing," Meg said. "Whoever she is, her family hasn't reported her missing."

And that, Matt knew, was a deal-breaker for Meg. Having an intensely close relationship with her family, Meg couldn't stand the idea of someone not being loved enough to be declared missing.

Matt? His years growing up around cops, listening to the war stories, and then his time as a homicide detective had hardened him to this sort of thing. The shitty truth was there were people that no one gave a damn about.

He'd learned early on if he got emotionally invested, the torment would destroy him.

Meg hadn't learned that lesson yet. Maybe she never would. Who knew?

Matt boosted off the credenza. "Let me know what you need from me."

Charlie appeared in the doorway. She wore black slacks and a gray blouse that blended with the wall color. The overhead light glinted across her dark red hair and, unlike her sister, her blue eyes were sharp, the makeup around them perfectly applied.

The sisters. Such a puzzle.

"Hey," Matt said.

"Hi." She propped one shoulder against the doorframe. "How are things with the senator?"

"I suggested he get his lawyer involved. Now that they have a body—or at least bones—the feds are gonna look hard at him."

Meg stopped messing with her sculpture and waved the carving tool she'd picked up. "Charlie, have we heard from your guy at the ME's office?"

"Not yet. What about your FBI contact?"

Having consulted on missing persons cases for the feds, Meg had earned a few favors from inside the Hoover building. Favors she never minded calling in.

"He confirmed the remains are Felicity."

This information wasn't a shock. Not with what he'd learned while at the senator's with Taylor. Whom he owed a text. Or better yet, a call because, case or no case, he'd spent a good portion of the night wide awake, imagining all the places he'd like to have sex with her. Imagining that mouth against his ear, once again telling him all the ways she wanted him to fuck her. Ooh-eee, the woman was wicked.

Thoughts of Taylor and her filthy mouth and amazing legs stirred him up, and God help him if he got a hard-on in front of the sisters.

He brought his focus back to the senator and his dead wife. "Not surprised. They found her rings with the bones. What about the baby?"

"Nothing on him."

Damn. Matt ran a hand over his face and reminded himself not to get caught up. But kids—babies, for fuck's sake—did him in. Children couldn't defend themselves and any crime, anything against a child, froze his blood.

At the time of her disappearance, Felicity had been eight months pregnant and about to give her husband a child.

"Which means," Matt said, "the feds are probably at the site searching for him. Do we know how shallow the grave was? If whoever buried her didn't go deep enough—"

Meg put her hand up. She didn't want to hear about animals getting to the remains. He couldn't blame her.

"They're out there now. Everyone available is on it. Hopefully, they'll find him. There's something else."

Matt met her gaze and her blue eyes, so like her sisters, held a hardness. Challenge. "What's that?"

"Taylor Sinclair."

Whoopsie. A sting shot through his shoulders. Whatever this was, it wouldn't be good. Not with the way Meg was looking at him. He cocked his head. "What about her?"

Meg slid her eyes to Charlie, who took the cue that her sister wanted her to amscray. She straightened up, tugging on her blouse sleeves. "I have calls to make. If I hear from the ME, I'll update you."

"Thank you," Meg said.

While waiting for Charlie to clear the area, Matt kept his gaze on Meg, wondering WTF. Why the hell would she be bringing up Taylor? Yes, he'd let her know he'd seen Taylor at the senator's and that he'd shared the dental records with her. Outside of that, there wasn't a whole lot to discuss.

Unless...

"Taylor Sinclair," Meg repeated. She set her sculpting tool on the worktable and faced him. "Make sure you know what you're doing there."

"Meaning?"

"Meaning the FBI has big plans for her. If someone is going to take a fall, it won't be her."

Whoa. Matt pursued his lips, considered his options. Although Charlie had been the one to hire him, he and Meg had always had a good—a great—working relationship. The thing he appreciated about her was her honesty. Her no-holds-barred approach to all things. She didn't have time for subtle, and preferred gut-wrenching, let's-get-shit-done truth.

"Meg?"

"Yes?"

"What the hell are you talking about? And since when do we not talk straight with each other?"

The corner of her mouth lifted and she let out a huffing laugh. "Matt, I do adore you." She leaned back on her work-table, stared down at her battered Crocs, the work shoe of choice. "A friend of mine was at the conference you attended."

Bingo.

"That friend saw you and Taylor in the hallway outside the room you went into together."

He ticked back to that hallway. His pressing her against the door. Nibbling her neck. Or was it her ear? Who the hell knew? All he knew was he'd clamped his hands over her ass, bringing her flush against him so she'd understand exactly how much he wanted her.

All in a public hallway.

Excellent.

For the first time in his adult life, Matt felt his cheeks fire. This was as bad as his mother busting him and Joelle Connors in the backseat of his car. He cleared his throat and blew out a breath. "I see."

"It's none of my business," Meg said.

"Actually, it is. The senator is our client. At the time, Taylor wasn't assigned to Felicity's case. *That* happened the following morning." He held up one hand. "God's honest truth."

"I believe you. I know your work ethic."

"But?"

"Lust is a tricky thing, isn't it? Makes us do things we wouldn't normally do."

"Like behaving unprofessionally in a hotel hallway?"

Meg held her hands wide. "You said it, not me. I don't know what your relationship is with her."

That made two of them. Meg stayed silent and Matt raised his eyebrows. If she expected him to comment, she'd be waiting awhile. Not because he wanted to protect his and Taylor's privacy. Pretty much, that had been blown out of the water when they dry-humped each other in a hotel hallway. His resistance to elaborate was more about his own ignorance on where exactly his relationship with Taylor stood.

"My only intention here," Meg continued, "is to make sure you have your head clear. The wife of a United States Senator is dead. More than likely, their baby also. We have a responsibility here, and the FBI does as well. Not to mention, the press will be all over this. Please, just be careful with Taylor. I hear she's a pitbull."

5

*T*oday wasn't a three-and-a-half-inch heel day. It was only eleven and Taylor's feet were killing her.

Thank you, Mad Dog.

She'd picked out the designer heels and the red satin bra and panty set this morning with Matt on her mind. Now her feet ached as she marched to the conference room, ready to get some answers from the good senator, and the underwires in the new bra felt like a vise around her chest as they lifted her matching Cs to epic heights.

Stupid. Even after she hadn't heard a word from Matt, she'd designed the day's wardrobe around the infinitesimally small chance she might see him today. Now, she was paying the price for letting her personal life get in the way of work. Meredith would cuff the back of her head if she knew.

Not for long though. The senator was hers to question finally and she was in warrior mode. No more of his dancing around. She wanted answers and he had them. He and his lawyer were about to learn that she wasn't one to mess with. She had her notes and her strategy outlined and Taylor, agent extraordinaire, was ready for battle.

The conference room was small and clean, but she pulled up short in the doorway. It was also empty. Taylor glanced at her watch and frowned. The senator should have arrived five minutes ago.

A fresh wave of annoyance hit her. Who did this asshole think he was? She'd been patient and understanding—at least as much as she could be when her gut was telling her flat out that Senator Jarvis had played a hand in his wife's disappearance.

Women and girls made up the bulk of the cases on her desk. From past experience and sheer numbers, she knew the majority of them had been hurt, raped, kidnapped, or killed by someone they knew. Someone who supposedly loved them. It made her absolutely sick.

Smacking her files down on the glass tabletop, she checked her phone for messages. None from the senator or his lawyer.

Dammit.

None from Matt either. *The fink.*

She straightened her pen next to her files and huffed out a breath. Her yellow notebook sat on top of the stack of files with her list of questions—a list she'd gone over a dozen times last night. Things did not add up with this case and she was sure the senator knew more—much more—than he was letting on.

Beckett Pearson blew into the room, fixing his Burberry tie with one hand while he balanced a white paper cup with the other. "Wait...no senator?"

Beck was her right-hand investigative specialist. Men like Senator Jarvis often opened up to him better than they did her —a female in a strong, high-raking position of authority. Beck would start talking about the Sabers or Jets and the next thing she knew, the person across the table would be telling him their deepest, darkest secret.

"He's late." Taylor drew a fingernail down the corner of the folders. She would have been pacing if not for her feet screaming at her. "I get the feeling he doesn't want to talk to me."

Beckett plunked down beside her and handed her the white cup. "Green tea with jasmine. It will detox your liver and open your crown chakra."

She'd rather have a scotch. "Thanks... I think."

"So old Walt is letting you know he's in control."

Beck had once been a defensive lineman in college. He kept himself in good shape and dressed like a GQ model. Rumor was, he'd modeled for Vogue during his college days as well. If Taylor had a guess, he finally got tired of people seeing him for his outward appearance only and not for the high IQ and natural analytical skills he possessed that they couldn't teach at Quantico.

"He thinks he is. He kicked me out of his house yesterday morning, insisted on having his lawyer present for the interview, and now, he's not here at the time his assistant cleared his calendar for. If he were innocent, why the power play?"

Beckett made a big deal about looking over one shoulder and then the other.

Taylor took a sip of the tea. It wasn't bad, but too hot. "What are you doing?"

The man grinned, those gorgeous cheekbones above his closely trimmed beard bunching. "Looking for your balls, boss."

"Haha, be careful or I'll have yours in a sling." She set down the paper cup and checked her messages again. Nada from any of the men she was currently waiting on.

Leo Wellington walked by the glass wall, saw her and Beckett, and backtracked. "Hey, I heard about the Jarvis case. I want in. Let me know when Walt gets here."

Fat chance. "You bet." She gave him a thumbs-up and he smiled before continuing on his way.

"Now there's a surprise," Beckett murmured, fiddling with

the digital camera set up to record the interview. "Fresh life gets breathed into an old, high-profile case, and *bam*, the shark shows up to catch a slice of the limelight."

Last week, Taylor would have admonished Beck for his insubordination. Today, she felt the same way. He was interested in her cases, including thinking he could solve Isabel's where she couldn't.

Fink number two.

At least Matt had redeemable qualities.

Yeah, like using me for my body instead of my mind.

She kinda liked that about him.

Once upon a time, she'd believed the biggest competition she'd ever have would be at Quantico. She figured once she made it into the Bureau, she'd proven herself. That she deserved to be here.

The reality was completely different. As a new agent, she'd had to prove herself time and time again, and the competition for the attention of the higher-ups had been fierce. Once she'd been placed in charge of the cold case unit, she'd encountered competition from the other supervisors and team leaders, everyone vying for funding, more staff, and/or a promotion.

Cutthroat and competitive. It was similar to that Survivor show on TV that she never had time to watch.

Everyone wanted to be a star inside these walls. Leo had done a mighty fine job of that, but now she wondered how many backs of his counterparts he'd used to get to that spot.

And now he wanted a lift on her rising star.

Screw that.

Taylor ignored the groan from her feet as she stood, grabbing her stack of files. "Have Janiece call the senator's office and see why he's been detained. We'll have to reschedule. There are 90,000 missing people out there waiting on me to find them."

That statistic made the green tea in her stomach turn to acid, but it was true. There were easily 200,000 cold cases in the United States and not all were unsolved homicides. Many involved missing persons, unidentified remains, and wrongfully convicted persons whose names might be cleared using new methods of analyzing evidence that had been developed after those crimes had been tried.

Not all cold cases were federal, but even one was too many in her book. At that moment, her team had 52 missing persons cases alone. Nearly half involved children. There were plenty more nonactive, unsolved cases in her file cabinets, just waiting for her team to take another look at them and find a new lead or witness.

Beckett jumped up and handed her the cup. "Maybe we should pay a visit to the senator's office. Bring a little heat on him. I volunteer to be your muscle."

Taylor would have loved to do exactly that. "I'm not chasing Walt Jarvis. If he thinks he can dick me around, I'll get a subpoena and drag his ass in here one way or another. He'll be breaking the law if he doesn't show up and give us his interview. I'm sure that will go over well with his constituents when he can't do his job because he's in a jail cell for impeding a federal investigation."

Beckett touched his tie again and grinned. "I think you just found your balls, TayTay."

"Do *not* call me that." The nickname was harmless, but he was forever teasing her, and part of the game was for her to act like she hated it. She didn't. Isabel had always called her that.

Now, Taylor's team was her family—her only one, really. They had nicknames for each other and they knew some pretty deep stuff about one another. That camaraderie was priceless, especially when working cases that sucked the life out of you. It kept them all from going insane. "Any word from the techs at the scrapyard about the bones? Have they found any that might be the baby's?"

Beckett shook his head. "Not that I've heard. I'll follow up with a call to the ERT."

Evidence Response Team. "Cora's in charge," Taylor told him. "See if you can get hold of—"

"Taylor."

The voice interrupting her came from the doorway. Taylor looked over to find Meredith standing there with a grim look on her face. "I know, Mer, the senator blew us off. I'll have Janiece check with his assistant and—"

Meredith cut her off again. "Come with me."

Definitely a summons. "Yes, ma'am."

As Mer took off down the hallway, Taylor exchanged a look with Beck. She handed him her files and cup. "I really should have worn my comfortable shoes today."

And maybe avoided that meeting with Grey and Mitch this morning.

Consternation showed in the lines on Beck's forehead. "Maybe they found the baby's bones."

She liked that guess better. A sinking feeling in her stomach, she took off to follow her boss to her office.

Only, Meredith didn't head to her office. She beelined to the elevator and was already inside when Taylor caught up to her. Mer pressed the button for the top floor and the shiny metal doors slid closed with a heavy *thunk*.

The top floor. Where the director of the FBI played God.

"What's up?" Taylor dared ask. She never liked being blindsided. "Is everything okay?"

Meredith eyed her in the mirrored walls. Looked away.

The silent treatment? What was this?

"Meredith, whatever it is, just say it."

"You and the PI?" Meredith sounded totally disgusted. "You told me you met him at the conference. You neglected to mention you slept with him."

Oh, that. "Who told you Matt and I slept together?"

"That doesn't matter. You *didn't* tell me."

Didn't matter? No one from the office but her and Leo had been at the conference. "So these eyes and ears you have everywhere go by the name of Leo?"

"Leo has nothing to do with this."

That was a bald-faced lie. "I didn't tell you that I'd slept with Matt because it has no bearing on anything."

The elevator compartment vibrated with Meredith's anger. "His client is the senator! Of course it has bearing!"

"Neither one of us knew about Felicity's bones until the morning after we slept together."

"So you're not continuing to see him?"

That was no one's business. "My personal life never has and never will affect my career, Mer." One bald-faced lie deserved another. "I promise you that."

The long hall to the director's office was carpeted in Federal Blue commercial carpeting. Just before they hit the end, Meredith directed Taylor into the large, well-appointed conference room next door.

The director wasn't in attendance, but Meredith's boss, the assistant director, was.

Marcus Cunningham skipped formalities, his steely gaze dropping to Taylor's shoes and back up to the TV screen on the far wall. "Agent Sinclair, what have you been doing?"

The question struck her as odd. She wasn't sure if it was rhetorical, but regardless, she felt the need to answer. "I've been waiting for Senator Jarvis to show up for his interview. He was due here fifteen minutes ago and hasn't arrived yet."

AD Cunningham pointed at the TV. "Perhaps because he's in the middle of a press conference."

Taylor followed his finger, realizing the 52" screen was filled with a picture that made her blood run cold. "What the hell is he doing?" she said, as much to herself as to the other two people in the room.

Cunningham turned his hard eyes on her, his lips a straight, unforgiving line. "Funny, that's exactly what I was going to ask you."

His attention went back to the TV where the senator was outside his home entertaining a group of reporters.

Cunningham hit a button on the remote and the mute lifted, Walt's voice filling the room.

"The Justice Department and FBI are making my life a living hell over this while I'm in the midst of grieving a second time for Felicity. My first wife is dead, and no one will tell me if my child is as well. So while the FBI should be focused on finding Felicity's killer, and determining what happened to my unborn son, they're wasting taxpayer money and the nation's time harassing a respectable, upstanding senator."

In the background behind Walt, Ann stood in an elegant two-piece suit dabbing tears from her eyes. Her husband pounded a fist into his other hand. "I want this case resolved and I want to know who killed Felicity and what happened to our child, but I will not stand by and let the FBI harass me and my current wife because they are too lazy to go after the real criminal."

Jarvis continued blustering, but Cunningham muted the TV once more and tossed the remote on the glass table in front of him. He intertwined his fingers and rested them on his stomach as he leaned back in the black leather chair. "Care to explain to me what the hell is going on, Sinclair?"

DNFU. Mitch's acronym rang in her head.

Meredith crossed her arms, her face mirroring Cunningham's. "I warned you about this. We need to solve this case and we need to do it ASAP. The thing we do not need to do is piss off the senator."

Another black eye, that's what Mer had called it. The first time around, the FBI had taken a beating in the media because of the high-profile case. Jarvis was playing victim to the press for the second time and upping the ante, making the Bureau look bad. Making Taylor, Meredith, and AD Cunningham look like schmucks.

Jarvis was going to be a more formidable opponent than Taylor had given him credit for.

Bring it on. Unbeknown to the good senator, his actions only confirmed Taylor's gut instinct—the man had somehow, someway been involved in Felicity's disappearance, and possibly her death.

And there was no way Taylor was backing down. He wanted to up the stakes and try to make her look bad? Tough shit. She lived to put bad guys away. All he'd done was make her more determined than ever to bring him to justice.

In order to do that quickly and quietly, Taylor was going to need some major resources, and by the looks on the faces of the two people who could give her those, she was shit out of luck.

The only card she had up her sleeve was a certain PI who could play outside the lines and also just happened to be in good graces with Senator Jarvis.

"I'm sorry, sir," Taylor said to Cunningham. "I thought the senator was going to play nice, but obviously, he's not. I'll—"

"Shut up, Sinclair." Cunningham rose from the chair and toyed with the remote for a moment before he set his sharp, unforgiving gaze on her. "You have embarrassed the Bureau and royally fucked this up after a day. One fucking day."

What? How was this *her* fault? She'd tried to interview the senator and he'd lawyered up, then blew her off to play victim to the press.

She started to respond and Meredith shut her down. "I put you in charge of this because I knew you could handle it, Taylor. Was I wrong?"

Having Cunningham jump on her was one thing. But Mer? The woman had been present at the Jarvis house and seen what had gone down. She'd always had confidence in Taylor's abilities.

Don't argue. Not now. Meredith was trying to save face in front of her boss. Later, they could have a heart to heart.

She'll throw you under the bus if it serves her purpose or the Bureau's, Grey had said. Taylor hoped he was wrong, but at the moment, she could feel the wheels of the bus bearing down on her.

"You were not wrong to put me in charge," she assured both of them. "I *will* handle this. The Bureau is going to receive plenty of good press, I promise, when I solve this case, just like the last three my team has closed in the past month." She couldn't help throwing out a reminder of why she was in charge of the cold case unit.

"I don't give a shit about what you've done up 'til now," Cunningham said. "I want the Jarvis case closed immediately and I better not hear or see one more negative press report, courtesy of the senator, am I clear?"

Plastering on a confident smile, Taylor looked her boss's boss in the eye. "Crystal, sir. I'm on it. I promise you, I'll figure this out. Whatever it takes."

Whatever it takes translated to asking Matt for help.

"You have 72 hours, Sinclair." The AD was no longer looking at her. He played with the remote, switching news channels. "Seventy-two hours. If you haven't cleared this case off my desk by then, I'll hand it over to Leo. Him, I can count on."

Ouch. Hustling out of the office before the lynch mob strung her up by her designer heels, Taylor went to work on damage control, dialing Matt as she hit the elevator. The red satin bra and panty set she had picked out that morning might get some action yet before the day was over.

"Hello, beautiful," Matt answered. "Honest to God, I was

about to call you. And before you take my head off, I didn't know Walt was doing the press conference."

The elevator dinged and Taylor stepped inside. "I need to see you. Now."

"What's up?"

She punched the button for her floor and rubbed her forehead where a headache poked at her. "I don't want to get into it over the phone. Can I meet you at the food truck in fifteen?"

"No can do. I'm tied up until after six tonight. How about dinner?"

Shit. She couldn't wait that long. "Matt, I'm serious. I need to see you now. It's important."

"Listen, sweet cheeks, there is nothing more I'd like to do than meet you for—eh-hem—*lunch*, but I'm on a case for the sisters. I'm also helping out a friend with another investigation. As soon as I'm done with this, I'll come by your place and take you anywhere you want to go. Or we can stay in. I'll bring the food to you."

Taylor kicked off the shoes and rolled her toes, sighing with relief, but also with annoyance. "Fine. Tonight. I'll see you then and bring Thai."

"You got it."

Thirty minutes later, Taylor and Beckett scanned the scene past the yellow crime tape at the scrapyard. Four CSIs were working a gridded area, while their leader, Cora, shook her head at Taylor's question. "No bones small enough to be an unborn child's, but we've recovered over 200 of the mother, so she's nearly intact."

All of Felicity. None of her baby. *Yet.* "Thanks, Cora, keep me posted. The wolves have their teeth around my neck, so I'd appreciate any info you can get me as soon as possible, especially in regards to that baby."

The CSI leader nodded and walked away. "You'll be my first call if we find any bones."

Beck eyed Taylor. "You've got that look, boss."

Taylor's fingers tingled with the adrenaline of a fresh angle on an old case. "No bones for the baby."

"Yet," Beck said, mirroring her thoughts.

"If our kidnapper killed her before she gave birth, the bones would be here."

"Or they killed her and the baby somewhere else, then dumped Felicity's body here."

Taylor bit the inside of her cheek, another option coming to mind. "Or she gave birth before she was killed."

"Could be that too. Or the kid is actually here somewhere, just not with his mother's body."

"That's what we need to find out. Let's get back to the office." She glanced at her watch. "We have less than seventy hours."

After work, Matt drove to the Columbia Heights address Taylor had texted him. Known as a yuppie neighborhood in the Northwest quadrant of DC, the area boasted a variety of restaurants and local shops as well as big retailers. Pretty much whatever you wanted, you could find here.

On his way up the concrete porch steps, he couldn't help notice how the freshly painted house, on a block stuffed with older, sturdy brick homes, stuck out like the new Cadillac on a street full of well-maintained Chevys.

The recently renovated home, according to Zillow, had been gutted and split into two units. The first floor and basement were Taylor's and the upper two floors some other lucky bastard's. How Taylor could afford a brand new place in DC on a federal agent's salary was a mystery, but good for her. He rang the bell and a light tinkling of chimes sounded from the other side. Such a foo-foo bell for the intensely passionate Taylor Sinclair.

The door opened and Taylor filled his very happy sightline in a skintight sweater that hugged her tits nicely, snug jeans, and bare feet. This woman, either dressed to kill in her federal agent wear or casual in jeans and a truly exceptional sweater, knew how to slay a man.

Namely him.

Down, big fella.

Depending on what this all-important meeting was, maybe Mad Dog and little Mad Dog would see another night of action. A vision of Taylor bent over a bed, gripping the comforter, popped into his brain and he didn't bother fighting the small smile tugging at his lips.

"Whatever you're thinking," she said, "knock it off."

She left him standing in the doorway, but waved him in. He followed her down a short hall keeping his eyes on her swinging ass as her feet smacked against pricey-looking tile.

"Nice place."

"Thanks. I bought it with an inheritance from my grandmother."

At the end of the hallway, she stepped into a large, sunken living room containing a giant gray sectional and a deep-cushioned chaise lounge. *Oh, honey, there are things we could do on that.* The surrounding walls were painted a deep, brick red and the windows covered in a sheer white curtain that his artist boss would most definitely approve of.

In his less than expert opinion, the whole thing shouldn't have worked. Shouldn't have. And maybe he was just a horny son of a bitch, but the place screamed of passion, heat, and long nights of truly amazing sex.

"Damn, that's hot," he said.

She scooped up a rock glass sitting on one of the end tables. "Thank you. This is my sanctuary from work. It's eclectic but Gram would have approved, I think." She jiggled the glass, making the amber liquid sway. "Can I get you a drink?"

"What are you having?"

"Scotch neat."

Apparently her drink of choice since she'd been partaking in the same two nights ago when they'd banged each other stupid.

"I'm good. I ordered dinner to be delivered."

She eased onto the sofa, her gaze on him as she slowly crossed one leg over the other and brought the drink to her lips. "I like seeing you in my place."

Opting for the safer route, he took the spot adjacent to her. "I like *being* in your place. Keep it up and it'll take a miracle to keep my hands off you."

"Maybe I want your hands on me."

At that, he smiled, but something told him Taylor wasn't ready for him. Not yet. The other night at the hotel, she'd been playful.

Loose.

One scotch beyond a light buzz. His mind ticked back to his mother, wooden spoon in hand while making dinner and giggling during a slow-dance with his father. Smack dab in the middle of the kitchen. It should have been a happy sight. Should have been. Instead, it had become something he'd grown used to when his mother hit the vodka bottle one too many times and Dad humored her rather than upset the grieving drunk.

Dysfunction at its highest level.

He brought his gaze back to Taylor and her thrown back shoulders. Nothing loose about her tonight. The federal agent had something on her mind and he wasn't interested in competing with whatever it was.

"Wicked woman, Ms. Sinclair, but I think you're distracted. And, if we're going to end this night the way we did our last one together, I'd like your full attention. Your call earlier have anything to do with it?"

"Your client." She set the drink down and rested one hand on the back of the sofa. "He's pissing me off and putting me in hot water with my bosses."

"I gathered that. What's the latest?"

She hesitated and—*here we go*—he'd lay odds they were back to the debate over sharing information and him stealing her cases.

"I shouldn't tell you, but"—she shrugged—"someone will leak it anyway."

"Gee, thanks for that trust."

"Don't give me that. I trusted you enough to call you this morning. I was going to have you meet me at the scrapyard for some detective work, but you were too busy."

"I do have a job."

The corner of her mouth twitched. "The CSI unit has been over every section around Felicity's bones and there's no baby."

No bones. Matt's brain tunneled, hyper-focused on Felicity and her unborn child. He held up one finger. "She was pregnant when she disappeared. How are the baby's bones not there?"

"Well, that's the question isn't it?"

She picked up the drink again, slugged it back and held up the glass, inspecting it under the shadowed light of a floor lamp.

He snatched it away from her. "Let's forget the drink a minute."

"Not likely. I've had a shitty day. My boss is unhappy because I've stepped out of her careful, very rigid boundaries on this case and I have the press breathing down the Bureau's neck—which is exactly what she told me not to let happen. I'm hoping you'll make it better for me. In a couple of ways."

For safekeeping, he tucked the empty glass out of her reach in one of the three square trays on the leather ottoman that doubled as a coffee table. "Have they finished searching? Could the bones have been...moved? An animal could have gotten to them."

"There's approximately a few hundred yards still to be searched once they've moved the pile of shit covering the ground, but if there was a baby buried with Felicity, the bones shouldn't be on the other side of the yard. No bones. They're still looking, but..." her voice trailed off and she shrugged.

"What, Taylor?"

"What do you mean, *what*? Where's the baby? I have questions about this woman's death and your *client* is not only being uncooperative, he's making the FBI, including yours truly, look incompetent. I want to know what Jarvis is hiding."

How the hell much had she had to drink? The woman was all sorts of fired up. Matt held out his hands. "He didn't kill her. He's *grieving*. People do stupid shit when they're grieving. Which would explain the press conference. Ever think of that?"

"You're awfully confident."

Bet your ass. "Yeah. I am. He loved her. And believe me, I looked at every angle. The marriage was strong. They respected each other. Her family confirmed it. Sure, they fought occasionally, who doesn't? It's not a smoking gun."

"I never said she was shot."

He gave his head a solid shake. "It was a figure of speech. What the hell's your problem?"

"*My* problem? I'm trying to figure out what the hell happened here!"

"And I'm not?"

For a few seconds she gave him the hard stare. The I-will-incinerate-you look his mom liked to level on them when someone suggested another rehab stint. *Well, have at it, sweetheart.* Over the years, Matt had become immune to that look.

Taylor may have spent her days bullying witnesses, but he wasn't having it. Any of it. Instead, he met her stare and the room filled with hot tension that could have sparked a fire.

The two of them sat locked in a battle of wills until, finally, she broke eye contact. She leaned forward, slapped her hands over her face then pushed them back through her hair. "I'm sorry. This case. It has me all twisted up. And the baby. My God. Where is he? Is he still alive?"

She was churned up all right. He could see it in the tautness of her cheeks, the stiff, iron grip she held onto her hair with. Taylor, as much as she liked to play the in-control federal agent, was at war. And it was something down deep.

Something ugly.

Matt knew all about that. The buried anger, the soul-evicting sorrow that bore into bones and held on. The unrelenting mental pounding.

This woman? She had it in spades, and after some digging, he suspected why.

"Is this about the baby?" he asked. "Or something else?"

She looked over at him, her hands now gripping the cushion, her eyes direct and maybe...what?...moist? "Of course it's about the baby."

He switched to the seat next to her and set his hand on her back, gently stroking. After a second, she met his gaze and he sensed the change. That crackle of lust sparking between them. Her pupils dilated and she lay one hand on his thigh, inched it higher, closer to his crotch.

All while he kept his eyes on hers, watching her battle demons.

He enjoyed sex as much as the next guy. Easy sex? Even better. Not from Taylor though. He didn't want her this way. No chance. He'd spent months thinking about her and, for once, he wasn't satisfied with a meaningless, easy lay.

He set his hand on hers. "Sweetheart, we have time for that."

She gave him a sexy little smile, but nothing about it moved him. Nope. This Taylor, this facade, left him cold. Even when she kissed him, that wicked mouth hungry on his, soul-kissing him and stealing his air.

Nothing.

He backed away and pressed the tips of his fingers against her lips. "Stop. What's got you worked up?"

Angling back from his touch, she rolled her eyes. "I told you. Bad day." She squeezed his thigh. "You're here to make it go away."

Looking down at her hand, dangerously close to his dick, he shook his head. What kind of idiot was he? Sex on a platter. Right in front of him. And he didn't want it.

No. He wanted it. Just not like this. "Talk to me, Taylor, and I'll fuck you until I split you in two. Is that what you want?"

That got her attention. Her gaze burned into his. Whether it was anticipation or her need to rid herself of the hell churning inside, she got hot and moved closer to him, her hand sliding from his thigh, over his belly to his chest. She tangled his shirt in her fist.

"I keep picturing that infant," her voice shattered like glass against stone. "Buried. In wet, cold dirt. That innocent baby, alone out there, away from his mother and father. Can you imagine? All alone, crying, waiting for someone to help him."

"There are no bones. He didn't die there. Don't torture yourself about something that never happened."

"But he might have died somewhere else, in the exact same way, or...or..."

"Shh." He cupped her chin, kissed her softly. She tasted like scotch and gut-rotting grief. "You can't do this to yourself. If the baby is alive, we'll find him. If he's not, we'll still find him and bring him home, just like Felicity."

In a heartbeat, she was on him. Swinging her leg over his lap, straddling him and kissing him with lip locking desperation and he started to get it. Taylor needed to lose her mind for a while. Cradling her face in his hands, he pushed her back half an inch. "Honey," he said, "this isn't about that baby. This is about your missing sister."

"Oh, God. Not that. Not you too. Just...just shut up, Matt."

"No. Hate to tell you, sweetheart, but I understand you."

"Fuck you. You've known me all of a few days."

She hopped off him, grabbed the glass from the tray, and headed for the kitchen.

"What you don't get," he said, "is that we have the same monster inside. Eleven years ago my sixteen-year-old sister was walking home from school and got snatched off the street. Just gone."

Midway to the kitchen, Taylor stopped and spun back, empty glass in hand. "Oh, my God. No."

He nodded. "We were lucky."

"You found her?"

"We found her."

She stood motionless, taking in the words. *We found her.*

"Please," she said, "tell me she was alive."

Matt stayed quiet. He had to. For a few seconds, at least. To get his head together. Talking about this never brought anything good, only madness, rage, and all those fucking thoughts about fucking evil things that fucking evil people did. So he propped his elbows on his knees and steepled his fingers against each other, concentrating on their perfect alignment. If he looked at Taylor now, he might pick up that kiss where they left off and all that would accomplish would be two people in a helluva hot mess of emotional puke. "It took six months, but we brought her home. They found her in the woods five miles from my parents' house. Those six months made us nuts. We didn't know where she was. When we got her back, at least we knew. She was gone, but we had her body to bury properly."

"That's why you became a homicide detective?"

"Partly. I wanted to be FBI. Just like you." He met her gaze. "Didn't make the cut."

"I didn't know that."

"It doesn't come up much. I wanted to tell you, though." He stood, walked over to her, got right into her space, cupped her cheeks in his hands, felt the warmth flood his suddenly freezing hands.

"When I tell you we have the same monster inside." He squeezed her cheeks, kissed her lips. "Believe it. I watched my mother turn into a grieving drunk and I can promise you scotch and sex won't make that monster go away."

6

———

"*V*ictimology," Taylor said, avoiding Matt's irritated gaze as she refilled her glass. If Matt had wanted to be an FBI agent, he knew the filters of profiling. In his past life as a detective, he'd used them too. "Let's start with what we know about Felicity."

"Really, Taylor? You're not going to talk to me about your sister? About mine? After everything I've just said?"

"Nope. Not talking about our personal shit."

Or his drunk of a mother because Taylor was *not* a drunk. She controlled herself when necessary.

Nope. No way in hell was she going down that long, dark road tonight. Not on top of everything else. "What I *will* talk about is how the hell we're going to find Baby Jarvis, which means we have to figure out who our kidnapper-slash-killer is."

He came up behind her, put his hands on her hips with a sigh. "Felicity Jarvis, age 28, eight months pregnant. Married to Senator Walt Jarvis. College graduate from Cornell, majored in dance. Financial donor to the Kennedy Center Ballet where she once was part of the troupe. She was loaded, thanks to her family's sunglasses empire. Sunglasses." His breath was warm against the back of Taylor's head. "Who knew you could become a billionaire from eyewear? We're in the wrong business."

In the midst of her pain, he was trying to make her laugh. Take the sting off. He really was better than scotch.

And here she was, being a total bitch. *What's new?*

"I'm sorry about your sister," she said softly, her mind jumping all over the place, trying to find something to land on to break the monstrous ice cube filling her chest. It was easier to talk about missing children—dead children—if she didn't have to look Matt in the eyes. "And your mom. Life can be so brutal and unfair."

"Yeah." His hands slid around her and he tucked her into his arms, resting the side of his head against hers. "That's why we do what we do."

Right. Back to business. She couldn't let emotions rule her while a baby was missing. "We have no solid motive for the kidnapping, but Felicity's wealth would be a strong possibility. The senator's position another. There was no ransom request, and the senator wasn't being blackmailed. That we know of," she added.

The selection of the victim often offered a possible motive of the offender, making it easier to get a clear suspect list. Taylor still believed Walt might be guilty; Matt disagreed.

It was going to be a long night.

Sucking down another shot of scotch, she set the glass on the counter and turned to face the devil's advocate holding her in his arms. "Initial contact site between victim and offender?"

"Felicity told Walt she had a stalker and the sightings were always at the same baby store. No statement from her—that he could remember, at least—that the kidnapper made actual contact, but according to Walt, Felicity did mention seeing the man in his silver truck on multiple occasions watching her."

If Walt was to be believed. "According to your client's statement, the stalker was outside the store, a retail place, at night, and Walt believes that's where she was kidnapped. Why there?"

"Felicity was a regular visitor to that store because of the baby, so the kidnapper knew her routine. He planned it ahead of time."

"So was he watching Felicity or the store and she just happened to catch his eye?"

"Good question. No one else reported any man in a silver truck watching them. Let's assume the stalker was specifically after Felicity."

He was good at this. Taylor reached for his belt and began undoing it as she talked. "The kidnapper probably knew the location well, though, if he'd been watching Felicity there. He might even have known someone who worked inside the store and knew the video surveillance was shit in the parking lot."

He didn't stop her eager hands, his fingers going to the buttons on her shirt in a tit for tat. "Which brings up the disposal site. Was that planned too? Did he have familiarity with the scrapyard or was it only after Felicity's death that he searched for a place to dispose of the body?"

The belt was undone. She pulled his shirt out of the waistband of his pants. "The bones were surrounded by a pile of junked building materials. The forensic anthropologist believes Felicity's body was most likely there for the better part of the eight years she's been missing, but actual date of death is unknown at this point. Cause of death is still unknown as well, so we can't confirm or rule out physical or sexual attack. There is even a slim possibility Felicity died of natural causes and was simply dumped. Highly unlikely, but we have to consider every single possibility, and at this time, we have nothing obvious from the bones. Still waiting on the tox screen, but since it's being pulled from bones, it may not be all that reliable. If our kidnapper/killer disposed of her body there, he intentionally used the building materials to hide her. That's planned and organized."

He finished the last button and drew her shirt down over her shoulders. He leaned down and kissed one naked shoulder, murmuring against her skin, "Any correlation between the store and scrapyard?"

She ran her hands under his shirt, feeling his tight abs. This is what she needed. To feel him. To have him feel her.

For both of them to be alive.

A connection between the initial crime site and the disposal site could offer a lead into the killer's personality. "None that I've found. One site is very public. The other is open to the public but secluded. Everyone goes to the store. Not many people go to the scrapyard. Background checks on all the employees of the baby store and scrapyard show no crossovers."

"The risk of being seen at the store indicates a lack of sophistication from the killer, but killing Felicity ensures there's no witness, which *is* a level of sophistication. Is it possible her death was accidental?"

"Anything is possible." God, it turned her on that she could talk work with him. She'd never been able to do that with anyone else. "She could have died accidentally, maybe even during or after the baby's birth."

He eased the shirt the rest of the way off her arms and let it fall to the floor as he stared at her breasts, heaped up like matching Mt. Everests. "Nice bra."

Score. The stupid underwires had been worth it from the way he was salivating.

"Thanks." She gripped each side of his shirt and gave a tug. Buttons flew, exposing his gorgeous chest. "Nice pecs."

He leaned into her, planting his hands on the counter behind her. His eyes were hard, not sexy and teasing like normal. "You sure you want to talk shop when I'm about to fuck you senseless?"

The scotch had taken the edge off of her heartache. Matt's attention had helped as well. "My two favorite things, sex and solving cold cases. Might be fun to see if you can work your magic well enough to make me forget this case for a few minutes."

"Is that a challenge?"

Of course it was. She longed for oblivion. Most nights, she found it in the bottom of a bottle. The alcohol blotted out the horrors of the day, the horrors of her past. Tonight, Matt might be the prescription to doing that. It had certainly worked two nights ago and she hadn't end up with a hangover the next morning.

She lowered his zipper and slid her hand inside, cupping him. He was hard and thick and his eyes momentarily went fuzzy as she gave him a squeeze. "Looks like you're up for it."

With a low growl, he caught her bottom lip between his teeth and kissed her, hard, pushing her roughly against the counter. "No more work talk," he hissed, undoing her pants and peeling them down her legs. He kneed her thighs apart and cupped her ass cheeks in his big hands, lifting her off the floor and onto the counter. "If we're doing this, I want your undivided attention. Forget the case."

He stepped out of reach and shucked his clothes. Took a condom from his pocket and put it on. Taylor stared in admiration and licked her lips. "What case?"

The teasing light finally entered those baby blues and he grinned, yanking her jeans the rest of the way off her legs. "That's more like it. The Mad Dog doesn't compete with anyone —or anything else."

"Are you referring to yourself in third person?"

He grasped her around the waist, lifted her slightly, and ripped her undies off. "Nice panties, but I like you better without them."

She laughed. She couldn't help it. He was...fun. Such a

different energy to this fucking bad day. Plus, she had the control. A part of her liked that. "Get inside me. Now."

He scooted her to the edge of the counter and drove himself inside in one fast movement. Taylor gasped. It felt so good.

No more thinking.

No more remembering.

Just feel.

She spread her legs wider, giving him deeper access and moaning as he accommodated her, his driving rhythm sending her toward a climax quickly.

Too quickly. She didn't want it to be over this fast. "Wait..."

He stopped, buried deep inside her. "What? Are you kidding me right now?" His breath was ragged. "Two, three more strokes, Taylor, and I'm gone. Done."

Her own breath was hit and miss. "I've been waiting for this...all day. Waiting for you. Don't rush it."

Tipping his head back to look at her through half-lidded eyes, he frowned. "But you like it fast."

Boy, did she. Usually. The faster and harder, the easier it was to fly apart and stay gone for a while. "Will you stay with me? All night?"

He brushed back a lock of her hair once again in her face. "Is that what you want?"

She didn't know what she wanted. Not really. What she did know with no uncertainty was that a part of her, the one who had listened to his confession about his sister, wanted to curl up in his arms and never leave that space.

If only she could tell him that. Be that vulnerable. She didn't want to use alcohol or sex to blot out the ugliness. They were simply all she had.

Now she had him. "I want lots of sex like the other night. If you're going to bail after dinner, then you better pony up a few orgasms between now and the time my doorbell rings, but if you stay...we can take things slower and enjoy ourselves."

A slow, wolfish smile curled one corner of his lips. "I can stay. No more scotch though. That's non-negotiable."

If he stayed, she wouldn't need it. The companionship, the distraction, would be enough. "No more scotch," she agreed.

He began moving again, deliberately, inch by inch, in and out, his mouth finding her neck, his teeth nibbling at the sensitive flesh there. "Good. And I'm up for seeing how many orgasms I can give you *before* the delivery boy shows up."

Taylor went lightheaded, succumbing to his mouth, his thrusts, *him*. Wrapping her legs around his waist, she arched into him and hung on as he increased the speed.

Freedom. For once, Taylor let go of everything. Her control. The pain. The need to be perfect. The need to be loved. The need to save her sister.

Gone. All of it. There was only Matt and his skilled hands, teasing mouth, and the way he made her feel.

The orgasm hit with shocking intensity, ripping up her spine. Taylor threw her head back and screamed.

It was a banshee yell, full of grief. At the same time, it was also one of absolution. Of liberation.

Matt froze. As the echo of her cry faded in the kitchen, he swore softly. Poor guy, she'd probably scared him.

But then one of his hands hit the cabinet behind her as he buried himself deeply one final time, every muscle in his body contracting.

As he went over the edge with her, Taylor wrapped her arms around him and tucked herself into his sweet oblivion.

Somewhere his phone was ringing.

Bad to the Bone. Tony's ringtone.

Matt's sleep-addled mind gently prodded his exhausted body awake. He rolled over, fought the heaviness of his eyelids only to receive a blast of sunlight for his efforts. Son of a bitch.

They'd forgotten to close the blinds last night. He slapped a hand over his eyes, plunging himself back into darkness before slowly peeling his hand away. All while Thorogood's *Bad to the Bone* continued to pound him awake.

If Taylor intended to keep up this sexual marathon, he'd need to put her on a schedule. As much as he liked to get laid, he required a certain amount of sleep. None of which had happened on the two nights they'd spent together.

Wasn't this the blessing/curse of falling for a nymphomaniac?

"Oh, my God," Taylor grumbled. "Shut that thing up. What *time* is it?"

He glanced at the blazing yellow numbers on the digital clock and scooped his phone off the bedside table. "Six-thirty."

Good Christ, man.

On the third ring, he punched the screen and flopped to his back. "Gerard, this better be good."

"Morning, sunshine," Tony said.

One thing about Gerard, he'd always been a morning person. Even back in their police academy days when most of the guys wanted to sleep all damned day, he was up and at it, working out, getting in a run, studying, whatever.

Pain in the ass.

Beside Matt, Taylor nudged backward, her warm butt connecting with his hip, followed by the rest of her body pressing into his side. Taylor. A snuggler. Go figure. He tucked his free hand under her, spooning her against him and inhaling that soft, floral scent that, after their first night together, had suddenly become a great way to start his day.

"Do you ever sleep?" Matt said to Tony.

"I do. Quite well, in fact. Listen up, can you run shotgun with me on a case tonight? Shouldn't be more than a couple hours."

"What is it?"

MISTY EVANS & ADRIENNE GIORDANO

"Gay bar. I need a beard. Or would that make you a reverse beard? Whatever. I need a boyfriend."

"I'm not kissing you."

At that, Taylor flipped over, shooting daggers at him. "Relax," he said. "It's my buddy."

That drew two raised eyebrows.

"Undercover work," he assured her. "For a case."

Apparently satisfied, she tucked herself back into his side and rested her head against his chest. She wound her hand through his chest hair and started moving south. At least until he locked onto her wrist. What he didn't need was little Miss Frisky playing with his hardening dick while he talked business with Gerard.

Still, this, he could get used to. And if it took marathon sex, well he supposed he could sacrifice his body for the cause.

"Who's with you?" Tony asked. "Did you get lucky last night? Let me talk to her."

Matt laughed. "Fuck off."

A male voice sounded from Tony's end of the conversation. "Wait. Is that Stephens?"

"Yeah," Tony said, "he's gonna come out and play tonight."

"I need to talk to him." The phone line went silent for a few seconds. "Matt? It's Justice Greystone."

Whoa. Greystone—Grey to his friends and colleagues. Not only was Tony awake, he was already at his office. Jesus. "Do any of you people ever sleep?"

"Only when the ME isn't calling me about a senator's dead wife."

Well, all right. That got his attention. Needing to not be in bed with Taylor and his healthy erection, he slid away from her, flipped the sheet off and set his feet on the floor.

"Why'd the ME call you?"

"She's a friend. Taylor dropped my name the other day. Since it used to be my case, the ME thought maybe I was consulting. I tried Taylor but her phone went straight to voicemail."

Matt glanced back at Taylor, who'd closed her eyes but wouldn't be winning any Screen Actors Guild awards because she was, without a doubt, dropping some eaves.

Such a tangled web.

He couldn't blame her. He'd listen too. And if the medical examiner was calling at dawn, something interesting must be in that report. "What's the news?"

"Felicity wasn't pregnant when she died."

"The anthropologist's report came back?"

"They're still working on the skeleton, but knowing she was pregnant they analyzed the hip bones first."

Matt had learned a few things from Meg, his boss and a forensic sculptor who'd taken classes and studied human bones more than the average artist. One of the lessons was that pregnancy alone wouldn't change a woman's bones.

Childbirth was another story.

Completely bare-assed, he hopped off the bed and headed for the kitchen where, the night before, he'd spotted a pad and pen by the phone. He swung around the breakfast bar, found the pad and snatched up the pen. "What'd they find?"

The sound of shuffling paper came through the phone line. "In layman's terms, they identified small linear indentations on the pubic bones. According to the anthropologist, those dents indicate a woman has given birth."

Which confirmed Baby Jarvis had been delivered after Felicity was kidnapped but before she was murdered. Was he alive when he was born? Or had he died in utero and she'd had to deliver a dead baby?

Jesus. "So, she gave birth. That probably explains why the baby's bones weren't with hers."

"Exactly."

Which meant...*missing baby.* As in alive.

Jesus. "So fucking twisted," Matt muttered.

"What?"

"Nothing. Talking to myself. If I say pretty please, can I get a copy of that report?"

"Only if you come and get it. I'm not emailing it or giving you the file. You get a hard copy. And you sure as hell didn't get it from me. Understand?"

Grey wasn't stupid. He ran his own ghostlike team of operatives and wouldn't put his team—or his operation—at risk for Matt or anyone else. The Justice Team was so far off the books only a handful of FBI big shots knew of their existence. Grey wanted to keep it that way.

"Absolutely," Matt said. "If it gets out, it won't be my doing."

"Then you can have it."

"I'll swing by this morning. Besides, Tony needs a date for tonight. I'll get the deets on that while I'm there."

He disconnected from Grey and jotted a couple of notes to himself. He'd need to research these indentations on the pubic bones. Maybe ask Meg about it.

"What's up?"

He glanced up, found Taylor standing in the opening separating the hallway from the kitchen. Her blonde hair was a tangled mess that she'd pulled over one shoulder and she'd slipped on a fluffy cotton pink bathrobe. This woman. So many sides. Last night it was red silk lingerie, this morning cozy cotton. Either way, he wanted her. Again.

"That was my buddy," he said. "He needs me to work an undercover op with him tonight."

She puckered her lips and a vision of all the places she'd put them filled his mind. He had to stop. Thoughts like this, with a woman like her—a lone wolf who self-medicated with booze and sex—would lead him nowhere good.

"Tony Gerard?"

"You know him?"

"The guy they call Moose? I'm aware he works for Grey's team."

Well, shit. Keeping his promise not to leak the anthropology report meant not leaking the Justice Team's existence. Obviously Taylor knew all about that. Particularly since Grey had allowed her use of his name to fast track a forensics report. But how much did she know about what the Justice Team actually did?

She smiled at the consternation on his face, obviously reading his thoughts. "I worked with Grey before he blew his career out of the water. And, yes, I know about his team of spooks and what they do. Sort of, anyway. I'm not sure anyone knows the complete truth, except Grey. Now, all you have to tell me is what he said about those bones that had you hopping out of bed at 6:30 in the morning. It must be something important."

"Honey," he said, "you're gonna lose it when you hear this one."

7

*T*aylor couldn't believe her eyes or the fact that Matt —*Matt!*—knew Grey's secret hideout when she didn't.

The armory looked deserted and tragic. The outside of the main building was dark, the bricks stained. Weeds grew in the cracked sidewalks and driveways around the place and the fence sported plenty of debris around the edges.

No lights shone in any of the windows, even though it was a cloudy morning, the sun completely hidden behind a storm system rolling in off the Atlantic. If Grey and his crew were inside, no one would know. There were no cars outside, nor welcome signs of any kind.

"You're sure this is the place?" Taylor said as Matt's car grumbled under her ass by the closed front gate. "I knew it was an undisclosed, hidden location, but I had no idea it was straight out of a *Mad Max* flick."

"Flick?" Matt made a face. "No one uses that term anymore. What century were you born in?"

"Shut up." Her sister had loved that word. She'd used it all the time after hearing it once on a rerun of that old show, *The*

Brady Bunch. They'd had a video player and tiny TV in their room and every Friday night, Isabel would haul her sleeping bag and stuffed toys onto the floor and ask Taylor to put in a flick for her. To this day, Taylor couldn't stand Brady Bunch reruns. "What I want to know is why Justice Greystone would trust you with this location."

Matt looked incredulous. "Why wouldn't he?"

Taylor hid her irritation. *Because he didn't trust me.* "So you're working for him, now?"

"I told you, I'm helping out a friend. Tony and I work well together, always have. Grey knows Walt hired me and that you're on the case. He's giving us equal time. When he couldn't get hold of you, he called me. Why is this bugging you so much?"

She'd let her phone die. Because of Matt. Hell on a stick, what was the matter with her? She never, *ever*, let that happen. Her team might call her with a break in a case. Mer might.

Her mom might call to say they'd found Isabel.

I will find Izzy, come hell or high water.

Matt was screwing with her. Taylor rubbed her forehead, fighting the tension there. Before she could come up with a witty retort, however, a voice came over the speaker at the gate.

"What the fuck do you want?"

Mitch Monroe. Perfect.

Matt held up his middle finger to the video camera overhead. "Your boss called me. Now open the fucking gate and let us in."

"No one enters until they answer the question. Superman or Batman?"

Matt rolled his eyes. "Batman, duh."

A moment of pause, then a buzzer sounded and the gate rolled open.

I will never understand men. "You know Mitch, too, huh?"

The car shot forward, rumbling as Matt jetted around

toward the back of the building. "Jackass? Yep. He's a real peach."

Taylor unplugged her phone from the car's charger. "He doesn't like you either."

Matt pulled up next to the back door. "You discussed me with Jackass? That's either incredibly sweet or really weird."

The engine cut off and Matt hustled around to open her door. She was already out, pocketing her phone, before he got the chance and he rolled his eyes again. With a possessive hand on her lower back, he guided her to the door.

A big, tall man with dark features met them. "About time. Did you have to do your hair and paint your nails, princess?"

Matt flipped him the bird. "Good to see you, too, Moose."

So this was Moose, aka Tony Gerard. His nickname fit—big guy, well over six foot and filled out like a football linebacker. His eyes missed nothing, taking in Taylor and her still-wet-from-the-shower hair.

She held out a hand. "Agent Sinclair, FBI."

His big paw grabbed hers and gave a firm shake, then he motioned her in. "So you're the Feebie I've been hearing about."

Matt pressed on her back and she stepped across the threshold, seeing a wide-open warehouse with a smattering of old Army desks and metal chairs. "And you're Matt's gay friend," Taylor said with a straight face. "I've heard about you too."

Gerard grinned and he and Matt exchanged a standard male-to-male greeting that involved some violent backslapping and knuckle bumping.

The sound of the door closing behind them echoed off the high ceiling. Mitch sat on the top of a desk where another former FBI agent, Caroline Foster—now Caroline Foster Monroe—typed efficiently on a computer. Caroline and Mitch, in a rather bold move, had gotten hitched in Las Vegas after closing a case together. Beck had told her about it, but Taylor had forgotten until now.

He Who Shall Not Be Named in Meredith's world was throwing a stapler up and catching it, over and over again. Caroline reached out and snatched it in midair, slamming it back onto the desk.

"You're no fun," Taylor heard Mitch mumble as he sent her and Matt the stink eye.

Grey walked out from behind a screen and hailed them, while a skinny guy in a tricked-out ergonomic office chair watched the three giant screens in front of him and ignored everyone.

The smell of deliciously dark coffee hit Taylor's nose and she realized she was running a quart low since they hadn't stopped for any. "Any chance I could get a cup of coffee?" she said to Gerard.

"Sure, Mitch'll get you one."

Mitch's response was a rude gesture. To Taylor, he pointed at his T-shirt. "Look! I got this after visiting the Smith with you."

The white letters on the black shirt read, "Black is my happy color!"

Taylor couldn't help it. She laughed. "Well, aren't you a ray of black?"

Grey, refilling his cup with some coffee at a counter across the room, shook his head.

Caroline stopped typing and glanced back at her. "You're responsible for that shirt?"

"Not really, but sort of," Taylor admitted. "We studied a Nevelson sculpture at the Smithsonian the other day that was all black. Mitch needed a reason for the color choice."

"Black equals greatness," Mitch told Caroline, pointing to himself, "and we all know how great I am. A natural match."

Caroline huffed out a patient sigh and stood to shake

Taylor's hand. "I wish I could say I remember you from my time at the Bureau, but I don't think we ever met."

Taylor shook her hand as Matt and Tony headed for the coffee maker, Grey saying something to Matt too soft for Taylor to hear. "I was a lowly field agent at that time," she said to Caroline. "Just getting started. I was lucky enough to work with Grey a couple of times. I knew all about you, though. Crack sniper, SWAT team, manager. You were—are—Wonder Woman."

Caroline smiled. "I hear you're filling that role now."

"Not even close I'm afraid." She lowered her voice and said to Mitch, "How is it that you're now buddies with Matt? I thought I wasn't supposed to trust him, and here he is with inside intel into the Justice Team's hiding place."

Mitch gave her a look that suggested she was stupid. "Moose and Grey think he's all that. Not me."

"Matt is a good guy." Caroline shooed Mitch off her desk. "Tony saved Grey's life and Matt is a friend of Tony's. Grey trusts him because he trusts Tony."

"Sinclair," Matt called to her from across the room. He was holding up a donut in one hand and bagel in the other. "Breakfast?"

God, he was handsome, his hair ruffled and his shirt untucked on one side. He seemed totally at ease in this abandoned armory with a bunch of renegade FBI agents and a former Supreme Court officer. Normally when working a case, she had little appetite. This morning, she was starving.

Maybe it was all that exercise last night. "Bagel."

Grey waved her over to the tech center and Matt met her there with the bagel and coffee.

"Matt explain why I called him?" Grey asked her.

"My phone died." She shot Matt a scolding glance, but he seemed completely clueless about why. "I apologize for being unreachable."

"No apology necessary. I was worried you might be bugged,

so this may have worked out for the best anyway."

Yeah, maybe.

Matt's hand was on her back again as he downed a long john and mumbled a hello to the tech guy who lifted a finger in return greeting.

The professional in Taylor wanted to scoot away from Matt's possessive hand, not let the others see that there was anything personal going on. Yet, it was apparently obvious they'd already figured it out from the way they'd all looked at her when she'd walked in.

A part of her cringed at that, Mer's voice chiding her. The rebel in her told Mer to take a hike. "You told Matt this had to do with Felicity's autopsy," she said to Grey, "and you didn't want to discuss it over the phone. What's going on?"

As if he had mental telepathy, Grey pointed at the center computer screen and the tech geek automatically hit two keys and *voila*, the ME's report appeared.

Grey's finger went to a specific line on the report. "We have confirmation that Felicity did indeed give birth before she died."

The ME had sent the report to Grey first. Or maybe Taylor had the same thing waiting in her inbox. "So the baby could still be alive."

Matt scanned the report. "The kidnapper could have targeted Felicity to get the child."

"I'd say it's more than a strong possibility," Grey said. "And if that's the case, my earlier suspicion that Senator Jarvis played a part in his wife's disappearance may have been wrong."

Her gut may have been wrong, too, and the baby might be out there somewhere alive. Her brain made the calculations— the Jarvis child was no longer a baby. He'd been missing for approximately eight years. "If I find the child, I can find Felicity's killer."

"She was definitely murdered." Grey pointed to another

section of the report and the tech guy zoomed in on it. "The forensic anthro found a nick on the hyoid bone in Felicity's neck."

A second screen showed a photograph with an enhanced view of a bone. A red arrow pointed to a thin scratch.

The coffee she'd sipped turned to acid in Taylor's stomach. "Her throat was cut."

Grey nodded, looking grim. "Official cause of death at this point is speculated as loss of blood from the throat wound. For a nick to happen that deep, her carotid was severed. Dr. Smith, our ME, believes it was more of a jab, causing a deep laceration and the cut on the bone, than say, a slice across the trachea."

Tony joined them, holding a plastic knife. His hand went up, the tip poking the side of the tech guy's neck, right under the jaw. "Like this?"

"Hey!" The tech guy jerked his head away. "What the hell's the matter with you, a-hole! I'm not your reenactment bitch."

"Jesus, Teeg," Gerard said, drawing the knife away. "Don't be such a pansy."

Grey waggled his fingers at Gerard and the man brought the plastic knife to Grey's throat in the same spot. "The weapon had to be sharp, but thin, and went through the carotid all the way to the hyoid."

The weapon could tell her a lot about the killer. "Did Dr. Smith have any idea what type of knife was used?" Taylor asked.

Gerard let his hand fall. Grey pointed at the report one more time. "She couldn't list anything conclusive, but she did have an idea."

"What?" Matt asked. He'd finished his donut and had a spot of icing on the corner of his mouth that Taylor wished she could lick off. "Must have been a skinny blade from the size of that cut. Either that, or only the tip of the knife made that nick."

Grey sipped his coffee as the third screen filled with

pictures of a particular type of blade that made Taylor's gut tighten. "Seriously?"

Matt's jaw jumped. "Is that a scalpel?"

"Sure is," Grey confirmed. "It's difficult from a single, tiny nick to determine a conclusive weapon, but I've found it's rare for Dr. Smith to be wrong about her hunches."

Matt blew out a long, slow breath. "Surgeons, the ME, all the medical teaching hospitals in the area...hell, even veterinarians use scalpels. Might as well be a hunting knife that Wal-Mart sells for all the good that does us."

Taylor didn't see it that way. "It's a starting point we didn't have before."

Grey wasn't a smiler, so when his lips twitched slightly, Taylor took it as a sign he agreed with her. From the look in Matt's eyes, he did too.

"I'll take a copy of the report to Walt first thing this morning," Matt said. "Taylor, you're welcome to come with me. Then I suggest we pay a visit to Felicity's OB/GYN. Start ruling out any and all medical personnel who came in contact with her."

Taylor already had her no-longer-dead cell phone out, hitting the speed dial button for Beckett as she walked away from the huddle around Teeg.

"Greetings, fair lady," Beck said, yawning. "I had a twenty on you calling before four a.m. You did stay up all night working on the Jarvis case, didn't you? I thought for sure you'd have orders for me before now."

She'd been up, all right, but not working per se. *Damn Matt.* She glanced back and saw he was still talking to Grey and Gerard. "We need to attack this from a fresh angle. Let's see what we find if we start investigating the missing child instead."

"But we don't know anything about the kid—what he looked liked, how much he weighed. Hell, we don't even know if it was a boy or girl."

"The Jarvises were expecting a boy. It's in Felicity's medical records that Grey got his hands on during the initial investigation. Check out that report. And we do know a few things about the kid based on his parents' genes. He was—*is*—"

"Is? You really think the kid is still alive?"

"I'd bet my badge on it and we can find him. He's a Caucasian child who most likely has blond or light brown hair and blue eyes. His father has a cleft in his chin; the kid will too —simple biology. And at Felicity's last checkup, the child was estimated to weigh nearly eight pounds. He should have been born in September or October of 2009. I want a list of every baby boy in this area born during those two months."

Beck let go of a whistle. "You got it boss. When will you be in?"

Taylor watched as Matt started striding toward her, the same look of grim determination on his face as she felt in her chest. "I'm going to pay Walt Jarvis a visit and then I'm heading to the hospital. I have a baby to find."

Walt was in a meeting. Despite his wife's remains being found and needing to plan a proper burial, the senator took his civic duty seriously and was up on the Hill with the Senate majority leader.

Which didn't please Matt, and certainly pissed off Taylor, but ballsy or not, she wasn't about to go busting into the highest-ranking United States senator's office to interrogate a grieving husband.

"He didn't kill her," Matt said, firing up the Mustang after they left Jarvis's office.

"I want to believe that, but he's not acting the grief-stricken husband he claims to be right now."

"First of all, she's been gone nearly eight years. Second of all, men grieve differently. We're all about distraction, keeping our minds active so we don't have to deal with pain-in-the-ass emotional crap. That's how ninety-percent of us operate." He whipped off a toothy smile. "Being the crack investigator you are, you should know that."

"I do know that. And, being the crack investigator *you* are, you know the husband is always a suspect." She returned the toothy smile. "So, I'm still looking at him even though my murder weapon may be a scalpel and I have a missing child on my hands."

Yeah, the husband always got a look. Matt himself had done the due diligence on that before signing on for this assignment. A dead woman was one thing. A dead pregnant woman was another. It made his insides boil and he had to be sure, before getting into Walt's corner, the man was innocent. Nothing in Matt's investigation indicated Walt could be a murderer.

Nothing.

And Matt had torn the guy's life apart. Then did it again. If Walt had secrets that Matt didn't find, the man had done a bang-up job of hiding them.

Taylor seemed so sure though. At least she had been until the scalpel had become their smoking gun. But even though Walt had no history of education or work experience where he might have used one, Taylor still liked the man as a suspect.

She was too professional to base her suspicions on simply disliking him. Not Taylor. Justice had to prevail, regardless of her own feelings about a person.

And her close rate was a thing of beauty. You didn't get to be the FBI's hottest closer by making mistakes.

Which made him wonder if he could have missed something with Walt. He drove on in silence, his mind whirling, working through every bit of intel he could remember.

He's clean.

Had to be. If he wasn't, Matt would be faced with another career failure and it would only compound the fact that he hadn't made the cut for Quantico.

No. The guy was clean. He knew it. *Knew* it.

He merged into traffic and headed for St. Mary's Hospital. "We'll hit Felicity's hospital first. Then we can visit the rest. The others are a long shot, but you never know. Hell, they're all long shots. If she was in labor, her kidnapper wouldn't bring her to a DC hospital, period, especially not where her OB is on staff. Not a senator's wife whose picture had been all over the news. He—"

"Or she. Could be a woman."

"Or she, would take Felicity some place out of the way where she wouldn't be recognized."

"Our unsub may have had medical training and delivered the baby himself, then killed Felicity and dumped her body."

Another possibility.

Taylor was in full-blown agent mode. "When you investigated, did you find evidence of marital problems?"

He glanced over at her. "Why are you harping on Walt if you think the killer had experience with a scalpel?"

"Walt had the finances to hire someone to kidnap and kill her. Maybe the baby was a bonus. White, male babies bring good money on the black market."

She had more experience with that then he did, but it still made his skin crawl. "That's a horrible suggestion. Do you have a reason I don't know about from your investigation that suggests Walt and Felicity weren't happily married?"

"No. Which is why I'm asking. Everything I have indicates they were happy. No mistresses, no boy toys. Just an up-and-coming power couple about to have a baby. These two were the modern day Kennedys. Everyone loved them."

"And that makes you suspicious?"

"Is anyone's life *that* perfect? He did remarry as soon as he could have her declared legally dead. Maybe Ann was waiting in the wings the entire time."

She had a point there. But he didn't want to believe the

Jarvis's marriage had been fucked up enough that Walt would hire someone to get rid of her and sell their child. "It seemed too perfect to me, too, at first. When I couldn't find any fucking around, I switched to the possibility of abuse."

"And?"

"Nothing. I went through bank records, credit card receipts, medical visits, everything. If either one of them was spending money trying to cover an affair or spousal abuse, I couldn't find it."

"Neither did Grey when he originally worked the case. I've reviewed all those avenues as well and found nothing suspicious." She reached into her briefcase and pulled out a thin manila folder. She flipped open the file and studied something inside. "According to Felicity's OB, her mother never went with her, and with Walt's schedule, he missed a lot of her prenatal appointments. We should probably talk to her doctor and any nurses who were on staff at that time."

"Good thought, but been there, done that. I spoke with her OB last year. He said Felicity went to the appointments with Walt or alone. She liked her privacy. From what I've heard, if she ever got bad news, she didn't want anyone else hearing it. She was worried about tabloids."

"Oh, Lord. It wasn't as if *People* magazine was banging down their door."

"Whatever, Taylor. Her husband was a public figure. She wanted her privacy."

Matt pulled into the hospital parking garage, grabbed the first available space and they made their way through the maze of security that would allow them onto the obstetrics floor. The various elevators and multiple entries with crisscrossing hallways should have scared off would-be criminals. A guy needed a damned map for the place.

"Now that we're here," Taylor said, "I remember how tight security is."

St. Mary's was a private hospital smack-dab in the middle of DC that catered to politicians, high-ranking White House officials, big shot CEOs, you name it. If they had pull in this town, St. Mary's Hospital was the place to go. It took private to another level.

The first time Matt had come here, he'd been shut down cold. Didn't even make it past the first security gate. Walt Jarvis had rectified that right quick by taking care of the necessary HIPPA forms that would give Matt access to his wife's files.

Taylor stepped off the elevator with him and was greeted by another security guard in front of the giant wooden doors leading into the OB unit. No commercial grade doors here. After a quick check of IDs, the guard pushed a button and the doors swung open.

"Nurse's station is on the left," he said.

"Thank you." Taylor hooked her badge on her waistband and adjusted it so anyone within three feet would see it. She knew the drill and Matt was equal parts turned on and envious.

Not so much the FBI part, but the badge. So much of his life had been spent around law enforcement that the badge had become a part of him. At least until the homicide rate in DC spiked and the emotional toll wore on him.

Still, he missed it. The ability to serve.

He followed Taylor to the nurse's station, a series of oversized counters and desks that formed a large circle in the center of the ward. An older woman, Marge, according to her nametag, in a pair of purple scrubs sat entering something into one of the computers.

"Good morning."

Taylor forced a smile, but the fatigue in her eyes, the puffiness, told a different story. The dead on her feet kind.

"I'm Special Agent Taylor Sinclair." She slid the badge from her waistband and let the nurse take a good long look. "This is Matt Stephens."

No badge for Matt, but Taylor wasn't stupid. Alerting the nurse he wasn't a fed would mess up a potentially good opportunity for fact gathering.

"How can I help you?"

"We're investigating the Felicity Jarvis case."

"Oh, that poor woman. I saw they found her remains. What a tragedy."

Taylor nodded. "We're re-interviewing anyone who may have had contact with her. I know it was a long time ago, but is there anyone here who might remember her?"

"Me," Marge said. "I've been here fifteen years."

Now this was lucky. "Great," Matt said.

"I can't really give you any information though. Not without permission."

Matt waggled a finger. "If you look it up, you'll see Senator Jarvis has given permission to share his wife's medical records with me."

Marge put her fingers to work on her keyboard, then studied the screen. "Can I see some ID?"

Matt whipped out his driver's license and Marge checked his personal info against the hospital's files.

Handing him back the license, she nodded. "I'm not sure how much I can tell you. I might have to get my supervisor."

"If you need to, you can do that, of course. In the meantime, Senator Jarvis indicated this was the hospital where Felicity's doctor—Morton—had privileges. Is that correct?"

"Still does. His office is right down the street at the TriCenter Birthing Clinic. That's where he delivers most of the babies. He's the best. The running joke around here is he should have top level clearance considering all the high-powered babies he's delivered."

"I see," Taylor said. "He wasn't her original doctor though. She switched to Morton."

"Well, I'm not sure about that, but I wouldn't be surprised."

"Why is that?"

The nurse glanced around, then lowered her voice. "Felicity came through here a couple of times toward the end of her pregnancy. I remember it because it was a few weeks before she disappeared."

"Yes," Taylor said. "I saw in her file that she was admitted."

Marge nodded. "She was having trouble urinating. They had to put a catheter in to alleviate the problem. It happened twice. She was admitted both times. She hated the hospital. Dr. Morton explained the advantages of having her baby at the birthing center and she decided to go there for her delivery. She signed up for the Presidential Suite, I heard. I used to help out with their Lamaze classes and I know Dottie Hernandez, the manager. She was thrilled to get Felicity signed up."

"Really?"

A tired smile quirked Marge's lips. "The Presidential Suite is big bucks, but it's the best money can buy. It's the one the VIPs use. They have to pay out of pocket for most of it because insurance won't cover the entire cost."

Taylor looked at Matt who rolled his eyes. Who cared what the room looked like as long as they got a healthy baby out of it? "So," he asked, "Felicity wanted to see the Presidential?"

"Yes. And the next day, I saw that Morton's nurse called and reserved it for October 12th."

Matt cocked his head. "Scheduled it? Like a dental exam?"

Poker face firmly in place, Taylor contemplated that. "She wanted a C-section."

Another nurse swung into the pit area and Marge paused. The second nurse grabbed a chart from one of the bins on the desk and walked off. Once the woman was out of earshot, Marge looked up at Matt and Taylor again.

"Some of these young mothers with their careers and powerful husbands schedule their babies like they do a haircut. Felicity was rich and wanted to be sure she had dibs on that suite, so she scheduled a C-section with the anesthesiologist, doctor, and the birthing team she wanted. I remember her the few times she showed up for the Lamaze group. She was likeable enough, but so spoiled. She had been a ballet dancer, you know. Said she didn't want to wreck her hips, even if she never danced again. She rarely showed up for the classes, but I guess when you can hire a team to make the birthing process fast and easy, you don't worry about learning how to breathe through a contraction."

This nurse had obviously remembered Felicity as more than the senator's missing wife, and a scheduled C-section at a posh, private birthing center only confirmed that Felicity had not been some disgruntled housewife who'd run away and ended up dead. They had her bones and confirmation that she'd been murdered after the birth of her child. But why? Was the murderer here? Someone who'd interacted with her, knew she was close to term, and kidnapped her to get to her baby?

At the exact moment the thought filtered through his brain, Taylor looked up at him, her eyes direct and...knowing. *Yeah, babe, right there with you.*

Without making a show of it, he tilted his head toward the door. They needed to get out of there, huddle up and figure out what their next move was.

But Taylor was one step ahead of him. "This birthing center —you mentioned it's just down the street, correct? And the person in charge? What was her name?"

"Dottie Hernandez."

Taylor gave him that look again and he felt it too—the tingle at the back of his scalp. Another lead to chase down. They were getting closer.

"Thank you," he said to Marge, tapping the counter before he followed Taylor, loving the cocky sway of her hips and shoulders. She smelled a lead.

And he was right there with her.

8

*D*ottie Hernandez was climbing out of her Cadillac with a bag from the corner deli when Taylor and Matt caught her in the parking lot of TriCare Health Birthing Center. The Center served three major area hospitals with specialized birthing units that catered to the wealthy and those classified as high-risk, such as twins and other multiples.

"Mrs. Hernandez?" Taylor called. She'd seen Dottie's photo on the Center's website on her phone and recognized the woman's thinning red hair and the flashy gold cross around her neck as the manager hustled onto the sidewalk, her large, designer handbag slapping against her dark green skirt.

"Yes?" Dottie looked over and smiled, the edges of her eyes crinkling. "Oh, you must be the Alexanders. I'm so sorry I'm late for your tour. Let's go on in. You're going to love it here when the time comes."

Matt started to correct the woman, but Dottie was already at the wide glass entry doors, struggling to balance her load. Matt ran to catch up with her and open the doors.

She looked over and winked at Taylor. "Chivalry is not dead! A fine, young man you have here."

Taylor winked back. "He has his moments."

Matt made a face at her behind Dottie's back and Taylor grinned.

Dottie might have been barely five foot tall and in her fifties, but the clinic manager could move. Taylor and Matt had to hot step it to keep up with her as she swept past the receptionist, throwing out their last name to the woman, and motioning them to follow her.

"They need to sign in," the receptionist called. "They need visitor badges!"

"I'll take care of it," Dottie called back. "I've already kept them waiting long enough!"

She had her keycard out and swiped it at her office door before Matt and Taylor rounded the corner. The clinic was done in soft pastels and lots of pictures of newborns floating in clouds. Taylor supposed the decor reassured pregnant mothers that birth was a heavenly experience.

Maybe it was here.

Matt motioned Taylor through the open door of the office, then followed. "I think there may have been a mistake," he said.

Dottie dumped her lunch and purse onto a credenza behind her desk. The wall above the credenza held multiple certificates and awards—she'd been a nurse in her younger years and had gone on to get her master's degree in business. Taylor also spotted an undergrad degree in family counseling.

The desk was cluttered with files, a computer, and a dozen or so pictures of various families. Dottie snatched a couple of visitor passes from a desk drawer. "No, I assure you, there's no mistake! We're the finest birthing center this side of the Mississippi, Mr. Alexander, and my tardiness is not the norm, nor should it reflect poorly on the center. I was at a meeting all morning and it ran over. I promise, we have the best doctors and birthing teams anywhere, including Johns Hopkins, and I'm going to make it up to you for being late for this appointment. We'll take excellent care of your wife and child. I'll see to it myself." Her big smile and crinkly eyes slid to Taylor. "How far along are you, dear?"

"We're not the Alexanders," Matt said.

"Oh, heavens, did I get that wrong?" Dottie shoved papers off her old-fashioned calendar blotter, a chubby index finger sliding along the days of the week. "I'm so sorry! You're Mr. and Mrs. Dillinger, aren't you? For some reason, I have you down for this time next week. Goodness, I apologize again. Please follow me. I read your intake form, and I truly believe that the Presidential Suite is the perfect room for you and your family."

Matt opened his mouth and Taylor jabbed him in the side. "We'd love to see it."

Dottie missed Matt's frown since she was already out the office door. "Right this way!" she sang out.

"What are you doing?" Matt murmured as Taylor snapped a visitor badge onto his jacket lapel.

She took the other badge and clipped it onto her own jacket. "It's called undercover investigation. Surely, you've heard of it."

He followed her out the door, still speaking sotto voce. "We have to identify ourselves."

"We will." *Maybe.* Taylor's gut told her she'd get farther with this woman if she played the part of an expectant mother, and time was of the essence. "Let's see the Presidential Suite first."

She expected him to continue expressing his dissent, but instead he patted her ass and gave her that wicked grin. "Well, then, after you, *Mrs. Dillinger.*"

It was a total fishing expedition, but playing an expectant mother for a few minutes was more fun than heading back to her office with no further leads. "I've found in the past," she said softly as they followed Dottie down the carpeted hallway, "that getting into the mind of the victim can be as effective as the criminal's when it comes to solving cold cases."

"The Presidential Suite is in the West Wing," Dottie called back to them as she rounded a corner. More cherub babies and clouds lined the walls. "Each of our suites offers a bed for the father, a seating area for family members, and a large birthing tub for the mother as another option."

A few steps ahead, she continued to chatter away as Taylor and Matt hung back, scanning the place. Here and there, they saw a nurse or other non-medical employee rushing in and out of doors.

Matt put his arm around Taylor's shoulders. She wasn't sure if he was simply getting into the part of her husband—God help her—or this was a continuation of that morning's need to touch her. Good or bad? She couldn't decide.

They passed through a set of wooden doors and entered the West Wing. *How appropriate.*

A sign on the wall indicated the Diamond and Platinum Suites were to the left. The Presidential Suite to the right.

The smell of cinnamon and chocolate filtered down the hall, as Dottie, still barreling ahead of them, pulled out her keycard once more. Just outside the suite doors was a small alcove with a sink, refrigerator, and coffee maker. The coffee pot was full, the scent of cinnamon and chocolate stronger here. A plate of fancy cookies sat next to the pot.

Dottie unlocked the suite, then beamed and held a hand out toward the tray. "Cookies are delivered fresh daily to the family. Can I get you a cup of coffee? It's my favorite flavor from Fresh Market. All organic and fair-trade, of course. We only want the best for our patients." She started pouring cups of coffee without waiting for an answer. "There's juice and flavored waters too, if you'd rather have something non-caffeinated."

Matt accepted a cup of the flavored coffee and eyed the cookies. "This really is the Taj Mahal for having a baby, isn't it?"

Dottie was still smiling, but managed to give him a serious

look at the same time. "We are *the* top-rated birthing center on the East Coast, Mr. Dillinger, and our twenty-one awards attest to that fact." She handed Taylor a cup of coffee. "It's rare that the Presidential Suite is open, but you picked a good day for your tour. Cookie?"

Taylor hadn't finished her bagel that morning so she grabbed a chocolate chip cookie from the selection. "Felicity told me you were the best."

Dottie's brows drew down as Matt helped himself to three cookies and gave her a questioning look. My God, the man could put the food away.

"Felicity?" Dottie looked confused.

The cookie was still warm, a chunk of dark chocolate melting on Taylor's tongue. "Felicity Jarvis. She recommended this place to all of her friends, you know, before..."

She let the rest hang. Dottie set the plate of cookies on the counter, her face going pale. She genuflected and rubbed a thumb across the gold cross at her neck. "God rest her soul. I heard the news last night. So you were friends with Felicity?"

Taylor stared at the cookie in her hand, acting sad. God would strike her down one of these days. "She was so young and beautiful. Just an amazing ballerina. I know she was glad you were here for her, to make the delivery easier. Such a shame she didn't get to use the suite."

None of it was a lie.

Dottie looked away. "I'm so sorry for your loss."

The art of undercover work was to know when not to raise suspicions. "So this is the suite," Taylor said, taking her cookie and coffee across the threshold. She needed to get Dottie back to her happy place, put her back at ease before she said anything else about a dead woman.

Dottie hustled past Taylor, lifting her arms. "This is it!"

The Hilton had nothing on the Presidential. Soothing earth tones and designer furniture met her eyes. The room they entered was set up like a living room/kitchen combo. There was even a fireplace with a large window on each side that showed a lovely view to the east. Two doors led off to what Taylor assumed were a bathroom and birthing room.

"Dang," Matt said, coming up next to her. "How much does all this cost?"

"The birth of a child is a blessed event," Dottie said with an admonishing tone. Taylor wondered how many soon-to-be fathers had signed on the dotted line, regardless of the cost, because of this woman's sales pitch. "We cater to our VIPs so they can enjoy it to the fullest."

She walked them through the three separate living areas and told stories about the wonderful staff and experiences the center offered. Taylor had a wistful moment, imagining a life where she wanted kids and could afford a setup like this to have them in. What was it like to live a charmed life full of volunteering and babies, and no thought of murder or missing children?

She would never know that life.

Matt, finishing up his last cookie, gave her a smirk behind Dottie's back and the wistful moment passed.

He thought they were wasting their time by the impatience on his face. Maybe they were. But having a more complete picture of Felicity's life, and speaking to some of the people involved in her pregnancy, was the best way Taylor knew to find the needle in the haystack that she needed to bring this case home.

The clock was ticking.

And there was no way she was handing this over to Leo.

"Is this your first child?" Dottie said to Matt.

Mad Dog didn't miss a beat. "Yes, ma'am. But I'm hoping to talk her into a whole passel of them."

Oh, he was good. Maddening, but good. Dottie laughed and Taylor felt heat in her face.

But a part of her wondered...

No. She didn't have time for a serious relationship or kids. Besides, she'd sworn a long time ago not to bring an innocent child into this world, much less a whole *passel* of them. The world was cruel and even parents with the best of intentions starting off could end up jaded.

Like hers. "One might be too many at this point," Taylor said under her breath, fingering the tweed on one of the rocking chairs.

"Don't be silly," Dottie insisted, patting her shoulder. "Children are a miracle. Believe me, once you hold your baby in your arms, you'll want more."

Taylor felt queasy and set her cup on the coffee table. "Well, thank you for the tour, Mrs. Hernandez. We really should be going."

"It was my pleasure." Dottie moved to the door, all business again. "I have a packet of information for you in my office, and if you're considering scheduling this suite, I encourage you to do so soon. It's always in high demand and availability fills up quickly. We're already pretty much scheduled out for the next eight months."

Eight months? Wow. That was a lot of pre-planned births.

Taylor and Matt paused at the alcove to wait for Dottie to lock up. "We do have several other suites," she said, "and I can always check their availability for you as well, but really, the Presidential is the way to go, especially since this is your first."

Matt nodded. "Looks like fun to me."

Fun, right. Probably was for everyone but the mother.

Dottie started off down the hall and Matt put that protective, guiding hand on Taylor's lower back as they fell into step behind her. "Even if you decide not to go with the Presidential," Dottie said over her shoulder, "you'll want to attend our information night tomorrow here at the center. We go over all the details of selecting your birthing team, the info about our

Lamaze group meetings, and we tour all of the available suites. We also set up your birth portfolio."

"Birth portfolio?" Taylor asked.

"Our VIPs always have a portfolio." They left the West Wing and turned the corner heading for Dottie's office. "For security measures, you know."

No, she didn't. "What security measures?"

Dottie raised a finger in the air and shook it. "The safety and security of our patients is our number one priority. Along with the birth plan for the medical team, the portfolio contains the necessary personal information about the mother and father, along with their picture IDs. We have a list of relatives and friends our parents have okayed to visit. This allows the staff to keep a close eye on everyone who comes and goes."

They arrived at Dottie's office door, and she turned to them before entering. "We run a large facility and have to keep track of every person entering and leaving for the safety of our patients and most especially, the babies. Some of our patients attract a lot of media attention and it wouldn't do for us to allow a reporter or some crazy fan to sneak into the clinic and breach the privacy of the families we serve, now, would it? It's happened at other facilities, you know, but never here."

Interesting. With all this security, and yet, she and Matt had just taken a tour under false identities. "Felicity didn't mention anything about a portfolio," Taylor said, following Dottie into the office and handing over her visitor badge, "or maybe you didn't have those when she booked the Presidential Suite?"

"Yes, we did." Dottie accepted Matt's badge and dropped both into her desk drawer. "I was the one to institute the portfolio system when I took over as manager in 2008. I raised the bar on the standards and security protocols the minute I was promoted."

The woman picked up a cheery yellow folder and handed it to Taylor. "You'll find all the information and forms you need in here, along with my card. Call any time. I'm happy to answer any questions you might have, and please consider attending the informational meeting tomorrow night. We can start your portfolio, sign you up for Lamaze classes, and get your insurance lined up, even if you aren't quite decided yet on which suite you prefer."

Matt gave Taylor that look again, suggesting she come clean. She ignored him. "Thank you. We'll be there."

"The meeting starts at 7 p.m.," Dottie called after them as Taylor took Matt's hand and dragged him out of the office. "There'll be cookies!"

Outside in the parking lot, Matt opened Taylor's car door. "What the fuck was that?" he said, but he was grinning.

She slid into the seat and stared at the building as he went around to his side of the car and climbed in. "If you wanted to kidnap a senator's pregnant wife and steal their child, where better to get all the pertinent information you needed than from their birthing portfolio?"

"You think it was someone here at the clinic?"

"Possibly." Taylor glanced over at him and he was still looking at her with that what-the-fuck face. "All my instincts are screaming that this is about the baby, not Felicity. I could be wrong, but I think it's worth pursuing. If I don't have any stronger lead by tomorrow night, I've got nothing to lose but to show up for that meeting. We can ask Dottie more questions and see if there's anyone else who remembers Felicity."

"What if the real Dillingers show up?"

"I'll make sure they don't."

"How are you going to do that?"

She gave him a confident smile. "I'm a crack FBI agent. I have my ways."

His grin widened. "I am totally turned on right now."

She reached over and stroked a finger across his jawline. "You should be."

Without warning, he reached across the seats, grabbed her by the back of the neck, and dragged her toward him. His lips crushed hers and his free hand fondled her breast through her shirt and bra.

The rush of playing pretend and pulling it off pumped hard in her veins, so Taylor felt him up as well, giving his thickening erection a good squeeze through his slacks.

Next thing she knew, they were in a full-on make-out session and she was about to climb into his lap when her phone rang with Beckett's ringtone.

"Ignore it," Matt said, his hand tugging on her ponytail as his teeth grazed her neck.

"Can't. I'm down to forty-eight hours to solve this case before it gets handed over to Leo the shark."

She shifted her body and answered her phone. "Make it quick," she said into the phone.

Matt shifted the lapel of her white shirt over and kissed his way down the top of her breast and she had to force herself not to moan.

"Got a list of the births during the timeframe you asked for, boss," Beckett said. "And I've got at least nine kids who match the profile you gave me."

Matt had found his way to her breast, pulling aside her bra and licking her nipple. "Good...job. I'll be...in the office..." She had to bite her lip as Matt sucked her breast into his mouth, twirling his tongue around her areola. "Holy shit—I mean...uh, shortly. I'll be in the office...shortly."

"Are you okay, Taylor? You sound—"

She didn't listen further, disconnecting the call and tossing the phone over the seat. "I hate you"

"No, you don't. Now, shut up and let me have my way with you, Mrs. Dillinger."

Taylor didn't argue.

· · ·

At exactly 7:00 p.m. Dottie strolled into the common area of the birthing center where four other couples had congregated with Matt and Taylor. Or, as they were currently known, Randy and Adela Dillinger.

Taylor, as promised, had done her thing and paid a little visit to the Dillingers, explaining the situation and the FBI's need to temporarily use their names for an investigation and voila, Matt and Taylor were suddenly six weeks pregnant and searching for options outside of a hospital birth.

Jeez, this was nuts. As a single man who'd had precisely two relationships he'd even considered possible long-term material, he didn't have a clue what kind of questions an expectant father would ask. And, Taylor? God love her, but she hardly seemed the type to be skilled in this area. Give her a Glock and a ripe murder and she was an ace. Motherhood?

He glanced at her, studied the curve of her cheek, the way she nibbled her bottom lip as she read one of the birthing center brochures. *Yes.* Definitely motherhood material. All that assertiveness and intensity, the need to right wrongs, she'd be fierce as a mom, but good. Protective.

She leaned over, slid a hand across the back of his shoulder and got close to his ear. "Relax, Mr. Dillinger. Before I kill you."

Shit. Apparently his apprehension about this whole thing was showing. He always hated undercover work. Too many things could go wrong at too many times. For some, it got their juices flowing, him? Nah. He enjoyed the puzzle of working a case, asking questions, figuring the angles.

Dottie breezed into the room. She wore a navy dress and had pulled her reddish hair back into a severe bun. Matt figured her for mid-fifties, but she could have been older. These days, with all the Botox and other treatments women put themselves through, who knew?

"Hello, everyone," Dottie said, her gaze moving to each couple as she offered up a cheery smile. "Thank you so much for being here." She looked over at Matt and Taylor. "Welcome back! Lovely to see you."

"Thank you," Taylor gushed. "We're so excited!"

Matt looked over at her, marveling at her ability to be a tough-talking FBI agent one minute and a gushing expectant mother the next.

A blonde woman across from them reached for her husband's hand and squeezed it. The two of them exchanged a look and the man nodded. Clearly they'd just experienced a non-verbal message, similar to what Matt and Taylor had done yesterday at the hospital. But that had been business. This? This was personal. What would it feel like to be here and not pretending? To experience the nerves and excitement of planning the birth of your child.

He tried to conjure an image of it. Of him coming home, to Taylor, her belly full and round with his baby. Would he rub his hands over her, maybe talk to his child? If it was a boy, he'd probably roll a football or baseball over that belly just to get things rolling in that direction. Couldn't hurt, right? A girl? Well, she'd get kisses. And maybe a softball. Daddy's girl.

"Okay," Dottie said, "let's head on back and we'll get started."

She led them to the back of the center to a sitting room large enough to seat ten. The muted paint and thick carpeting gave the place a homey feel and Matt immediately understood why they used this room for open houses. Everything about the place screamed upscale, comfort, and luxury.

Right up Felicity's alley.

Dottie waved them all to the cluster of sofas and chairs near the fireplace she stood in front of. Matt moved to the one closest to Dottie, spotting the dark blue binder with the birthing center's logo on the front—fancy-shmancy raised lettering—sitting on his chair.

"If you would," Dottie said, "open your binders to page one.

This will tell you a bit about our process. There are forms to be filled out and given back to us so we may reserve your spot in one of our amazing birthing rooms. From there, you'll be assigned a caseworker who will help you put together your birthing team."

While Matt opened the binder and skimmed the first page, Taylor raised her hand. "Can I ask a question?"

Such a polite little girl. Matt nearly rolled his eyes.

"The caseworker," Taylor said. "Is she a medical service provider?"

"She is actually a social worker with a master's in social work. She's working on her PHD so she is more than qualified."

"Excellent," Taylor said.

The blonde woman once again shot Taylor a look, clearly irritated over the interruption to Dottie's spiel. *Well, sister, get used to it.*

An older woman wearing giant diamond stud earrings stuck her head in and Dottie stepped away to speak with her. A minute later, the woman left as quietly as she'd entered and Dottie resumed her pitch, highlighting items contained on the first page, top doctors, nurses with a minimum of ten years experience in labor and delivery, Lamaze coordinators, all of it handled via the caseworker.

Ever the curious one, Matt skipped ahead and flipped the page. Page two listed ten anesthesiologists. Ten. Looking into all of them would probably take more time than Taylor had. Although, depending on how long they'd been working with the center, one of them could have been Felicity's choice. They'd have to look into that.

Taylor raised her hand again.

If Dottie was irritated with the interruptions, she hid it under a gentle smile. "Yes, Mrs. Dillinger?"

"The anesthesiologists, are we able to pick anyone from the list?"

"Of course. On the next pages, you will find full bios on each doctor. Our caseworker is happy to facilitate a meeting, if you would like."

A meeting? With the drug guy? What did it matter if you liked him or not as long as he got that epidural rolling before the woman nearly broke in two?

"Excellent," Taylor chirped again.

Sweet, cheerleader Taylor was almost too much and Matt couldn't contain his smile.

"What?" she said. "You know how I am. I want who I want."

"I hear you, girl!" the dark haired woman on the other side of Taylor said.

"Right? I mean, we're the ones doing the work, we should get to choose."

Matt and the husband exchanged a glance and both shook their heads.

"Unless," the blonde snipped, "you're doing a natural birth. Then it's not an issue."

"Wow," the dark-haired woman said, "you're brave. I want the drugs. Load me up."

Taylor high-fived the woman.

Good God, he needed to get her out of here before she exchanged numbers with the dark haired chick. Or got clocked by the blonde.

"All that can be decided later," Dottie said. "For now, I'll give you a few minutes to peruse the books. We have two case-workers and our Lamaze coordinator here tonight to answer questions. To save time, we'll split up and have two couples meeting with caseworkers, one touring the facility and the other with our Lamaze coordinator. We'll rotate everyone through."

"Excellent!" Matt said, mimicking Taylor.

She smacked his arm, but grinned and, shoot, she was damned cute like this. Something in his chest hitched. All this baby talk and pretending to be a couple was making him soft. Still, he leaned over and kissed her. Barely a peck compared to the make-out sessions they tended to have, but Taylor squeezed his arm and let the kiss linger for a few seconds.

Yep, that was them. Just a happy couple in love.

"Oh, you two," Dottie said. "I knew you were special the minute you walked in here."

Ninety minutes later, Matt escorted Taylor from the birthing center, blue binder in hand. Right now, that item might be their biggest lead.

In the darkness of the parking lot, he opened the passenger door for his bride, swatted her very fine ass and waited for her to slide in before walking around to the driver's side.

"You're pretty good at this husband thing," Taylor said as he fired up the Mustang.

"Ha. Good one."

"No. Really. Just the right amount of attentiveness balanced with teasing. You're a natural."

"You're not so bad yourself with all the excited new-mother questions."

"I thought that blonde was about to throttle me. She had a monster stick up her ass."

Bye-bye cheerleader Taylor.

He pulled out of the lot while Taylor used the light on her phone to read through the binder. He shot a look at the page she stopped on—the anesthesiologist list. "We need to cross-check all these doctors and see if any of them are Felicity's. It might be a lead."

"It says two of the caseworkers have been there since '05 and '07, respectively."

"That's good. We'll look into them too. And the Lamaze meetings. I saw somewhere in the case notes that Walt and Felicity had attended a class the night before she disappeared. That might be something."

"Did you notice the woman talking with Dottie?"

"The tall one with the diamonds?"

"That's her. Who the hell was that?"

Taylor pursed her lips. "I wondered that too. She didn't stay long, but I assume she works at the center. All in all, Mad Dog, I'd say this little excursion netted us a few possible leads."

"Yep." He held his hand up to high-five her. "Good work, Special Agent Sinclair."

"You too, Mad Dog. We make a good team."

He waggled his eyebrows. "In more ways than one."

9

"*W*hy Walt and Felicity?" Matt said, nuzzling Taylor's ear as she stuck her key in the lock of her condo. "What was special about Baby Jarvis?"

It was a question they'd already hashed over at dinner. After the meeting, they'd both been starving and hopped up on adrenaline from their little undercover sting. Matt had driven her by her place to change clothes and then he'd taken her for a bite to eat at a hole-in-the-wall diner where they'd both consumed copious amounts of breakfast foods, of which the place specialized in serving any time of day.

"Comparatively speaking, nothing," Taylor said, letting them in and entering the code in her security system. "When you look at the type of people that attended the open house tonight, none of them stood out in respect to the others. There were two politicians with their spouses, the weather guy from Channel 6 and his wife—she was the blonde. Next was the lead actress from that new hit Fox TV show with her equally famous actor boyfriend, and a guard from the Wizards basketball team with his wife. If the group Walt and Felicity attended these meetings with was anything like tonight's rich and famous crowd, I don't know why the Jarvises, or their kid, would stand out to a kidnapper."

She tossed her keys on the side table and kicked off her shoes. Matt, ever the gentleman, helped her off with her jacket. She unstrapped her gun holster and placed the weapon next to her keys.

It felt good to have someone take care of her. To feed her, to chauffeur her around. To talk cases and brainstorm ideas about her unsub with. She sighed as he tugged her shirt out of her waistband and ran his hands under it, skimming over her stomach.

"There was no ransom note, no phone call." He kissed her neck and brushed his thumbs across the undersides of her breasts. "Cementing the idea our perp was going after the baby, but why take it before it was born? Why not wait until Felicity gave birth and then kidnap the child?"

Taylor had already given that some thought. "Too much security around the baby once it's born. It was their first child, they'd be watching it every moment, and would probably have a nanny with her eyes on the kid as well. Felicity, however, didn't even have a bodyguard. Snatching her out of a parking lot was a cinch compared to nabbing that baby once it entered the world."

Matt undid the button of her jeans, grazed her hipbones with this thumbs. "Messy, though, having to dispose of the mother once the baby arrives."

Maybe it was sick that they could talk about dead mothers and missing children while undressing each other, but Matt had taught her in the past few days that using sex as a way of dealing with the barbarity of her job was better than alcohol. "Messy, but not that difficult, as evidenced by what happened."

Matt backed her up against the side table, planted his hands on either side of her hips and hit her with his pretty blue-eyed gaze. "You think Dottie is in on it?"

For the first time in her career, she could talk shop with a lover, not only because he was working the same case, but also because he wasn't turned off by the gruesome details that were part of her everyday life. "Whoever targeted the Senator and Felicity had a golden opportunity to gain all the information they needed through the birthing center's setup. Those binders, complete with pictures of the parents, as well as their medical histories and personal information, are goldmines."

"So what's our next step?"

She traced the line of his jaw. "*My* next step is to go back tomorrow morning and question Dottie in an official manner."

"What, no Lamaze class?" He grinned. "I was looking forward to coaching your heavy breathing."

"You don't start Lamaze until you're farther along. Like six or seven months."

"No more Mr. and Mrs. Dillinger, then, huh?"

"We still have tonight," she teased, although she wasn't sure why she'd said that. Acting like a married couple for the undercover op was fun, sure, but continuing that act now was silly and dangerous. They weren't in a serious, long-term relationship.

Were they?

She shook off the thought. No way. Mad Dog Stephens didn't do long-term relationships. Neither did she.

The nature of their long workdays and inability to share details about their jobs were to blame. Burnout was high, the people they worked with knowing more about them than their own families.

Plus, Matt was a player. She'd done enough digging on him to know his reputation with women preceded him.

And Taylor never let anyone get close to her. Not anymore. Not after Isabel.

Matt kissed her, long and slow, pulling her out of her tangled thoughts, and she melted a little. He could be rough and aggressive with her or soft and careful. Like he could read her mind and knew exactly what she needed at any moment.

"I think I could get used to coming home to this every night," he murmured against her lips.

A little thrill ran through her, and she automatically squashed it.

But that didn't feel right either. She liked having Matt in her bed, eating meals with him, having someone to talk to. She'd never dreamed they'd still be together after that one-night stand at the conference, much less working on the same case as partners. But here they were, and damn if they weren't good together. Who knew what other craziness they could share?

"I kinda like it, too," she admitted, threading her fingers through his hair.

He drew his face back a few inches. "But?"

She started to say, "but we both suck at relationships" and a dozen other pat excuses that formed on her tongue. Instead, she just smiled at him. "No 'but'. If you want to keep this arrangement going for awhile and see where it leads, I'm game."

Another grin, complete with smoldering eyes. "Are you talking our working arrangement or our personal one?"

How could she resist those eyes? "Either. Both."

"I notice a definite lack of scotch since we had our chat the other night."

"Crack investigator, you are. I heard what you said. There are other ways to deal with pain than with a bottle. I'm working on it."

He swept her up in his arms, lifting her off the ground. "You just made my night, Agent Sinclair. My whole week, in fact."

She let out a surprised whoop and wrapped her legs around his hips as he carried her toward the bedroom. As they passed the living room, an inkling that something wasn't right hit her.

A blade of light cutting across her leather ottoman in the otherwise dark room.

"My laptop is open."

He stopped, flipping on the hall light. "So?"

"I always shut it down and close the lid before I leave in the morning."

"Maybe you forgot today."

She never forgot. "Set me down."

He did and then proceeded to follow her into the living room to her desk. The lid of her laptop was up, the screen lit with the mountain scene she used as wallpaper. "Even if I didn't shut this down, the screen saver should have kicked in and put the computer in sleep mode."

"Maybe it ran an update or something."

"I have it set up to do that in the early morning hours when I sleep."

She glanced around at the rest of the room. Nothing else seemed out of place. Plunking down in her office chair, she noticed her file on the Jarvis case was minimized but open. She clicked on the blue folder and the mountain scene morphed into a document with her notes on the case. "And I never leave a file open."

"You've been stressed out and distracted, Taylor."

But it was her routine. She checked emails while she drank her coffee, scanned the latest news, and jotted down notes on things that had popped into her mind overnight. Then she always—always—closed out all the files and shut down the computer. "They got around the password."

Matt peered over her shoulder, arms now crossed. "You think someone was here, in your place, looking at files on your computer?"

The tone of his voice suggested she was paranoid. Spinning in the chair, she nearly knocked him over as she took off for her bedroom. First, she snagged her gun from the hall table. "Let's check the basement."

Matt—good man—didn't question her further, drawing his own weapon and making the circuit with her, going from one room to the other in silence, then down to the basement level in case the unwanted visitor was still there.

No visitor, but Matt did gawk at her Isabel wall. Who wouldn't? It contained every newspaper article, every lead the cops—and Taylor—had ever chased. Pictures of Izzy, a map of their neighborhood, Izzy's profile, along with lists of possible suspects, none of whom had ever panned out.

Matt studied it in silence, took her hand and led her back upstairs. When he continued not to say anything about her Izzy wall, she pulled him into her bedroom and showed him the window that led to the alley. "The curtain is pushed back."

He still wasn't convinced. "Still doesn't prove anyone was here. Is anything missing? Broken?"

"No, which leads me again to the fact they were searching my files."

Her gaze caught on her chest of drawers. One corner of the top drawer stuck out a fraction, as if someone had opened it, and then when they tried to close it, it had jammed. The chest of drawers had been her grandmother's and often stuck on one side. Being used to it, Taylor knew to give it an extra push to close it.

Her stomach dropped. She flew across the room to the drawer and jerked it open.

"What is it?" Matt asked, once again looking over her shoulder.

Her relief came out in a whooshing sigh as she picked up her badge. "I store my badge here when I'm home. I left my credentials tonight since I was pretending to be Mrs. Dillinger."

"And they're still here."

"But someone was in this drawer, Matt. They were on my

computer, and they went through my things." A shiver of repulsion went through her, the old memory about Isabel and *that* night rearing its ugly head. Her chest filled with ice.

She stumbled toward the bed and Matt caught her arm, easing her down to a sitting position. He kept holding onto her as he sat next to her and pried the gun from her fingers. "Taylor, look at me. Breathe."

The panic kept rising, crushing her, filling up her throat. "I...I can't."

Strong hands tipped her head down between her knees. "Who's your favorite FBI badass ever in the history of the Bureau?"

What? Why was he asking her that right now? "I don't know."

"Yes, you do. Tell me who you idolized."

Her brain tried to focus, the memory of the night Isabel disappeared losing its hold. "I guess...I guess it's Grey."

"Really? All the directors and fancy profilers, and you choose a guy who lasted less than five years and quit?"

He was teasing her, but she felt the ice melting. She could swallow again. "Yeah, so? He was the best behavioral analyst I ever met. I only worked with him a couple of times before he and Mitch torched their careers, but I learned a lot from him. He always has a system, a process. It works. I use the techniques he taught me. That's why my close rate is so high."

Matt helped her sit back up, his forehead creased with concern. "Better?"

She was.

"Remember what I said about those demons?"

Brushing hair out of her face, she nodded.

"That little reaction you just had to the idea that someone broke into your place is related to your demons, isn't it?"

Absolutely. "Someone was in here, and it wasn't a street burglar. It was someone who worked around my security system, looked at my notes on the Jarvis case, and found my badge in that drawer."

"We kicked the hornet's nest tonight and one of them came flying out."

She nodded. "And it wasn't Dottie. Whoever this was had the tools and expertise to almost get away with it."

"Whoever it was now knows you're not Mrs. Dillinger."

Her legs shook when she stood but she went for her phone anyway. "I'll call one of my friends in forensics and have her dust for prints. I doubt we'll find any."

Matt followed her. "Aren't you going to report the break-in?"

"No. I don't want whoever it is to know that I'm aware they were here, but you're right. The jig is up. I also don't want my bosses to know that I went outside FBI procedure, played undercover agent without their okay, and let a potential kidnapper and murderer break into my place where he got by my security system and password protected laptop to read my notes on the case. God, Mer will kill me."

There would be more hell to pay if that happened, and as it was, she was nearly out of time on her 72-hour deadline.

She started to make the call when Matt stopped her, already speed dialing someone on his phone. "I've got this."

He spoke to one of the sisters he worked for, and twenty minutes later, a gal in ratty designer jeans and boots that cost more than Taylor's paycheck, showed up on her doorstep. "Charlie," Matt said, introducing them, "this is Taylor. Taylor, Charlie."

Charlie nodded at Taylor in passing, yawning her way into the place with a black bag in hand. "You owe me," she said to Matt, snapping on gloves and laying out her tools on the kitchen table.

"Add it to my tab," he replied.

Taylor felt a spurt of jealousy that quickly left. It was

evident as the two worked side-by-side that there was nothing between them except a friendly camaraderie.

An hour later, Charlie Schock confirmed that the only prints inside the condo were Taylor and Matt's, but Matt had found faint pry marks on the bedroom window where the intruder had forced it open.

After showing Charlie out and promising to buy her two tickets to the next Washington Capitals hockey game, Matt turned to Taylor. "Pack your bags. You're staying with me tonight, and first thing in the morning we're going back to the TriCare Health Birthing Center to talk to Mrs. Hernandez and everyone else involved with that group."

It took a serious set of balls—not to mention skill—to break into an FBI agent's place, bypass said agent's security on both the home and laptop and not even take anything.

Except information. Which further complicated things because there was no way to analyze what the intruder garnered on the excursion.

At least Taylor hadn't walked in on it. Images of her popped into Matt's mind. Opening the door, surprising the perp, her chest blooming red from a bullet and...nope. Not going there.

Emotions, right now, wouldn't help him. Logic. That's what he needed.

He unlocked the front door of his bungalow, a foreclosure in Farimount Heights he'd nabbed at a great price. He waved Taylor in.

"It's not fancy," he said, "but it's home."

She strode by him, stepped into his small living room with the oversized windows and fireplace and spun back to him. "Matt, you surprise me."

"Why's that?"

"I pegged you for a city apartment guy. You know, footballs

laying around, milk crates. Instead I get a tidy bungalow in the burbs with comfy looking furniture, stained wood trim and hand-scraped oak floors."

Before he'd bought this place, he had been that guy. On his 31st birthday he came home alone, wasted from a night out with the boys, and something changed. Call it maturity or boredom. Being unsettled. The revolving door of women in and out of his life didn't make for emotional stability.

In short, he'd had enough. The hangover the next day didn't help.

He set Taylor's overnight bag down and walked to her. "For the record, the trim and floors were here when I bought it and my mom helped with the furniture and curtains. I was fine with bare windows, but apparently that's unacceptable. As for the tidy part," he shrugged, "I don't know. I guess I'm not a pig. I like order when I come home."

She seemed to like that answer—*score*—because she ran her hands up his chest, brought them to rest on his pecs. "Another thing we have in common."

Oh, they had things in common all right. He dipped his head and kissed her, softly at first, but Taylor had something on her mind and it clearly required use of her tongue. And what an amazing one it was. She swept through his mouth, worked her way over his jaw and down his neck and his body responded. Her being so close, she hadn't missed that response, and brought her gaze to his while a wicked smile lifted her lips.

Damn, she got him hard.

She cupped his crotch, adding a squeeze. "Hi."

"Hi."

"Bedroom. Now."

Then she was on him again, kissing, arching into him, taking everything up a notch in that Taylor way.

"Or," she said, "maybe we won't make it to the bedroom."

If he wanted, he could put her against the wall and ram

himself into her. That's what *she* wanted. He saw it in her hot gaze and the way she touched him in ways his mother would definitely not approve of.

But something felt...off. Forced. Not on his part. On hers. Completely fucked up, that. Between their crazy chemistry and how good they were together, the last thing a roll in the sack should have been was forced.

He stepped back, holding his hands wide. "Whoa, babe, slow down."

She went for his shirt buttons and slammed her lips against his. "No. This'll be good. I know it."

A woman on a mission.

He didn't doubt it would be. He wanted her, she wanted him. One plus one made two. A grand, stupendous, supremely amazing two and suddenly he felt the need to analyze?

Yes.

Shit.

Still with his hands up, he didn't move. Just let her have at him, kissing, dragging her hands over his body, getting him harder and harder until his skin almost burst. This wasn't right though. Intellectually, he understood that if he touched her, he'd be cooked. He'd shove her pants down, bend her over the couch and that would be it. They'd rock each other's world, for sure, but as much as she believed it, she didn't need sex now. Sex, in his opinion, was currently her replacement for a scotch neat.

And he wasn't having it.

Not so much the sex, but the being used part.

Finally, she backed away, flapped her arms. "Jesus, Matt, am I kissing a stone? What's the problem?"

"*I'm* not the issue."

"Well, it sure seems that way."

"Talk to me, Taylor."

"About?"

"Your sister for one."

She huffed out a laugh. "Again with this? I want you to fuck me stupid and you want to talk about my missing sister. A man not interested in sex. Is it me? I mean, I have no family and my only friends are coworkers. It's me, isn't it? I'm a freak."

Fuck her stupid. Interesting word choice.

"Don't be ridiculous. You're not a freak and I'm extremely interested in having sex with you. Believe me. I'm just not your whipping boy."

"What does *that* mean?"

"If I handed you a scotch, would that suffice?"

Her jaw locked and her green eyes turned stormy, the wave of emotion she'd been struggling with for two hours letting loose again.

Bull's-eye.

She poked her finger at him. "Fuck you, Matt."

Anger, he realized, was Taylor's friend. Anger, she knew what to do with. It hid the pain, the torment.

The rest of it, all that shit sitting below the anger was what he wanted—needed—to see. He'd been there. Knew what it felt like to obsess over a missing sister. How the pain and guilt burned under the surface, eating away like acid from inside. For him, the not knowing had lasted six months.

Then his sister was found, her body wrapped in a sterile bag, which was all kinds of wrong, and his anger shifted to rage. Rage that didn't play nice with a guy about to join the police force and carry a gun.

A year of therapy didn't cure him, but it helped him figure out how to process his emotions. How to channel the negative energy into something positive.

Taylor whirled away from him, heading for the door. Nuh-uh. They were getting somewhere here and, as much as peeling back her anger would suck, he wanted to know her. What drove her. What *tormented* her.

And that meant dealing with the feelings about her sister.

He caught up to her and blocked the exit. "No way. You're not running."

"I'm not *running*. I'm pissed."

"Fine. Whatever. I won't give you sex or scotch so you're taking off? That's healthy."

She curled her fingers, shook her fists at him, gritting her teeth. "What do you want from me?"

"I want to know what the hell this is."

The blast of his words, or the yelling, forced her back a step. "What are you *talking* about? Last I checked, you liked sex. With *me*!"

She didn't know the half of it. "I love sex with you. It's like Christmas every day."

"So, why, all of a sudden, are you Dr. Phil? Newsflash, Matt, I'm not your patient."

"Never said you were, but I'll be damned if you're gonna use sex with me to transfer your pain and anger. Do us both a favor and tell me what was going on with you back at your place. The panic attack."

"My house was broken into!"

"Yeah, but you're a crack FBI agent. I've seen you in action and you don't panic. You're always on and sharp. Your house or not, you get the job done first. So, yeah, I'd like you to admit that you use scotch and sex and, well, me, to work out your rage."

10

---

*T*aylor tried to find the right words. The ones that would get Matt to stop talking and let her have her way with him.

Except the way his bright blue eyes had gone steely gray, she knew there were none that would accomplish that feat. She could strip naked and do a pole dance right here and he'd keep pestering her to talk about her *demons*.

It had started to rain and the *tap-tap-tap* of drops hitting the window echoed loudly in the strained silence between them as she stared Matt down. Why couldn't he cooperate? When was the last time a man had turned her down when she was trying to jump his bones?

Maybe I'm losing my touch.

Not only did her ego smart, her pulse beat an erratic staccato, fear and loathing cramping her stomach. She chalked it up to the break-in; a home invasion violated a person's feelings of safety.

Vulnerability. She hated it. Hated feeling violated.

"It's been another long, shitty day," she said to Matt. "I want to forget about it for a few minutes, that's all."

He leaned on the back of the couch. "It's more than that and you know it."

Anger. She needed to hold onto her anger since she couldn't drown it in scotch or sex. Keep him away from the truth. "You think prying into my mind, trying to force me to confess some deep, dark secret, is going to make me all better?"

"The guy who kidnapped your sister, did he break into your childhood home? Is that why you had the panic attack?"

Two strides. That's all it took to close the distance between them and slap his face.

The shock of it startled her—she'd never slapped anyone before—and she jerked back. Rubbed her hand. "Oh, God, Matt. I'm so sorry. That was...that was... Oh, hell, I don't know what that was."

He didn't seem shocked at all. Not even vaguely surprised as he rubbed his cheek. "Not the first time I've brought out the violent side in someone, sweet cheeks."

Standing, he grabbed her hand and ran his thumb across her smarting palm. "Look, it's none of my business, I get that, but I care about you, Taylor. You're driven, successful, and at the top of your game. But underneath that, you've been shoving a lot of pain away and I *know* that pain. That little panic attack at your place, the alcohol...this need to blot out the past and cases you work on. It's not healthy. You're going to explode one of these days or have a nervous breakdown."

An intervention. Great. Just what she needed. "My reaction at my place was a mild anxiety attack, not a full-blown panic attack. Believe me, I know the difference. I had them until I was 21."

His face actually showed a modicum of surprise. "So you've suffocated your pain enough to function until something like the break-in occurs. What happens when it rears its ugly head during a shootout or hostage situation? You could be endangering your team as well as yourself."

"We work cold cases, not hostage situations."

"Stop with the excuses. You're not immune to life-threatening job circumstances because you do most of your work behind a desk. You're in the field plenty, interviewing people and digging around, like tonight."

"I haven't been undercover in years."

"Fine." He threw his hands skyward and started walking away. "You win, Agent Sinclair. Your tough outer shell is in place, because God forbid you allow someone who cares about you to get close enough and discover you're human."

...someone who cares about you...

How much did he care?

Anger resurfaced as she watched his back recede. "Hey." She followed him down the hall to a closet where he grabbed a pillow and blanket. "Just because I don't want to talk about my missing sister doesn't mean I'm not human. I do have feelings, you know."

"Bedroom's that way." He pointed offhandedly and started back toward the living room. "I'll take the couch."

She trailed behind him, the cramping in her gut intensifying. "Matt—"

"Don't." He dumped the pillow and blanket on the couch and pointed a finger at her. "Just don't. You don't have the same feelings for me, and you've made it clear you only want me around because I have resources for this case. Oh, and sex. I'm a good distraction, right? Worth a couple of solid orgasms, at least. So you don't have to deal with your emotions. I've been there and done that and watched the people I love destroy themselves over it. I know where it leads. I have no interest in going there again."

The words were like blows. He might as well have struck her like she'd done to him. "That's what you believe? That I'm using you to solve this case?"

He met her eyes. "Aren't you?"

Oh, my God!

But she could see the hurt in his eyes. He wasn't just saying that. He believed it.

"I'm working with you because you're a damn good investigator." She stepped toward him and reached out to grab his shirt lapels, but he backed up. "Come on, Matt. You know I..."

Oh, boy. She was in a pickle now. If she admitted how she felt about him—how *did* she feel? That alone was scary—their relationship would spin off into something completely different. A deeper relationship.

Commitment.

She'd have to tell him about *that* night. About Isabel. Because that's what people did in relationships, real ones at least. They talked about their pasts, their families.

Was that why she never got close to anyone? Had she blamed her job all these years for being the culprit, when in reality, it was just an excuse to keep from having to explain what happened that night?

Damn straight she had.

Did it matter? If she didn't admit to Matt that she cared about him too—a fucking lot—he'd continue thinking she was a cold-hearted bitch who'd used him for his *resources*.

Taylor bit the inside of her bottom lip. Matt continued to stare at her, waiting.

Shit.

"It was my fault." The words bubbled out. "That night... Isabel was kidnapped because I left her."

They were such simple words. Such terrifying words. Tears sprung to her eyes and she dashed them away.

"That's the child in you talking," he said softly. "You know, as an adult, that it wasn't your fault. No matter what you did or didn't do that night, you were only a kid. There's nothing you could have done to prevent what happened."

Completely true, but so goddamn false. "I left her, Matt. I left her alone."

She paced to the far end of the room where photographs of Matt and his siblings hung. In one picture, he couldn't have been more than six or seven, but she knew it was him from that grin. From those crystal blue eyes.

Even back then, he'd had the Mad Dog charm.

She touched the frame, staring at six-year-old Matt. "All I wanted for my ninth birthday was a tent. Not a kid's tent with Barbie or Tinkerbell on it. I wanted a grown-up camping one so I could sleep outside and pretend I was a great explorer. I had a little telescope to look at the stars and everything."

She felt Matt come up behind her. He didn't touch her, just stood looking over her shoulder at the same photograph.

Taking a deep breath, she went on. "I begged Isabel for weeks to stay outside with me. Our dad offered to but I knew he hated the idea. He and mom weren't campers, not even back-yard stuff. Isabel was seven and scared of the dark, so I teased her relentlessly about being a baby and tried bribing her with all kinds of things. She loved this one stuffed animal I had, a rabbit, so I told her she could have it if she slept just one night out in the tent with me. She wanted it pretty bad."

The memory of Isabel's face lighting up when Taylor had handed her that old, floppy rabbit surfaced, making Taylor smile. "She was fine until the sun went down, then she wanted to go back inside. Mom and Dad wouldn't let me stay out there alone and I was furious that she was going to blow that perfect night for me. I told her to give the rabbit back and that I was never going to speak to her again. I made other threats too. Like she couldn't come in my room during storms and stuff when she was scared anymore. So she gave in."

The old anxiety rose in her throat, cutting off her air. Tears leaked down the sides of her face.

Matt turned her around, wiping at her tears, his brows

furrowed. "That's normal sibling stuff, Taylor. I did far worse with my brothers and sister when I was that age."

Taylor couldn't meet his eyes. A part of her wanted to fall into his arms and accept his support. The other part—the one she'd used for years to guard against breaking down—needed distance.

Run.

She stayed rooted in place, not doing either but clamping down on the waterworks. Her nose was already running, and her mascara was probably all over her face by now. In a minute, she'd have to make a mad dash for the bathroom or use Matt's shirt as a tissue.

"Once she finally fell asleep, I had to pee, so I ran back in the house. While I was in there, I stole some cookies from the pantry, thinking I'd put them under her pillow as an apology because I was feeling guilty. When I got back out to the tent, she was gone. That fast."

Matt pulled her into his arms, his embrace reassuring as he rubbed a hand up and down her spine. "Did the police have any leads?"

She put her face in the crook of his neck, knowing she was ruining his shirt with mascara and probably a little snot, but not caring. "I thought at first she'd gotten up and followed me inside, so I went back in to check. When I couldn't find her, I looked out her bedroom window and saw a silver pickup driving away from our side yard. It was an old Ford, beat up and listing to one side. I thought I saw a blond head through the passenger window. I didn't get the plate number on the truck. I'm not even sure it had one. I underwent hypnosis when I got older, trying to recall anything about it that would help the police find her, but they never did. They found the rabbit, though. She'd dropped it on the sidewalk right outside our property near the hedge."

"I'm so sorry," Matt whispered. "You're lucky the bastard didn't hurt or kidnap you too."

"I've gone over the old case files a dozen times and investigated every sexual predator and criminal who lived within a mile radius of us during that time. I can't find him, but I know he's still out there." The one thing she never said out loud formed on her lips. "Isabel might still be alive. Even if she…"

Her throat tightened again, and she swallowed the fear away, focusing on Matt's hand, so gentle, so reassuring on her back. "Even if she's not, I have to find her. I have to know what happened to her."

They stood together for a long moment, then Matt took her hand and led her to the bathroom where he turned on the shower and helped her strip off her clothes. Under the warm water, she bawled like a baby, letting all the years of grief and guilt have their way with her while Matt soaped her up and washed her off.

After dressing her in one of his old T-shirts, he tucked her into his bed and disappeared into the kitchen. When he came back a few minutes later, he handed her a cup of tea and crawled into bed next to her. They sat, side by side, Taylor sipping the tea and listening to the beat of her heart, normal once more. "I care for you. A lot," she admitted. The room was dark. It was easier to say things in the dark. Isabel had taught her that. "I care for you more than anyone I've ever been with. Just so you know. And that for me is terrifying."

Matt hugged her close. "I know."

As her eyelids grew heavy, he took the cup from her hands and let her fall asleep in the solid protection of his arms.

The following morning, Matt dropped Taylor back at her place to grab her car and followed her to work making a request along the way. Yes, he'd *requested* rather than told her to call him when she planned on leaving the office. Telling a woman like Special Agent Sinclair to do anything would only get him in a shit-ton of trouble. And he already had his hands full with her.

He headed out of DC and jumped on the 495, hauling ass toward his office. Nothing about this case was coming together. Sure they had bits of information, but none of those pieces fit together to form a picture.

His puzzle was far from complete. It happened sometimes. He simply needed to sit down—alone—in a quiet room and study what he had.

The morning sun was high in a blue sky, glaring off the vehicle in front of him. A silver truck. Of course. According to his research, twenty-three percent of pickup owners chose that color, making it the most popular color in America. With pickups making up eighteen percent of the total vehicles in North America, that was a whole lot of silver trucks to run down.

That little factoid hadn't made him happy. Taylor either, considering her sister was snatched away in a silver pickup. Even back then, the color had been popular.

He left the expressway, making use of the shortcut he'd discovered and pulled into the lot behind the building. Both Charlie and Meg's cars were in their normal spots. He'd have to sneak in. Maybe hide for a while to keep the distractions to a minimum.

That plan failed the second he opened the door and found both sisters standing in the hallway, steaming mugs of coffee in hand.

"Well, good morning," Charlie said.

"Ladies."

Charlie wore her typical skirt—she called it a pencil skirt—with a silk blouse while Meg opted for baggy, clay covered jeans and a T-Shirt that said, Kiss Me I'm Irish. Funny thing was, she wasn't Irish.

Meg held up her mug. "Coffee is hot. Some new blend Charlie worked up. I think it's a winner."

In her downtime, Charlie liked to tinker with coffee blends. Matt supposed the coffee thing was Charlie's version of his building cars. Whatever. As long as they all got through the day, it worked.

"Thanks." The sisters made room for him to push by. "I'll grab some in a bit. I'll be in my office."

As casual as he'd tried to sound, Charlie fell into step behind him. He didn't have to look to know Meg wouldn't be far behind.

He flipped the light on in his office and tossed his messenger bag on the desk.

"How's your new girlfriend?" Charlie asked, a sly grin on her face.

In his mind, he sighed. Tenacity made the sisters good at their jobs. Unfortunately, that quality painted all aspects of their lives. Including keeping up on what their investigator did in his personal life.

He unloaded his bag, neatly lining his legal pad next to the three file folders he'd brought to the office with him. Everything else had been scanned and stored on his laptop, but the contents of the folders had been collected over the past few days and he hadn't had a chance to catalog them yet.

"He's not going to answer," Meg said.

True 'dat. "Nope. But, if you need me, I'll be here working on the Jarvis case."

Charlie blew on her coffee and took a sip. "Good. Anything new?"

Dropping into the chair, he propped his feet on the desk. "Funny you should ask. How much do you know about this birthing center the Jarvises picked?"

"I know they'd planned on using it, but Walt said they weren't completely committed. On her last doctor's appointment, Felicity's blood pressure had spiked."

"I remember Walt saying something about that."

"Yes. At the time of Felicity's disappearance they were considering doing a hospital birth in case the blood pressure became an issue during delivery. Walt wanted to be at the hospital, just in case."

"Did the birthing center know that? Because everything I have indicates it was all-systems-go with them."

"Not to my knowledge. Felicity went missing before they'd made a final decision. Why?"

Matt sat up and set his feet on the floor. "I visited the birthing center. Call it an undercover mission."

Meg's perfectly arched eyebrows rose. "You..." She shook her head. "Huh?"

"Special Agent Sinclair and I posed as a married, pregnant couple and toured the facility. It's a helluva setup. Before that, we visited the hospital where the nurse told us Felicity had everything lined up. She'd scheduled a C-section so she could, without question, lock in all the doctors she wanted." He held up the folder with copies of the birthing center welcome kit. "These are copies of the forms from the birthing center."

"Felicity's? How'd you get that?"

"Not hers. I'd need a warrant for that. These are the blank forms. It's pretty involved. Everything buttoned up. I think Agent Sinclair might be working on a warrant, but I'm gonna head over and see Walt. See if he has copies of their paperwork."

While Meg stayed in the doorway, casually leaning on the doorframe, Charlie grabbed a coaster from the holder on the corner of his desk and set her mug down. He eyeballed the mug. That right there meant his plan for quiet study just flew out the window.

Charlie wasn't going anywhere.

"Something wrong?" Matt asked.

"I'm not sure."

"Okay. Want to elaborate?"

"Your association with Agent Sinclair."

Yep. Here we go. The whole thing was sticky business, riding the edges of ethical because Walt was his client. One he'd signed a confidentiality agreement for stating he wouldn't discuss his wife's case outside of Schock Investigations. Taylor was an outsider. A federal one currently investigating said client.

His only net was the fact that Taylor had been with him at the hospital and birthing center and had heard everything first hand. So far, he hadn't revealed anything she didn't already know.

A stretch? Totally. If Jarvis took him to court, he'd be screwed. No doubt. If it meant finding Felicity's killer and her missing baby, he'd, without question, hand over his investigator's license.

Matt held up his hand. "I haven't gone outside the boundaries of confidentiality."

Charlie scoffed. "Really? Going undercover with a federal agent working the same case is exempt?"

"I didn't tell her anything she didn't already know. And, yeah, before you do that you're delusional thing again, I get it. It's under control. If there's heat, I'll take it. You two will be out of it. I'll be the rogue investigator you reprimanded and fired. In fact, draw up the paperwork and backdate it. Fire me. Then you're in the clear."

"Don't be stupid," Meg said. "No one is getting fired. We're having a conversation."

Charlie didn't say anything. Not unusual for her. She liked to process, get her thoughts aligned before speaking.

Finally, she picked up her coffee mug. "Meg is right. No one is getting fired. But you're on a short leash with this, Matt. I trust you, but this is a United States senator. Don't fuck this up."

Ewww-eeee. Charlie dropping an f bomb. Pissed. Royally. "Yes, ma'am. I got it."

"Good."

She nodded and headed toward the door.

"Before you go," Matt said, "something about the silver truck Walt claimed was following Felicity is bugging me."

"What about it?"

"I don't know. Can I take a look at your notes again? See if I missed anything."

"Sure, but all Walt said was Felicity spotted a silver pickup with a window decal."

Whoa. Window decal. Walt had never told Matt about that. "Wait. What decal?"

Charlie swung her head from Matt to Meg and back. "A bald eagle on the cab window. It said God Bless America on it."

"He never told me about that. I don't have a decal in my notes and he sure as shit never mentioned it."

"He probably forgot who he said what to. I'm sure the FBI has it."

They'd see about that as soon as Matt asked Taylor what she knew about that vehicle.

With a world full of silver pickups, how in the hell could a man leave out that detail when his pregnant wife had gone missing? That was the best lead they had.

Unless, of course, Walt Jarvis was hiding something.

11

———

"Your house was broken into last night and you didn't call me?"

Taylor tried not to squirm under Meredith's stern glare as she sat across from her in Meredith's office. "They didn't take anything and I wasn't home. Nothing was damaged."

"What were they after?"

Goosebumps rose on Taylor's arms from the air conditioning. Meredith must have had another hot flash and cranked the thermostat down to sub-arctic temps. "Most likely information on the Jarvis case. My laptop was up and running when I entered the place and my file on the Jarvis case was open. I always close out everything and all my stuff is password protected. Whoever broke in disarmed my security system and got around my laptop's security."

"Damn it." Meredith's face grew even more grim. "I can't believe how this case is spinning out of control. Cunningham is going to have my badge before this is over. You should have called me."

"Yes, ma'am, I should have, but I was exhausted and all I wanted was some sleep." Mostly the truth. "I locked up and went to a friend's for the remainder of the night. I didn't see any reason to wake you and put a lot of other people out that late. I came here first thing this morning to inform you."

Meredith's lips worked. "You didn't call me because you knew I would chew your ass out about this."

Taylor decided to take the 5th and stay silent.

"Well, at least you were smart enough not to stay at your place afterwards. Tell me you didn't touch anything." Mer leaned forward and grabbed her phone. "I'll get a tech team over there right now."

There was no way Taylor was confessing that she'd already had Charlie Schock at her place dusting for prints. Better to keep quiet about that. Besides, the place had been a mess with fingerprint residue and she'd wiped everything down after Charlie was done. There were no prints to find. "Don't waste FBI resources on me. There won't be any prints, trust me. Whoever did this is good. I kicked a couple of rocks yesterday on the Jarvis case and someone obviously didn't like it. I'm sure the break-in is related to that. I want to bring Dottie Hernandez in for—"

Meredith held up a finger as she spoke into the handset. "Yeah, Cora, it's me. I need a team over at Taylor Sinclair's place as soon as possible. It was broken into last night. Nothing was damaged, but I want you to dust for prints and collect any evidence you can find."

Cora said something, Mer gave her an affirmative, and the two disconnected. "Who's Dottie Hernandez?" she asked, dropping the handset back into its cradle.

Oh boy. Mer was forcing her to come clean about the fingerprinting. It was either that, or Cora would figure out that Taylor had already wiped everything down. "Look, Mer. The tech team won't find any prints other than mine. I already had a friend check."

"You *what?*" Meredith looked like she was about to come out of her chair.

And, wow, Taylor had to admit, she'd never seen her boss look so completely vexed at her. That was saying something since Taylor had a way of vexing most everyone.

"Like I said, this break-in is the direct cause of my investigation yesterday, I'm sure of it. I'm also sure the perp was too good to leave behind fingerprints, so let's not worry about that. Dottie Hernandez is the manager of the TriCare Birthing Center where Felicity and Walt made plans to have their child. It caters to the rich and famous and, according to what Mrs. Hernandez explained to me yesterday, they create binders for each mother that contains numerous pages of personal information on everyone involved, right down to the people who might visit after the kid's born. They say it's for security, but that kind can backfire if it falls into the wrong hands."

"What does that have to do with Felicity's kidnapping?" The words were clipped. "And who is this friend you had fingerprint your place? Please tell me it wasn't Grey."

"Believe it or not, I do have law enforcement friends outside of this office, and no, it wasn't Grey." She didn't have any friends in law enforcement outside of Matt, but Mer certainly didn't need to know that. "The Jarvis baby could still be alive and Felicity may have been picked by our perp because of a dozen things, all listed in her TriCare birth planner. He learned all he needed to know about Felicity and Baby Jarvis from it. They were handpicked for a reason, and if I can figure out what that is, I can track down our killer."

Mer tipped back in her chair and studied Taylor. Taylor could almost see the imaginary steam pouring from her ears. "You have less than 12 hours to take solid findings to AD Cunningham, or he's going to pull the plug on your investigation. Do you really want to waste that time talking to this Hernandez woman?"

There were two types of FBI agents. Guys like Mitch who always had a smartass comment and their own agenda for solving cases, and guys like Justice Greystone, who were level-headed and smart when dealing with superiors.

The Mitch Monroes typically didn't last long, but for a moment, Taylor sympathized with them. She wanted to rail against the injustice of AD Cunningham's demand and Mer for taking his side in their last meeting. Meredith knew Taylor was a damn good agent and would bleed for the Bureau. This case, because it involved a United States senator and the media, was interfering with the search for justice.

A dozen reasons why questioning Dottie Hernandez was *exactly* what she wanted to do in her last 12 hours skittered through Taylor's head. In fact, they damn near begged her to channel Mitch Monroe and say them out loud. Instead, she chose the smart, professional, Justice Greystone route, "Yes, ma'am. I do."

Grey would be so proud.

Meredith shook her head, her gaze dropping to her desktop as she let go of a pained sigh. "I can't fucking believe this, but it's your neck, Taylor."

Disappointment hung in the air between them. Resignation.

Red-hot anger underneath it all.

Taylor wasn't the shining star in Meredith's crown anymore and the realization stung, but it was just another wound in her growing list of them.

I need a drink.

Or Matt. Mad Dog had a way of soothing her like nothing else.

If she stuck her neck out too far, she would get her head cut off. Which meant no more Jarvis case. No more grooming to take over Mer's spot.

One mistake. That's all it took in the cutthroat world of the Bureau to ruin a career.

Mitch had done it. So had Grey eventually, because he was loyal to Mitch and their friendship.

Taylor wasn't throwing her career away for a friend or any other noble cause.

Except justice.

Is there anything more noble?

"I'm going to find that child," Taylor said, standing up. "And when I do, we'll have our killer."

"You better hope so," Mer called as Taylor exited her office. "Because you've definitely murdered your career over this."

For half a second, Taylor hesitated. Then she turned back. "This job used to be about bringing criminals to justice and handing them over to the courts for retribution, not how many likes the Bureau gets on Facebook or the spin a bunch of reporters put on a story."

Mer did come out of her seat this time. She balled her fists and leaned on her desk, eyes nearly bugging out of her head. "Don't lecture me on the morality of this institution, Agent Sinclair, or I will personally take your badge and gun and escort you from this building."

Fidelity, bravery, integrity. Taylor wasn't quite sure where those principles were hiding these days in the halls of the FBI. But she took a step back and gave her boss—her *used to be* mentor—a nod of acquiescence. Meredith wasn't just threatening to take the case away; she was threatening to fire her lead cold case closer.

That took some giant-sized balls.

"Yes, ma'am." Taylor fought to keep the Mitch Monroe tone out of her voice. "I'll get back to work."

In the elevator on the way down to her office, Taylor felt a certain euphoria, which was weird, considering she'd just pissed off her boss for the third day in a row.

On the plus side, she had Mer's grudging approval to bring Dottie in and question her officially.

Things are about to get real.

Leaving the elevator, she checked her messages. Matt had called three times, all voicemails short and succinct. "Call me."

From the terse urgency in his voice, Taylor's euphoria dissipated.

Something was wrong.

She closed her door and dialed his number. "Hey, what's up?" she said when he answered.

His voice lacked his usual calm. "The sticker on the truck. Do you have anything in your files about it?"

"What sticker?" Taylor went to her desk. Files and half-empty coffee cups littered the top. She cleared away a couple of piles and dragged out the fat Felicity Jarvis folder. "I assume we're talking about Felicity's kidnapper's truck?"

"Walt said in an interview with Charlie that Felicity mentioned a sticker on the truck. Charlie talked to Walt initially, before she handed the investigation over to me last year. Do you have anything in your file about it?"

Taylor frowned, flipping open the main folder and skipping to the transcript of Walt's initial interview with Grey. "I don't remember anything about a sticker on the truck. Why? What's got you all fired up about a truck sticker?"

"Walt never told me about any sticker, but he told Charlie about it in detail, including that it was an eagle with a God Bless America sentiment written on it. It was located on the lower right back window."

"O-*kay*." She wasn't sure where this was going, although any lead at this point was good with her. "And you believe this has some significance?"

"Not sure what, but it seems weird to me that Felicity noticed the sticker and Walt mentioned it to Charlie and the

PD detectives, but then didn't say anything to me about it. I don't know. I may be reaching. It could be nothing."

She read quickly, skimming over Grey's notes inserted in the transcript. "There's nothing in the transcript I have about a sticker. Nothing that Grey added in his notes. Walt said Felicity told him it was a silver pickup, but she didn't mention the make or model. No other details, other than she'd seen it more than once following her. I can look through the rest of the notes if you want."

A heavy silence came from his end of the phone. "Do it in the car. I'll pick you up in fifteen."

"Where are we—"

The line went dead.

"...going?" she finished to the sound of dead air.

She was running low on time, Dottie's interview still waited, and a small detail like this seemed insignificant.

But Matt was an ace investigator, and this seemingly insignificant detail could blow the investigation wide open. She'd seen it before. Her own team had solved a crime from 1978 with a parking ticket.

Cramming the Jarvis folder and her stack of notes into her briefcase, she went downstairs to wait for him.

Matt and Taylor sat in front of a giant whiteboard in Grey's office. Well, the office being made up of a recycled metal desk, squeaky chair, and a large decorative screen separating his workspace from the rest of his team. The giant rolling whiteboard now sat in a large open area near the windows on the south side of the room.

Justice rolled his desk chair over, but didn't sit. He went straight to the board and drew four columns. "What exactly do we think we have here?"

This from Mitch who stood beside Taylor, feet at shoulder-width, arms crossed over his chest. For whatever reason, Mitch didn't like Matt.

Ask him if he cared.

Maybe it was because Matt had gone to the dark side and become a private investigator. Cops didn't like PIs. They saw them as wannabes, people who didn't have the stones to get through the academy or, if they did graduate, couldn't survive the job. In the world of law enforcement, you were either in or out. He'd, according to many of his former law enforcement brethren, sold out. When he'd left the PD, most of his friends and acquaintances dropped away. The true friends though, they'd stayed and he'd always be grateful for their loyalty.

The rest? He'd given up worrying about it. Working cold cases with the sisters allowed him to do the work he loved, to make a damned difference. Allowed him to sleep at night. In his mind, that's all that mattered.

Matt wandered to the whiteboard and picked up a marker. "I don't know what we have. That's why we're here. We figured with Grey's history on the case, maybe he could help us piece it out."

At the top of each column, Matt wrote Felicity, Walt, Baby, and Birthing Center.

"The sticker," Taylor said. "Grey, do you remember anything about a sticker on the rear window of the truck?"

Grey shook his head. "No. And I'd remember. The small details make cases like this and with the number of silver trucks out there, I'd have chased that."

Recapping the marker, Matt tapped it against the board. "And, we're talking more than seven years ago. What are the chances that silver truck is still owned by the same person *and* has the sticker?"

"It's a stretch." Taylor held up the blue folder from the birthing center. "Grey, I don't know if you've seen this, but it's the welcome kit Dottie Hernandez distributed at the open house. If all the forms are completed, the birthing center basically has an entire family history. Including medical and photos."

"And they need all that, why?"

Matt shrugged. "They say it's preparation for medical emergencies and security. If family members want to visit, they check the photos on file to make sure it's really them. I get it, but it's not sitting right with me."

Once again, Taylor held up the folder. "If this information landed in the wrong hands, say a kidnapper's, they'd have an entire medical history for the baby."

Grey's lips tipped into a frown. "Makes black market adoptions a cake walk."

Matt poked his finger. "Bingo."

"So let's start running it down."

On the board, Matt added a column for the Silver Pickup. "Justice, can you pull a list of silver trucks in say, a hundred mile radius? We'd need current and from eight years ago."

"Teeg," Grey yelled, "did you get that?"

The Justice Team's resident Geek Boy was already pounding away on his keyboard. "I'm on it."

"And," Taylor snapped her fingers, "how about we run a crosscheck on vehicles owned by employees of the birthing center?"

Good thought. Matt waved the marker. "We could pull employment records for the center to get a list of employees. If they have any illegals, it won't be accurate, but it's a start."

"Good luck," Monroe said. "It'd be an early Christmas if you guys scored on that."

Matt angled back, shot him a look. "Hey, it's a start. Are you gonna help or be a dick about it?"

"He's gonna be a dick about it. That *is* his way of helping," Grey cracked.

Whatever.

Mitch flipped Grey off. "All I'm saying is it's a long shot. I didn't say I wouldn't help you sort through the list."

Well, that was something. Matt met the man's gaze and nodded. "Thank you. Appreciate it."

"If the truck is a bust," Grey said, "what then?"

Taylor held up her hand. "The employees. We run backgrounds on all of them. See if there's even a sliver of impropriety."

"Easy enough," Matt agreed. "We can start on that while we're working the list of trucks."

"I can do that," Taylor said. "The clock is ticking on my deadline. Monroe, if you'll start on the trucks, Matt and I will run down the employees."

"Dottie Hernandez," Matt said. "Let's start with her. See what's what there. Then we'll run financials on everyone."

"I'll take those," Grey said. "I can do it on the down low."

"Thank you, Grey."

"No sweat. This case has bugged me for the past eight years."

"Got it!" Teeg said. "I'm printing you a list of silver pickups."

"How many?"

"Not too bad. Only twenty-five hundred."

Twenty-five hundred? What the hell did he consider bad?

"Teeg," Matt said, "the window decal was a bald eagle. What's the chance you can figure out if any of the owners of those trucks are former military?"

Teeg glanced at Grey. Yeah, Matt knew what he was asking. He wanted Teeg to hack into military databases and crosscheck the names against the list of truck owners. Another option would be the IRS, but the military databases might be a whole lot faster.

With barely a nod, Grey approved the request.

"Oh, goodie," Teeg said. "This should be fun."

"Before you do that," Matt said, "can you grab that list of

employees from TriCenter? I'd like to take a crack at that while you're working the military angle."

"Sure. Any idea how many employees they have?"

Taylor flipped open the welcome kit and shuffled through pages. "Yes, I saw it in here. There's a page that has all the stats about the center, history, number of births, employees, that sort of thing. Here it is." She tugged the page out, set the folder on her lap with the information sheet on top and ran her finger along the margin as she read. "Looks like...twelve full-time staffers. But then there are all the doctors, including the anesthesiologists and nurses. We have the lists of all the medical personnel who have privileges at the center. I haven't counted them, but I'd say it's around fifty all combined."

"Okay," Matt said. "We need Teeg to pull us the full-timers. See if anything pops. Then we run the list of medical personnel in the welcome kit."

Grey held out his hand and waggled his fingers. "Let me scan a copy of the medical staff. Teeg, if you have social security numbers on the admin folks, that'll help."

"No prob. What the hell, I'll grab their tax returns. We've only broken a few dozen laws so far today."

As whacky as this was, it was coming together. "We're good to go then. I'll work with Taylor on criminal backgrounds, Grey runs finances, and Monroe starts on the trucks."

Taylor smacked her hands together. "Let's do this, people."

12

---

*I*t was well past midnight when Taylor left her office in the J. Edgar Building, heading for home. Mer didn't seem to care what time it was since her voice on Taylor's cell reached similar levels to the karaoke singer from the cold case conference last weekend.

"I need your report by eight a.m.," Meredith said. "Not a second past."

"I'll have it to you."

That would be a minor miracle, but what the hell. She was already in deep shit. At this moment, a slight exaggeration with her boss was the least of her worries.

And she was damned tired of Mer's lack of faith in her.

Damned tired, period.

She needed a finger of scotch and eight—no, make that twelve—hours of uninterrupted sleep.

Not gonna happen.

She had a case to solve and a deadline to meet. She'd have to sleep when it was over.

By then, she'd probably be out of a job, so there'd be plenty of time for catching up on her ZZZs.

Matt didn't want her to stay at her place tonight, but she'd be damned if she let someone scare her off for a second night.

Ditto on the not gonna happen.

She'd already had the security system company upgrade her alarm, and added motion sensors to all the windows. If anyone paid her another visit, she'd be waiting for them.

"Did you interview that woman, yet?" Mer continued. "What did she say? The birthing center is a dead end, isn't it? I told you it was a waste of time."

Oopsie. After the brainstorming party at the armory with Grey, Taylor had been anxious to keep digging and Matt had dropped her off at the Bureau so she could check in with her team and update them on the investigation while he went to check in with his bosses. Taylor got the feeling from the little he'd said about the situation they were none too happy that he was mingling work and pleasure with her.

Tough cookies. All these procedures and rules clamped down on their investigation when a child's life might be hanging in the balance. For that, she'd risk it all.

No hesitation.

The parking garage was hot and humid even though the outside temp had dropped into the 70s. Her car was one of the few left on Parking Level C and her heels clicked on the concrete floor, echoing around the gloomy space.

The paperwork on the employees and military records of silver truck owners had been extensive and convoluted. Hours of weeding out possibilities Grey, Mitch, and Matt provided had narrowed it down to fewer than ten leads. More than manageable. "I'll have all of my findings in tomorrow's report," she told her boss. It was the best she could do considering she hadn't interviewed Dottie yet.

Mer went off on another tangent and Taylor tuned her out. Matt had promised to meet at her place in twenty minutes to go over her list. She didn't plan on getting much sleep tonight anyway since her 72 hours were almost over. Unfortunately, she couldn't line up interviews until morning, but maybe if she went over the ten solid leads she had with Matt, she could reduce them further. Come morning, she and Matt could divvy them up and go to town. She had already primed her team for a 7 am meeting where she would lay out her plan of attack like a football coach going over the team's playbook. The only thing she had yet to decide was whether to do a man-to-man defense or zone blitz. That would be determined on how many solid leads she and Matt decided on tonight.

If she ever got Mer off the phone...

Keys in hand, she passed the center pylon with a big C on it and spotted her car in the end slot. Another long, brutal day, but her adrenaline was pumping. They were close, so close.

"Mer," she interrupted, "I really need to go."

Her eyes burned from too many hours staring at her computer screen and she wished she had an extra hand to rub them. But with her briefcase in one hand, keys and travel mug in the other, and the phone tucked between her ear and shoulder, she fought back a yawn and blinked the irritation away as best she could.

"AD Cunningham will be at our meeting. Don't let me down, Sinclair."

Her vision blurred for a second, the shadows around her car seeming to stir and ripple. She blinked again and pulled up short, her adrenaline-fueled limbs getting another jolt.

Someone had just crawled out from under her car.

A man in black rose quickly to his knees, then jumped to his feet, eyeing her through a black ski mask.

"Taylor?" Her boss's voice seemed far away. "Did you hear me?"

Taylor stopped, wondering if she should drop the stuff in her hands and go for her weapon.

Unarmed. At least she didn't see a gun. "What the fuck are you doing?"

She couldn't be sure, but it looked like he grinned behind the mask. She kept an eye on his hands, but he didn't reach for any weapon.

"*What* did you just say to me?" Meredith screeched.

She took a step forward, shifting her keys to her briefcase hand. "I don't know who you are or what you're doing, but you're messing with the wrong woman."

The man pivoted and started to run.

Meredith said something else, but Taylor let the phone fall.

Bastard! Heady anger roared through her. First her house, now her car? Who was this fucker and who did he think he was dealing with?

Dropping the briefcase and keys, she threw the stainless steel travel mug as hard as she could. The mug smacked the man in the back of the head, knocking him off balance. He threw his hands out as he hit the wall, giving Taylor the chance she needed to catch up to him.

He pushed off the wall; she jumped on him, taking him to the ground. He wasn't much taller than she was, but outweighed her enough to flip her over, the back of her head smacking into the concrete floor.

She sent a fist into his nose, hearing the crack of cartilage. He grunted and jumped up, ready to take off again, so she snagged his foot and tripped him.

His body crashed to the floor and he kicked back, trying to shake off her grip. She held on, jackknifing her legs around and nailing him square in the kidneys with the toe of her boot.

He arched from the blow and cursed, the word low, guttural. One of his fists came out of nowhere, nailing her in the stomach.

The pain was intense but she didn't let go, wrapping her

legs around his and flipping them both over again, her on top, pinning him facedown on the floor.

His weight once again worked in his favor as he did a pushup and unseated her. She fell beside him, rolled away from a hard kick, then used her momentum to spring back up.

Could this be Felicity's killer? The baby's kidnapper?

She drew her weapon, the sound of Mer's hysterical voice on the ground behind her. "Come on, asshole," she said, licking her lips. "Let's see what you've got."

He came to his feet, chest heaving. "Get the fuck out of my way."

A dozen comebacks and questions ran through her mind. "You're done. This ends here and now. Put your hands up."

Yep, that was a grin behind the mask. Same as before. "Fuck you."

And oh, she needed to wipe that grin off his face. Her firearms training kicked in and she held the gun aimed at center mass. "Go ahead. Give it a try."

He roared with anger, rushing her low. She fired, nailing him in the shoulder, but it didn't stop his charge. He took her to the ground, knocking the weapon from her hand.

He reared back, sitting on top of her and Taylor sent a fist to his chin. His head snapped back and he jumped up, holding his shoulder and staggering.

She rolled to her feet and saw his gaze land on her gun.

The man went for it and Taylor tackled him this time, knocking him onto the trunk of her car. He bounced left and Taylor spun and kicked out, landing a heel to his knee before he could regain his balance.

She heard a pop, her spin taking her back around to connect a fist to his temple.

But he didn't go down.

Who is this guy? The Terminator?

He swung at her head. She ducked, breathing heavy. He snatched up her briefcase and hit her square in the kidneys.

Damn, that hurt.

Don't let him steal the briefcase!

Her job, as well as the life of an innocent boy, depended on the information she had in it.

Of course, Ski Mask could be the key to both as well.

She sent another roundhouse kick at him, knocking the briefcase from his hands. The case slid under her car.

Safe.

It might be safe, but she wasn't.

It was time to end this escapade.

Another growl erupted from Ski Mask's mouth as he lunged at her. Taylor had just enough time to send an elbow toward his face, connecting with his cheek.

He saw it coming and deftly avoided the worst of the jab, knocking her onto the trunk of her car.

"Hey!" she heard a man yell from the area near the elevators. "Let go of her!"

The security guard must have seen them on the video feed.

Better late than never.

Ski Mask grabbed her ponytail and jerked her head back, his mouth coming close to her ear. "You're screwed, bitch. I'm going to make you pay."

He slammed her forehead down onto the car twice in quick succession. As Taylor's vision whited out, she heard the security guard's footsteps running toward her as the heavy thud of Ski Mask's boots went the other way.

Her legs wouldn't hold her and she slipped to the ground, blackness taking her under.

Taylor was banged up good. At least she'd had the sense to call him. She sat in the back of an ambulance summoned by the security guard, arguing the whole time with an EMT surveying the damage to her forehead.

"I'm fine," she said. "It's barely a scrape."

"You could have a concussion."

"I don't. Not even dizzy."

"Taylor," Matt said. "Quit breaking the guy's balls and let him do his job."

"I'm not going to the hospital. This is silly. I'm sure someone, somewhere in this city, just got shot. You guys should be treating *that* person, not me."

The corner of the EMT's mouth quirked. Encouraging her pissy behavior by laughing wouldn't help.

"Look," the guy said, "I can't force you to go to the hospital. All I can do is recommend it. Which I do. Strongly."

Taylor waved a hand. "Yep. Got it. You're off the hook. Now let me out of here."

The guy looked at Matt, his face a cross between frustration and good-luck-pal. "She's all yours."

Matt whipped out a toothy smile. "Thanks for that."

The EMT helped Taylor off the back of the bus and she immediately started moving toward her car where a DC cop waited.

"We put out a BOLO," the cop said, "but..."

"I know," Taylor said. "It's not likely my guy is running through the streets of DC in a ski mask, leaving a nice breadcrumb trail of blood from his bullet wound for us to follow."

"We'll pull security video. He probably took the mask off and maybe we'll get a look at his face. You never know."

"Thank you, Officer. I appreciate it."

He handed her a business card. "Call that number if you think of anything else."

"I will. And thank you."

The cop nodded then faced Matt, gesturing to Taylor with his chin. "She shouldn't drive."

"She won't. I'll get her home."

As soon as the cop left, Taylor whirled on him, then obviously having moved too fast, swayed sideways. He grabbed hold of her, wrapping his hands around her shoulders to steady her. "Take it easy. You've got a head injury."

"I'm fine." She closed her eyes. "Moved too fast."

"I see that. I can also see that your eye is swelling. You're going to have a nice shiner from this to go along with that bump."

"We need to get out of here."

"What's the hurry?"

"My boss is the hurry. I was on the phone with her when all this went down. I texted when I regained consciousness to tell her I was fine, but now she's on me. She's called five times."

On cue, her phone rang. "Make that six. I'm not answering it."

"You can't ignore her. She's gotta be worried."

"I texted her. If I talk to her, she'll scream at me. That I can deal with. It's the pulling me from this case, which she will most likely do, that terrifies me."

The grand plan was to avoid her boss? That made zero sense. "Uh, babe, she can still pull you from the case whether you talk to her or not."

"She won't do that. That's not how she operates." Taylor dipped her head, let out a sigh. "I don't know how I went from being a rock star to..."

"You're still a rock star."

She looked up at him, pointed to her face. "*Not.* But thanks for saying that."

"You've had a few setbacks."

"Ha!"

He set his hands on her shoulders again, stroking them with his thumbs. "You're tired. And you just kicked some guy's ass."

167

That brought a smile out of her. When Taylor gave him that smile it was like Times Square at night.

"Now you're sucking up. I like it."

He squeezed her shoulders and turned her toward his car. "I'm taking you back to my place. I probably have a can of soup somewhere. It's the cure-all. We'll get some food in you and I'll put you to bed."

"We need to go over the leads. I have it down to ten."

Jeez, the woman didn't give up. "We can do it in the morning."

"I have an 8 a.m. meeting that will either save my job or put the final nail in my coffin. I'm meeting with my team before that. If I have to eat, then you have to review the leads with me."

He glanced over at her, took in the muscle throbbing in her clenched jaw and knew he wouldn't win. Part of being a smart man meant knowing when compromise was in order.

Like now.

"Deal. But I'm limiting the time. Forty minutes."

"Forty!"

"Yes. And that's generous. I mean, how long does it take to eat soup?"

They reached his car and he opened the door for her.

She looked up at him and the already blackening bruise on her forehead brought him back to some guy kicking the shit out of her and his blood fired hot. Damn. He'd never considered himself a hero and had no illusions about the filth he'd seen in this world. The kooks. The crazy methheads and murderers. He'd seen enough of it to know he couldn't save the world.

And he sure as shit couldn't save Taylor. She could take care of herself.

Most of the time.

Tonight though, given the break-in at her place, he should have been with her. Still with his gaze glued to her, he reached up, ran his thumb down her cheek and dipped his head, kissing her gently, already feeling his body stir when she responded. Unlike most of their kisses, this one didn't pack that urgent punch. The get-your-clothes-off-NOW anticipation that typically sparked their sexual marathons.

He liked it. The slow, easy pace. The lack of rushing. They'd have to explore that. Not tonight, but sometime soon. He pulled back, let his hand wander over her chest, across her breast and torso until landing at her hip where he patted her ass.

"Watch your head when you get in."

At that, she smiled, a lusty mix of grateful and seductive.

"You're slowly killing me, you know."

"Ditto that. It's shaping up to be a wild ride."

Matt checked his watch. "Thirty-nine minutes." He swirled one finger. "Wrap this shit up."

Across from him at his kitchen table, Taylor shoved her half-eaten soup aside and spread three file folders in front of her. One contained her list of birthing center employees, the other of people who owned silver pickups and the final her most recent notes on the case.

"Oh, come on!" she said. "We're not even halfway through the list. You can't be serious with that forty minute time limit."

"Honey, I'm as serious as a heart attack." He grinned. "Or a *parking garage* attack."

Because, yeah, he was the guy sitting across from her watching the bump on her forehead grow and that bruise expand. She was definitely going to have a black eye. She needed rest and pouring over case files wouldn't do it. Still, he understood her drive, her need to find Baby Jarvis.

If she was scared from the attack, from her home being violated and her person being assaulted, she wasn't showing it.

Except by throwing herself even more into her work.

Damn, the woman tripped him up. He sat back, let his shoulders press against the ladder-back chair and folded his arms across his chest. With Taylor, he needed to present a calm, yet definitive demeanor. Otherwise, she'd own him.

And that wasn't happening.

"I'll make you a deal," he said. "You go to bed and I'll work on the files. That's my final offer."

"Puh-lease. That's your *only* offer. What kind of negotiation is this?"

"It's not. That's my point." Shoving his chair back, he stood. Was it lame that he was assuming a power position by standing over her? Absolutely. Taylor was stubborn—bullheaded even—and he'd use any tactic necessary to make sure she got some rest. "Leave the folders. I'll deal with them."

Working on a theory of momentum, he cornered the table, eased her chair back, clasped her elbow and guided her to her feet. For once, she didn't argue, but that may have been a fatigue-induced lucky break.

"Five more minutes," she countered.

"My house. My rules. You're going to bed."

Determined not to think about her in his bed without him, he led her down the hallway, flipped on the bedroom light, grabbed her one of his T-shirts to sleep in, and pointed to the bathroom. "Go change. I'll get the bed ready."

"Matt, I can put myself to bed."

"I know, but..."

"What?"

He shrugged. "I like helping you get ready for bed."

"Oh, my God," she said, her eyes hot on his. "I'm totally doing you."

"Which is why I will sleep on the couch."

She whipped the T-shirt from his hand and spun away. "We'll see about that."

In the five minutes it took Taylor to do her thing in the bathroom, he turned down the bed and changed into basketball shorts and a sleeveless T-shirt. Later, he'd ditch it all because he turned into a furnace when he slept and any clothing on his body made him seriously uncomfortable.

Across the hall, the bathroom door opened and Taylor stepped out wearing only the T-shirt that dropped to mid-thigh on her much shorter body. He dragged his eyes over her long, shapely legs.

Stay strong.

If he let her, she'd easily talk him into a quickie. Which wouldn't be bad. Except, one quickie led to another and four hours later, they'd both be without sleep. In her current condition, he couldn't let that happen.

She sauntered by him, swinging that amazing ass and dropping a kiss on him as she went.

"Come to bed, Mad Dog. It'll do us both some good."

"No."

She made snoring noises.

Snoring noises? *Really?*

After fluffing the pillows, she sat on the edge of the bed. And lifted the T-shirt over her head, tossing it at him as his eyes fixed on her tits like locked-on radar. Her nipples poked out from the sudden cold and Matt couldn't stop looking. He stood there like a horny teenager getting his first peek at Playboy, his mouth literally watering and his dick hardening. She was so damned beautiful and all he wanted, constantly, from the first time he'd put eyes on her, was to touch her. Everywhere.

Now was no exception.

"You," he said, "don't play fair."

"You've just figured that out? Come to bed. Make me happy. I'm begging you."

Begging. Jesus, she was a master at this. At getting what she wanted. The seduction. If it was even that. This right here? This was her putting it out there in typical aggressive Taylor style and, guess what? He didn't want it.

Not the sex. He always wanted that. With Taylor. What he didn't want was being her target. Being some random man on top of her, under her, behind her, ramming himself into her so she could forget her problems.

"No."

She let out a hard huff, grabbed the covers and whipped them over her as she rolled to her side. With her back to him. "Fine. You're right. It's been a rough night. I need some sleep. Don't mind me, I'm just the woman who threw myself at you."

"*What?*"

She roared to a sitting position again, ran both hands through her long hair and wrapped them around her skull. "Matt!"

What the hell was this about? "You're pissed now? Because I want to take care of you? You've got to be kidding me."

She dipped her head, still holding on to it. "Yes. No. My head hurts. I'm exhausted and..." she dropped her hands.

This is it. He hoped. Right here. That moment when she hit rock bottom and had nowhere to run and hide.

He took two steps but she held her hands up. "Don't come near me."

"Okay. You're exhausted and what? Finish what you were going to say."

"No."

"Why?"

"Because it hurts. Is that what you want to hear?"

"If it's the truth, yes."

"Damn you."

He closed the distance between them. When she didn't argue or shove him away, he perched on the edge of the bed and set one hand on the comforter covering her thighs.

Twisting her fingers together, she refused to look at him so he tucked his finger under her chin and nudged it up. "You're exhausted and what? Tell me."

Tears filled her eyes and she swiped at them, digging her palms into her eye sockets before furiously circling her hands in front of her chest. "I don't know what to do with all this... this...crap...inside me. It's like..."

She balled her hands until her knuckles popped, slamming them onto the bed and kicking at the blanket until her legs came free. Before he could stop her, she slipped out of bed and paced the room, stopped at the wall, came back and did it again, her feet slamming against the carpet.

"It's a monster," she said. "A mean, rabid dog, caged inside me and if I open that door, that fucking, goddamn door that has kept the monster away, I'll go crazy. I'll... I'll... I don't know!" She spun back to him, waved her fists. "But you know that, which is why you called me out on drinking. So, what do you want? You want me weak, humiliated, and unsure? Gotta tell ya', that's *not* me."

Slowly, he got to his feet, but didn't move toward her. As keyed up as she was, getting close to her right now might land him on his ass.

"No. That's not what I want. Admitting you're hurting doesn't make you weak, Taylor. It makes you human."

"Then I guess I'm human because this sucks." She growled at him, literally baring her teeth. The monster at work. "Feeling *vulnerable* sucks."

"Sometimes, yes. Right now, I think it's okay. I'm hoping you allowing yourself to be vulnerable with me means you trust me with it. That's an amazing gift."

Their eyes connected for a few long seconds, but she remained quiet, looking at him with those green eyes that had, in the last few minutes, softened. Finally, he'd broken through the wall that kept Taylor emotionally distant.

After shutting her down a few minutes earlier, he walked over to her. She stood vulnerable, still naked except for a pair of white lace underwear.

"I'm sorry I upset you," he said. "I just...want you. All of you. We understand each other. If you'd let me, we could be great together. And not just the sex. All of it."

"I don't know how to do that, Matt. I don't. I'm *empty*."

"Honey, you are far from empty."

He slid his arms around her, his hands settling on the upper curve of her ass as a shot of cold zipped up his fingers. "You're freezing."

"I know. I've been cold a lot the last few days."

He pulled her into him, felt the press of her breasts against his shirt and all thoughts of her getting rest flew right out of his mind. Rest? What rest?

Yeah, he was a pig. Somehow, he didn't think she'd mind.

"Matt, you confuse me. I thought you said..."

"I'm an idiot."

She grinned. "Most men are."

That tore it. The woman was irresistible. He kissed her, long and slow, tentatively touching his tongue to hers, waiting for her to respond and then, there it was, her yielding, the stubbornness giving way and she arched into him, took the kiss up a notch as their tongues played tag.

He eased her backward, toward the bed, gently lowering her, determined to make this go slow. No slam-bang. No random guy she needed to unleash her rage on. This time, it had to be different. *He* wanted to be different.

He rolled beside her, dragging his hands over her hips, thighs, ass, and finally her tits where he pressed his thumb over one of her nipples. She hissed at him, drawing a hard breath and he clamped his mouth over her other one, drawing it into his mouth, sucking until she arched her hips up.

She wanted him.

Good.

Groaning, she set her hand on the back of his head, holding him in place. "Talk about not playing fair."

He released her, then blew on the wet nipple. "You don't seem to mind."

"Not in this lifetime."

When she wrapped her hand around him, he rolled to his back, let his mind drift. To Taylor, under him as he rocked himself into her. When did he turn into such a pansy when it came to sex? Before her, all he wanted was the release. The fast orgasm that would reset his system.

Now, he wanted everything. Slow, fast, hard, gentle. All of it.

And crazy Taylor Sinclair could give it to him.

Fantasies roaring, he reached over to his nightstand and slid the drawer open. "Condom," he said.

Taylor let go—a shame that—and moved over him, her inner thigh rubbing against his engorged dick. He needed inside her.

"I'll get it," she said, rummaging in the drawer.

He opened his eyes, watched her tear open the foil then took it from her.

"Between the two of us, we might be a disaster."

She laughed. "Like you said, we're good together, but it's a weird good. We're our own kind of crazy."

She smiled down at him and the air in his chest vanished. Gone. He sat up, cradled her face in his hands and kissed her. Never one to waste time, she angled to her back, bringing him with her and hooking one leg around him.

He gazed down at her, propped himself on his elbows and touched the edge of the bruise marring her forehead. When he found the fucker that put it there he'd kill him.

"Matt, please."

She arched against him and he shifted right and—yes—he

was inside her. Slowly easing into her as she smiled and her eyes rolled back.

"Oh, that's good," she said.

"Different?"

She locked her legs around him and cupped her hands on his cheeks. "Perfect."

13

$\mathcal{T}$he morning did not go at all like Taylor planned. Her usual morning of coffee and more coffee morphed into coffee and pancakes with Matt in his kitchen. At some point during the early pre-dawn hours, he left her and his bed and finished paring down their leads to three, so as he served her a hot breakfast, they hashed over how to divvy up their prospects.

The plan was for him to check out Kristina Caldwell, the Lamaze instructor whose income barely registered as middle-class but who lived in an expensive townhouse and drove an $80,000 vehicle. Not a silver truck, unfortunately, but she sure hadn't received her cushy living arrangements from her divorce six years ago, nor from any family money. That alone raised suspicion.

The other two she would take lead on, bringing her team up to speed at their 7 a.m. meeting. She would have Beck pick up Dottie and bring her in for questioning while she hunted down a prospective silver truck owner.

Her second morning surprise was Matt chauffeuring her to the office and dropping her off in front of FBI headquarters with a kiss that scorched her down to her toes. Yeah, they'd shared plenty of intimate kisses, but none felt quite like this. Somewhere in the past twenty-four hours, Taylor had lowered her guard. She'd fallen head over heels for Mad Dog. Her partner.

Her off-the-books, shouldn't-be-working-with-you partner.

Even now, as she headed for the front doors of the Bureau building, her heart fluttered like a manic butterfly. She couldn't wipe the smile off her face. Before entering, she actually turned back and waved at him as he drove away like she was some silly schoolgirl.

He tooted his horn and rumbled off and her heart fluttered even harder.

She pushed the glass doors open, and there was Beck waiting for her on the other side of the metal detectors, his tablet and a hot tea in hand.

"Hey," she said as she walked by the security guards and accepted the tea. "Ready for our big day? I have some leads for us to check out. We're close. I can feel it."

His suit was a beautiful dark blue and his tie the color of a pumpkin. Not many men could pull it off, but Beck looked like a GQ model even in old jeans and a T-shirt. He fell into step with her, heading for the cold case offices at the rear of the building. "You look like shit. Are you okay? Why didn't you call me last night?"

"I'm fine." Taylor sipped the tea and made a face. "What the hell is this?"

"Wildcrafted hercampuri. Detoxes your liver and balances your cholesterol. Which you're going to need after you see who's in your office."

Oh, jeez. She handed back the tea and slowed her pace. "Meredith? She's up early. But no surprise, since I didn't take her calls after the attack last night."

He held the door for her and they started down the long

corridor, one of the other agents giving Taylor the evil side-eye glance.

Damn. She thought she'd covered her black eye and bruise pretty well. Maybe not.

Beck waited for the agent to pass, then caught Taylor's elbow. "AD Cunningham is in there too."

Cunningham in her office. That had never happened before. "Is he slumming these days?" she joked.

"Taylor, this looks serious. Are they removing you from the case?"

Probably. Taylor handed him her briefcase. "All my notes and the leads on the Jarvis case I was going to assign to you and the team today are inside."

Beck frowned as he accepted it.

"It'll be okay," Taylor said, but her happy mood was dwindling fast. "Even if they do remove me, you guys can take over."

God, they better not remove me.

Stopping in front of the glass wall of her office, her eyes landed on the one person that made what was left of her good mood evaporate. "Or not."

"I can't work with him," Beck said.

Meredith must have felt their stares. She turned, saw Taylor, and for a brief moment, her face showed sadness. Whatever was about to happen, Meredith felt regret about it.

Makes two of us.

"Leo is the best profiler around," Taylor reassured Beck. *Besides Grey anyway.* "You'll be fine working with him."

Plastering on a fake smile, Taylor opened the door and entered her office.

And met the solid wall of Meredith Sardana, Marcus Cunningham, and Leo Wellington head on.

"Good morning," she said, feigning cheeriness. "I thought we were meeting at 8."

Leo gave her a smug smile. Cunningham shot a look at

Meredith and Taylor's boss stepped forward. "Agent Sinclair, after what happened at 12:24 this morning in the parking garage, Assistant Director Cunningham and I are concerned for your safety and your..."—she cleared her throat—"*perspective* with your current case."

"I'm fine," Taylor lied, skirting the three of them and taking her seat. "I know my deadline on the Jarvis case is up today, but I have new leads on what might have happened with the baby. I'm meeting with my team to bring them up to speed in two minutes. We have several people to interview, and—"

Leo held out a hand. "I'll take your Jarvis file."

Taylor caught sight of Beck, still outside her office, her notes tucked safely under his arm. Janiece had joined him, her face a worried mess of lines.

Taylor hid her own worry. "May I ask what's going on here?"

AD Cunningham sunk his hands into his pants pockets and looked bored. "What Agent Sardana is trying to say is that you're on suspension, Sinclair. Hand in your service weapon and badge."

"What the hell?" Taylor said to Mer, a sudden sourness in her mouth. "You're kidding, right? I'm suspended? Because I was attacked in the parking garage last night?"

Meredith crossed her arms. "You're lucky that's all it is. Every step of the way you've broken protocol on this case, and you know it."

Mer didn't know the half of it.

Or did she?

I have eyes and ears everywhere.

Damn spies.

"Broken protocol?" Did this have to do with Grey? Matt? Or was this Bureau speak for *you embarrassed us in the media?* "Could you be a little more specific?"

"Do I really need to?" Meredith shifted her weight and tapped a foot. "From the moment you started working with that

PI, you've violated procedure after procedure. You went under-cover without permission. You let someone break into your apartment and gain confidential information."

"*Let* him? I didn't let the perp do anything. He circumvented my security and figured out my laptop's password."

She continued as if Taylor hadn't spoken. "Last night in the parking garage, you discharged your weapon."

"A man attacked me!"

"We're looking into it, Taylor. Meanwhile, go home, get some rest, and forget about this case. Leo is taking over."

"Like hell he is."

Leo snickered.

Which made the anger she hadn't felt since last night emerge fresh. She jumped from her chair and started around the desk to get in his face—very Mitch Monroe-style—but Meredith grabbed her arm. "Don't make things worse for your-self, Taylor."

Taylor shook her restraining hand off and cut her gaze between Mer and Cunningham. In her peripheral vision, she saw the rest of her team gathered outside the glass wall of her office. "Is this because I went to Justice Greystone? He worked the original case. Why wouldn't I interview him and get his insight?"

Her boss's lips firmed and she seemed to choose her words before she spoke. "You're a loose cannon right now, just like Greystone was at the end of his time with the Bureau. I won't have those on my team."

She held out her hand. "Turn over your notes, Taylor."

Technically, the information contained inside her briefcase was the property of the FBI.

Good thing Beck was FBI.

"I don't have them." Taylor removed her gun from its holster and her credentials from her bag, stacking both on top of her desk. "Guess you're on your own to solve the Jarvis case."

Her legs shook but she held her head high as she moved past the threesome toward her office door. Beck opened it before she could and held it for her. She thanked him, moving down the hall, her team huddling around her.

"Did they fire you?" Beck asked.

Taylor kept moving. She needed her car. Needed to get out of here. "Suspension, that's all."

"Suspension?" Beck swore softly. "What now?"

"Leo's taking over. Don't let him have my notes. You guys are to investigate the two leads outlined on page three and four. I'll check into the third one outlined on page two. We're going to find Baby Jarvis and solve this case. We just have to be creative in the way we do it."

They started to follow her into the elevator that lead to the parking garage. Taylor held out a hand and stopped them. "Go back to your desks and get to work. I'll be in touch."

Mer hadn't even told her if the forensics team had cleared her car. For all she knew, the man last night had planted a tracking device. Hell, maybe he'd put a bomb on it. How had he gotten past security?

A dozen questions filled her head, the anger in her gut sizzling.

She'd shot the prick. Had they called the hospitals? Were they even looking for him?

She punched Matt's number in and he picked up on the first ring as she left the elevator and headed for her car.

"Miss me already?"

"I'm heading to Grey's. Meet me there?"

"I thought you had a couple of meetings."

"They were cancelled."

"What happened? Is it your head? Do you feel dizzy?"

She smiled. At least one person in the world cared about her. "Thank you."

"For what? Another amazing night of sex?"

The teasing did it and she laughed. Her career was in shambles, she was cut off from her team, and she was laughing.

Because of Matt.

"For worrying about me." She hated to get serious on him, but she wanted him to know. "Thank you for caring about me."

"Wait... Are you *crying*?"

She dashed at the tears on her cheeks. "Don't be ridiculous. How soon can you get to Grey's?"

She heard the screech of tires through the phone. "On my way. Should be there in fifteen minutes or less."

Her car still had crime scene tape around it. Was it safe to drive?

"Taylor!"

Meredith's voice echoed in the garage. Taylor turned slowly. "I've got to go," she said to Matt. "I'll see you in a few."

"Are you going to tell me what this is about once we're there?"

Meredith was stomping toward her, her forehead a thunderstorm.

Beck and her team must have played dumb about her notes.

God, she loved them all.

"Did my car clear forensics?" she called to Meredith.

"Yes, but it hasn't been cleared by me." Mer pointed a finger at her. "You're not leaving until we finish our discussion."

"I'm officially off the case," Taylor murmured to Matt. "But hell if I'm going to take this lying down."

"Jesus. What the hell happened?"

You happened.

Ignoring Meredith, Taylor smacked the crime scene tape out of the way and got into her car. "Nothing I can't handle. But trust me, Grey's going to love this."

"They *suspended* you?"

Matt sat in front of Grey's desk with Taylor beside him, her fingers gripping the arms of her chair while the Justice Team leader's eyes damned near exploded from his head. Add to that his face turning a violent shade of purple and whatever was going on inside him wasn't pretty.

"Yes," Taylor said. "I went to work this morning and they told me to hand over my badge and creds."

"Goddamn typical." Grey waggled one finger. "They had no intention of letting you keep this case. Should have seen that when Meredith gave you that ridiculous deadline. They wanted that asshole Leo to have this."

"Why?"

"Who the fuck knows. They're the FBI. They have reasons for everything."

"Guys," Matt said, "can we figure out a plan here? I mean, Tay, getting booted—"

Taylor gasped. "Oh, ouch, Mr. Sensitivity."

Ach. Shit. Maybe he should think once in a while before speaking. He reached over, squeezed her ice-cold hand still clutching that chair like a lifeline. "I'm sorry. My mouth moves faster than my brain sometimes. All I meant was, you don't need an FBI badge to keep investigating." He whipped off a happy smile. "You can be my assistant."

Grey snorted. "My ass. Everyone sit tight a minute."

He scooped up his desk phone and hit a button.

Taylor watched him with a sense of awe and hero worship most men would find intimidating. Matt? Well, idiot that he was, he found it inspiring. Getting Taylor to look at him that way might be his new goal in life.

She leaned forward, set one hand on the edge of Grey's desk. "What are you doing?"

He held up his finger. "Good morning. It's Grey. Is he in?"

"Grey," Taylor said, "it's okay. Like Matt said, I can work

with him. I already gave my team assignments. They have my notes. They won't give Leo a damn thing."

Justice kept the phone to his ear, a wry grin quirking his lips as he sat back, enjoying whatever he was about to do. "Watch the professional, Taylor. I'm exacting revenge for you. Actually, scratch that. The revenge is for me, you're the bonus. I hate the fucking backstabbing bureaucracy. I went through it, as did Monroe, even Caroline as well. Half my team has been jerked around by assholes who earned their stripes by sucking up inside the Hoover building."

Whoa. Justice was fired up. Based on what he'd heard so far, maybe his rejection from the FBI wasn't a bad thing. Even if it did still sting.

"Look man," Matt said, "don't get crazy here. Tay can fly under the radar with me."

"No. I'm getting crazy." He held up his finger again. "Good morning, sir...yes, thank you. It was an interesting case. I'll let Caroline know you're happy." He shot Taylor a smug look and hit her with a thumbs up. "Sir, there's another case I have an interest in. With your permission, I'd like to get my team on it. It might coincide with another of our investigations."

Five minutes later, after Justice laid some heavy bullshit on his boss, whoever the hell that was, and explained his history with the Jarvis case and how he'd left the Bureau before he could find Felicity, blah, blah, blah, he hung up and smacked his hands together.

"Tell me," Taylor said, "you did not just hijack the Jarvis case."

"Sweetheart, I just hijacked the Jarvis case. Thank me later."

Matt laughed. Taylor wasn't looking too thankful at the moment.

"Grey, seriously," she said, "are you trying to get me fired?"

Mitch's head popped around the side of the decorative

screen separating Justice's "office" from the rest of his team. "Who's getting fired?"

Taylor held up a hand. "I am."

"No shit?"

Matt rolled his eyes. "She's not getting fired."

Monroe's gaze pinged from Taylor to Grey. "What'd you do?"

"We're now on the Jarvis case."

"No shit?"

Did Monroe not have any other trite responses? "Dude, you gotta come up with something more original."

"Fuck off, Stephens."

"Children," Taylor said, "can we focus on my disintegrating career?"

"Technically," Matt said, "I think our friend here did you a huge large. If this case goes bust, the Justice Team—and not you—are on the hook for it. If we find Baby Jarvis, the Justice Team"—he looked at Grey—"I assume, will give you proper credit."

Grey nodded. "Bingo. You sure you don't want to come work for me?"

"I'm good where I am. Thanks."

Waving her arms, Taylor pulled their attentions back to her. "I can't believe you did this. Grey, if we blow it, you'll be in the fryer."

"Wouldn't be the first time. Besides, we don't exist, remember? If we do, I'll get an ass-whipping from my boss, he'll do what needs to be done to save face inside the Hoover building, and we all get back to work."

"You seem pretty confident of that."

"Taylor, this isn't my first rodeo. I don't care what my superiors say, they like that I piss people off. This team gets shit done when no one else can. We handle the cases the Bureau is afraid to touch. That's what I'm confident of. Now, are you going to shut up and help me solve this case or do I have to throw you out of here?"

Matt cleared his throat. "She's going to help you solve this case."

"But... I already had my team on it. Now I won't have them, and—"

"Shut up, Taylor," Monroe said. "Quit being such a tightass and roll with it. For the first time in your career, you get to go rogue. This is the fun part."

She narrowed her eyes at him. "I *was* going rogue. Why do you think I got suspended?"

"Getting suspended is for pussies. You're not really rogue until you get fired."

For once, Matt and Mitch actually agreed on something. Matt lifted one hand and high-fived his archenemy. "Why is it we don't like each other?"

Monroe shrugged. "Hell if I know."

Good enough. Matt turned back to Taylor. "We've got this. If you're not comfortable with the Justice Team angle, ride shotgun with me. You can act as a private citizen now and my firm has asked for your expert opinion on a case we are independently working. No feds, no Justice Team. Just you and me."

"It's not..."

"What?"

Wherever her thoughts led, she shook it off. "Nothing. I'm just...grateful." She reached for Matt's hand and squeezed it. Their eyes held for a few long seconds until Monroe cleared his throat.

"Knew it," he said to Grey. "She's banging him. After I told her not to. Unbelievable."

Taylor rolled her eyes. "Shut it, Mitch." Still holding Matt's hand, she turned to Grey. "Thank you. You have your own reasons for doing this, but I also know you partially did it for me. You know what this case means to me and I appreciate what you did."

"It's all good," he said. "But now we need to find this baby."

"Yes, we do." She pulled a file from her backup briefcase and handed it over the desk to Grey. "This is all I have with me. I have more at home I can send you."

Grey flipped the file open. "What's in here?"

"The Lamaze lady. Her name is Kristina Caldwell. Matt had planned to look into her this morning before we both got sidetracked."

Grey rolled his desk chair so he could look at Teeg behind the screen. "Nerd Boy, see what you can find on Kristina Caldwell."

"I heard her," Teeg said. "I'm on it."

Grey rolled back to his desk. "This is why Teeg makes the big bucks."

"My ass!" Teeg said. "Hang on. Here we go. She pays her taxes on time, has a big mortgage and some small credit card debt. Now, this is kinda interesting."

Taylor pushed out of her chair and swung wide of the screen so she could see Teeg. "What is it?"

"She's registered as a volunteer at Hearts of Love Adoptions. Call me crazy but I'd say that's some interesting irony. A Lamaze teacher working at an adoption agency?"

Matt joined Taylor. "What kind of volunteer work?"

"Give me a minute. I'm good, but not that good. All I've got is art. And it's buried. Here we go. It's a photo of her at an event. The caption says she's a volunteer."

"Teeg," Grey said as he jotted notes, "is Hearts of Love on that list of agencies Mitch and Caroline are working?"

While Teeg's fingers flew, Mitch shook his head. "Not ringing a bell. We may not have gotten to it yet, though."

What was this about Mitch and Caroline working with

adoption agencies? Matt held his hands out. "What are we talking about?"

Grey sat back in his chair and stacked his hands on his head. "My statement about the Jarvis case crossing paths with one of ours isn't far off the mark. We're investigating a black market adoption ring. We're using Mitch and Caroline as prospective adoptees."

Mitch as a father? Now that was scary.

"Nada!" Teeg shouted. "Hearts of Love is clean, so far. All positive reviews. That doesn't always mean anything. I'll dig around in the law enforcement databases. See what I can find."

Grey wrote himself another note. "Timing?"

"Am I Chris Angel here? This shit takes more than 3.5 seconds."

Holy hell. If Matt talked to one of the sisters that way—not that that would ever happen—they'd crucify him. The Justice Team definitely had their own set of whacky rules.

Matt glanced at Taylor. "Let's give Teeg time to sort this out. Meantime, you ride shotgun with me."

"Where?"

"Kristina Caldwell's. We've got a baby to find and you said she's at the top of your list. Let's go talk to her. See what she remembers about Baby Jarvis."

14

a make-out on a stakeout—it was a first for Taylor.

Stakeouts generally ranked right up there with hell in her opinion. A stakeout with Matt, however, wasn't all that bad.

In fact, it was currently rocking her world.

Through the windshield of his car, the setting sun hit him right along his strong jawline, growing stubble showing as he sucked her tongue into his mouth and stuck his hand up her shirt.

What had started out as a simple kiss while they waited for Kristina Caldwell to come home had turned into a full-on make-out session.

Taylor had tried to process all the emotions churning in her gut and blowing up her heart while staying focused.

Right. Like that was happening.

Grey went out on a limb. You have to solve this case, come hell or high water. Don't let Matt distract you.

Fat chance that. Matt had been doing that ever since he'd walked up to her at the bar that night at the conference. Even at the armory, surrounded by Grey, Mitch, and Teeg, she'd struggled to keep her mind focused on the investigation instead of sneaking Matt off to one of the empty rooms and doing him right there.

The FBI had employed plenty of closers over the years who were top-notch. Each knew how to kick over the smallest pebble to find the lead that would solve the case.

Taylor had a gut instinct that rivaled the best of them. Hers had told her to switch the focus of the investigation and follow every avenue Baby Jarvis might have taken. Grey had agreed.

None of the legal adoption agencies in the area had turned up anything fishy, and the TriCare Birthing Center didn't cater to women who wanted to give up their babies, but the overlap of Kristina Caldwell and Hearts of Love Adoption agency was a red flag. Much like the sticker on the silver pickup truck, this could be the small, seemingly insignificant element that could blow the case wide open.

Taylor and Matt had a list of questions to ask the woman, but Kristina wasn't home. She wasn't at any Lamaze meetings either—none were being held in the area, according to all the calls Matt had made.

Teeg was investigating black market adoption agencies. They couldn't stakeout any of them, so Grey and Teeg were working on a cyber investigation, using Mitch and Caroline as prospective adoptees.

Matt had mentioned what a scary idea it was for Mitch to procreate. In a way, Taylor thought it might be cool. He could be an ass, but she bet if you put a baby in his arms, he'd turn all soft and gooey.

Somehow, Taylor was sure she and Matt had gotten the safer, less fun assignment, and yet, it didn't feel that way. Matt had loaded them up with food from a hole-in-the-wall Greek restaurant, plenty of drinks, and he'd shared some funny stories from his childhood before they'd gotten sidetracked with that kiss. A few of his stories even involved his sister, but there was no sadness when he talked about her. He'd obviously loved her deeply and still missed her, but he focused on the happy times they'd spent together.

He'd managed to find that gap between devastation and survival. Taylor hoped that one day she could do the same with the memories of Isabel. She wanted to talk about her and remember how much fun they'd had together before her entire family's lives had gone to shit.

At some point in the past hour, she'd made a decision—once they were done with the Jarvis case, she was hiring Matt and the sisters to help bring closure to her own family. One way or another, she needed to know what had happened to Isabel.

And maybe if she didn't have an FBI job to return to...well, she'd have extra time on her hands.

Unless she kept Matt in bed...

"Heads up." Matt had somehow kept one eye on Kristina's place. "Black Lexus pulling in."

Taylor slid off his lap into her seat, buttoning her shirt. Sure enough, Kristina was finally coming home. Maybe they could get answers and figure out if she'd had any connection to Baby Jarvis.

Taylor shuffled napkins and empty pop cans out of the way and grabbed her binoculars. "Thank God, we didn't have to sit here all night waiting."

Matt took the binoculars and dropped a kiss on her lips. "I would have kept you entertained, sweet cheeks."

No doubt about that. "How exactly are we going to do this?" Taylor checked her makeup in the visor mirror. Her cheeks were flushed and her black eye was even more pronounced. "I'm not FBI anymore. I have no badge to flash, and she'll obviously remember us from the birthing center, so if we come clean, she'll know we duped her and Dottie. Not the best way to start our visit."

Kristina's car pulled into the garage and she hustled out,

grabbing the rolled up newspaper lying on the wide, concrete driveway.

"Hold up," Matt said. "She's got company."

Taylor squinted into the sinking sun. From what she could make out, a brand new white Escalade was sliding into Kristina's driveway.

"Damn. Guess we're sitting for a while longer." She edged over, shading her eyes from the sun to get a better look at the woman getting out of the Escalade. Kristina took a step back, looking left then right before she said something to the woman and waved the newspaper in front of her like she was trying to shoo her away. "Hey, isn't that the gal from the other night? The one Dottie and Kristina were both talking to in the back of the room?"

"Blond hair, fancy threads, enough diamonds to weigh down a cow?" Matt lowered the binoculars and nodded. "Check, check, and check."

The woman said something to Kristina and the woman once again waved her newspaper, looking completely flummoxed as she responded.

"Kristina doesn't seem too happy about seeing her." She wasn't a doctor or other birthing center staff member from what Taylor could recall. "Who *is* she?"

Matt reached into his backseat and pulled out a small parabolic microphone. "Let's find out."

The blonde moved closer to Kristina. In her high heels, she loomed over the smaller woman and Kristina reared back slightly, as if afraid she might catch something.

Matt stuck the earpiece in his ear and rolled down his window. He adjusted a few controls and then cocked his head.

"What are they saying?" Taylor whispered.

Matt took the earpiece out and held it up so both of them could listen. "Babies, what else?"

As Taylor leaned close to the black earpiece, she heard

Kristina snarl, "...told you the other night, this is on you...that baby...the whole thing." She pointed a finger. "...your fault, not mine."

The blonde's bracelets jangled on her arm as she raised a finger and put it in Kristina's face. She was facing them, so her voice came through clearer. "Just keep your mouth shut."

Blonde turned on her fancy heels and stomped back to her Escalade.

Matt threw the mic over the seat and started the car. "Stay with Kristina or follow blondie, Agent Sinclair?" He threw her a look, his hands gripping the steering wheel. "Your call."

He wanted to go after the blonde. Taylor looked between him and Kristina Caldwell, now hustling inside her garage, the door already starting its downward descent. The Escalade left the driveway and jetted up the street.

Taylor looked back at Matt. "I'm betting Kristina's not going anywhere else tonight. We can always come back."

He grinned and Taylor's insides did funny things. "I was hoping you'd say that. Put on your seatbelt."

They followed the blonde to the Adams Morgan area of DC where she slowed in front of a white stucco, corner building and then scored street parking in the middle of the adjacent block. Matt pulled into the fire lane on the opposite corner and waited as the woman parked and headed across the street toward the main entrance of the three-story building.

Lush flowerbeds filled the four-foot area in front and a leafy red bush added vibrancy to the long city block. Add to that the ornate overhang with red scrollwork covering the entry door and the whole place screamed of old-world elegance and money.

A man stood under the overhang keying in a code while Taylor snapped photos.

"Let's send this address to Grey and Teeg. See what they come up with."

"Send them her plate number, too. Might as well do the full workup."

"I will." She fired off a text and dropped her phone into her lap. "Here we are, chasing a hunch and following a woman who could be a total waste of our time."

"Eh. If it is, we cross her off the list. You never know."

Taylor chuckled. "She wasn't even *on* our list."

"She is now."

A car three doors down vacated a spot—lucky break there —and Matt hit the gas. "Parking space. Let's grab it while we're on ice."

"We're parking? We have no idea who this woman is or if she's important to our case. How long do you plan to wait?"

"No idea."

"Yeesh."

"Welcome to grunt work, babe."

They sat for ten minutes, stringing theories about the blonde and her possible connection to Kristina Caldwell and whatever baby the two women had been arguing about.

In the middle of their brainstorming Matt received a text from Charlie. The message contained a link to the local cable news station and he clicked it. A video popped up showing a reporter standing in front of a cemetery where Walt Jarvis had just held a private burial for Felicity. The reporter cut to Walt and Ann, their heads high, but grim faced and looking appropriately sad behind dark glasses.

"What is it?"

Matt closed the screen and set his phone on the dash. "Felicity's memorial service. Charlie sent me the link. Let's hope we don't have another impromptu press conference from my client."

Taylor's phone beep-beeped. "It's Grey." She punched the screen and put him on speakerphone. "Hey. What's up?"

"The Escalade is registered to a Rush Gardener, spouse of Rosalind Gardener."

Matt nodded. "Let's assume the blonde we followed is Rosalind. How about the address we sent you?"

"Owned by Rush as well. He's a lawyer. Civil litigation. Mostly car accidents, workplace injuries, that sort of thing."

How a civil litigation lawyer played into this, Matt wasn't sure. And apparently neither was Taylor because she curled her lip. "What do we know about the wife?"

"Thank you," Grey said to someone on his end. "Teeg just handed me a file and...oh, suh-weet."

"What?"

"Remember Hearts of Love adoptions?"

Taylor met Matt's gaze, eyebrows lifted. "The one Kristina Caldwell volunteers for? What about it?"

"Rosalind owns it. I knew there was a reason that place rang a bell with me."

What the? Matt's head damned near blew off his body. "She *owns* it?"

"You heard me. She's known in the adoption world as the Baby Matchmaker. Her agency—which she runs from her home—is private, quite renowned, and caters to the rich and famous who can't have kids or want to be seen as socially conscious and adopt, rather than adding to the world's over-population. Her agency's motto is 'Your perfect child is waiting.'"

"But she does everything legally, right?" Taylor asked.

"That depends on your interpretation of a certain incident in her background." Grey sounded almost gleeful. "Hearts of Love was involved in a controversy several years ago with a couple in Seattle. Some tree-hugging entrepreneurs with a billion-dollar cell phone recycling business wanted to adopt a couple of kids and contracted her agency to handle it. Something went sideways and the whole thing got hushed up and settled out of court. I don't have the details, but Teeg will keep digging."

Taylor held two hands up. "That's it. I want to talk to this woman. Something is definitely not copacetic in this whole thing. I want to know what her connection is to the birthing center, outside of Kristina Caldwell, and I want to know what baby the two of them were arguing over."

"Baby?" Grey asked.

Matt pointed at Taylor. "Relax a second. Let's think this through before we go knocking on her door."

"What baby?" Grey repeated, his voice carrying that don't-piss-me-off edge.

Taylor rummaged in her bag for something so Matt jumped in. "Rosalind showed up at Kristina Caldwell's when we were watching the place. We listened in and Kristina was bitching about some screw-up not being her fault."

"What screw-up?"

Wasn't that the million-dollar question? "We don't know. It involved a baby, which is why we tailed Rosalind."

Taylor smacked Matt's arm. A quick slap-slap-slap and *ow*.

"Heads up," she said. "Rosalind is on the move."

Across the street, Rosalind quick-walked from the building to her car, clearly in a hurry as she darted into traffic and almost got pancaked by an oncoming vehicle. A horn sounded and she raised a hand offering a distracted mea culpa.

That didn't last long because she hopped in and cut into traffic raising the ire of an old guy cruising the block in his ancient Ford LTD. How that land yacht even fit on the narrow street eluded Matt.

"Someone's late," Taylor muttered.

"Grey," Matt said, "which unit do the Gardeners live in?"

"2B. Why?"

"We'll call you back."

Taylor punched off and waved her hand. "Hit it. Let's see where she's going."

But Matt didn't move. He sat, staring at the front of Rosalind's building, his mind spinning. This was why he loved cold case work. The hunt. Chasing leads, failing, and trying again, all of it revved him up.

"Matt, come on. She's turning."

"I know," he said. "We're going to plan B."

"We have a plan B?"

He grinned at her. Couldn't help it. How cute was she? "We do now." He pointed to the building. "We're doing a sneak and peek."

15

"*H*a!" Taylor said. "Good one. Or did I not just hear you say you wanted to break into the Gardener's home?"

"You heard me, sweet cheeks. Rosalind isn't likely to volunteer that she's running an illegal adoption center out of her home, so we'll check it out ourselves. See if there's any meat to this theory." He whipped the key out of the ignition and dangled it at her. "Unless you'd rather wait in the car."

If he understood Taylor at all, there was no way on God's green earth she'd sit by and let him search the Gardener place alone. FBI agent—even if on suspension—or not, her competitive edge ran just as sharp as his. She'd want to see for herself what secrets the Gardeners kept.

She eyeballed the keys in his hand. "You're crazy if you think you're leaving me out here."

Yep. Just like he thought. "Alright then, Special Agent Sinclair, let's see what we've got."

Out of the glove box he snagged a soft leather pouch that fit nicely in his back pocket. His lock-picking tools. Next came a couple pairs of latex gloves. He handed one set to Taylor and shoved the other in his pocket with his tools.

"Handy," she cracked.

"I like to be prepared."

"Right. Because who knows when you'll be required to break into someone's house."

"Exactly."

After hopping out, he locked the car and held his hand out to Taylor, who grabbed on as he led her across the street.

Shielding her eyes against the sun with her free hand, she scanned the upper floors of the building. "Oh, look. Third floor. The corner unit has a for sale sign." At the curb, she pulled him to a stop and tugged on his sleeve. "Oh, honey. I love this building. Please, baby, let's go look at the unit for sale."

Taking her cue and for the benefit of the two women strolling with their toddlers, he lifted his hand to block the sun and stared up at the top floor.

"It's a great neighborhood," one of the moms offered.

"See!" Taylor gushed. "It's perfect for us."

"Eh," Matt said, again enjoying playing the role of Taylor's better half. "Why not? If it'll make you happy."

"Oh, sweetheart," she purred, "it will. And you know what happens when I'm happy."

The not-so-subtle innuendo wasn't lost on him. Or the moms. They wandered by, giggling at Taylor's hijinks, and Matt narrowed his eyes. "Go easy, killer, or I'm gonna be walking around with a chubby."

"Ha!" she said. "I think I'd enjoy that."

"And, you know, it wouldn't kill you to try to blend. I know you're not used to ditching rules, but seriously, let's not call unnecessary attention to ourselves."

He led her to the entrance, found the door indeed locked and pushed one of the buzzers. 1A.

No answer. He tried another—nada—then stabbed at the next one. Sooner or later, he'd get a response. 2D.

"Hello?"

Bingo. "Hi. My name is Brian Foggerty. My wife and I are here to look at the unit for sale, but the realtor—"

Bzzzttt. A buzzer sounded followed by the immediate click of a lock disengaging. Huh. If he'd known it was going to be that easy...

"He didn't even let you finish," Taylor huffed. "For the love of God, we could be serial killers and he just buzzed us in. People really need to be more careful with their personal safety."

Was she really complaining about this?

"Yeah, well, it worked for us."

He swung the door open and waved her through.

Once inside she headed for the elevator and punched the button. The elevator doors whooshed open and he set his hand on her lower back, guiding her in front of him. "You're funny, Tay."

"I am funny. Sometimes I don't appreciate that about myself. I'm too serious. You've helped me lighten up though. So, thank you."

Wow. Now there was a compliment of all compliments and it left him...stunned. Not stunned enough, however, to ignore an opportunity. A grand one. He waited for the doors to close, then hooked his hand around her neck and hit her with a kiss that had him contemplating the benefits of the emergency stop button. As usual, she responded, arching into him and playing hide-and-seek with her tongue.

Thoughts of pressing her against the elevator wall and sliding into her raced through his mind. Damn, he was crazy about her. She upped the ante on the kiss and slid her leg up his calf.

God, this woman was exceptional. Wicked, wicked woman.

Ding. The elevator cruised to a halt and Taylor angled back, pressing her hands against his cheeks. "Oh, my," she said. "I think we'll have to finish this later."

They sure would. "You can count on that."

He and Taylor had been competitors for months. That sense of competition had driven his lust for her to another level. From the second he'd seen her, he wanted her. Then when she opened her mouth he wanted to shut her up. By kissing her. Kissing that mouth.

Kissing everything. Taylor, pain in the ass that she was, did it for him. Intellectually, physically, emotionally, all of it. The highest of the highs.

But with the highs there had to be lows. That was life and sometimes it sucked. In fact, life sucked a lot. He'd learned that when his baby sister had been murdered and his mother became a drunk. The trick was making the most of the times that didn't suck.

He and Taylor? They'd yet to experience the lows with each other. Sure, she'd curtailed the drinking, but maintaining that sobriety was a different animal. Could she do it long-term and maybe give them a shot at an actual relationship? At commitment, dinners, and the mundane trappings that came with being a couple?

He hoped so.

The elevator doors slid open and straight ahead, against a stark white wall, an ornate brass sign indicated units 2A and 2B to the left.

Taylor, having perfect vision, hooked a left. "Look around," she whispered. "Check for security cameras."

"On it."

He did a visual sweep of the corridor, his eyes darting up and down, checking the corners and ceiling for any overhead cameras. "You see anything?"

"Nope."

"Me neither. I think we're good."

"Really, the security is extremely lax in this building."

"Good for us."

He stopped at unit 2B tucked in the corner. Another lucky break given that he only had to worry about nosey neighbors from one side. He knocked on the glossy red door and waited. Nothing.

"Try again," Taylor suggested. "Just to be sure."

Matt rapped on the door again, harder this time, but not banging. No sense alerting the neighbors to the B&E about to happen.

He leaned closer to the door, his ear almost pressed against it. No sound came from inside.

Satisfied no one was home, he nodded. "Huddle up here. Block the view in case someone comes into the hallway."

Taylor did as he asked and the scent of her perfume, something soft—jasmine?—distracted him for a few seconds. *Focus here, dumbass.*

Sliding the tension wrench into the lock, he turned until the inner cylinder moved then inserted the pick, finagling it until he'd moved each pin, one by one and...*done.* Lock popped.

Working quickly, he pushed open the door, heard a chime and halted. Door chime. *Security system.* But the chime went silent so Matt slipped inside with Taylor behind him. The keypad on the wall told him the alarm was inactive.

The fading aroma of fresh baked cookies tickled his senses. He locked the door behind them, then held his hand out, blocking Taylor from moving as he listened. Just in case someone was home, maybe in the shower, about to walk out and *hello, strangers.*

"I don't hear anything," she said.

The ultra-neat living room with walls the color of a stormy sky and a bright white sofa looked straight out of a decorating magazine. It led to a hallway that stretched across the front of the building. At the end of it sat what looked like another large, open area that must have been the kitchen and dining area.

Taylor snapped on her gloves. "I think we're good. Let's see if there's an office."

Three open doors, two on one side, one on the other lined the corridor and Matt hustled along. First door. Bedroom. He popped his head in. No one. Next door. Bathroom. Also empty. The third door was ajar and he noted the exact position before pushing it open and finding the office. Bingo.

Before they left, he'd reposition the door, but for now, they were going in.

A huge mahogany desk served as the focal point in the room. A large bookcase held what looked like vintage books and various knickknacks and framed photos. No photos of babies, though. It struck Matt as odd.

None of that, for the moment, mattered. What held Matt's attention was the three-drawer filing cabinet wedged in the corner.

"I'll take the desk," Taylor said. "You deal with that filing cabinet. Let's be quick."

Rosalind was Type A.

The top of her desk held little except for a thin laptop and single red file folder. The file had an elegant stamp on the front with the Hearts of Love logo. Inside was a birth certificate and adoption papers. Taylor had just snapped a picture of the birth certificate when she heard the squeak of the apartment door.

What the hell...?

She glanced at Matt, her blood rushing loudly in her ears. Someone was home.

He gestured at her as he tucked himself behind the open office door. It looked like he wanted her to get down.

Behind the desk? Was he kidding?

Knew this was a bad idea.

But, oh the rush of it! Breaking in, sneaking around, finding evidence...

Breaking the law.

We're so dead.

"Yes, I know I'm late," Rosalind's irritated voice cut through Taylor's racing thoughts. Matt was waving at her wildly. High heels clicked in the hallway. "I forgot the damned file. It's right on my desk."

Taylor shoved the birth certificate aside and shot a photo of the adoption papers. Slamming the folder closed, she dropped behind the desk and shifted the office chair in front of her, knowing it was a wasted tactic. No way they were getting out of this unnoticed.

Damn it! If she hadn't already incinerated her career, this would definitely do the job.

She fired off the two pictures to Grey and wondered how bad her arrest photo was going to look with her black eye, unwashed hair, and total lack of makeup.

Pretty damn bad. When the press got hold of this, AD Cunningham was going to string her up but good. He'd probably line up the firing squad. At least Matt and Beck would visit her in prison.

Rosalind blew into the office, bracelets jingling as she kept talking on her phone and headed for her desk.

Taylor held her breath. How had she gone from elite FBI agent to running shotgun on an illegal B&E in less than twelve hours?

Mad Dog. It was all his fault.

Again.

Rosalind closed the space to the desk and picked up the folder from the other side. Taylor made herself as small as she could, sure Rosalind would hear her heart slamming into her ribcage.

Game over.

"Here it is." Rosalind paused and tapped the folder on the desk. "Give me twenty. I promise you, it will be worth it. This baby is going to rock your world."

She turned and Taylor squeezed her eyes shut, waiting for Rosalind to see Matt behind the door and scream.

"No, I told you," she said, "this one is special. I handpicked her out of several children who fit your exact parameters. Her parents come from very elite stock. Like I promise every client, she is your perfect child."

Stock? Were people cattle now?

Rosalind's footsteps faded, her voice growing distant as she went back down the hall toward the front door. A moment later, the door squeaked once more and Taylor heard the click of it closing.

No way.

No. Frickin'. Way!

She hadn't seen Matt.

She hadn't realized Taylor was under her desk.

Taylor shook from head to toe. She couldn't even push the chair out of the way to crawl out from under the desk.

This was why she shunned undercover work and stayed safe in her Bureau cubicle.

"It's safe," Matt said. "You can come out now. She's gone."

"No shit, Sherlock," Taylor murmured, kicking the chair away. She climbed out on shaky legs and found Matt holding out a hand to help her up.

Ignoring it, she stood on her own, locking her knees. "What the hell did we just do?"

"Avoid an uncomfortable confrontation?"

He smirked and Taylor wanted to slap him.

What was this man doing to her?

"We shouldn't be here." She pushed past him, every cell in her body screaming for her to run. "I need air."

"Taylor." Matt reached for her, but she blew him off, beel-ining for the front door.

After making sure no one was around, she hustled outside, her pulse erratic and her head a mess. Matt's footsteps pounded behind her.

He didn't say anything else, just followed silently behind her. At his car, she planted her hands on the hood and tried to catch her breath.

"So that was fun," he said, leaning next to her. "What were you taking pictures of in that folder?"

"Fun?" She shook her head and ground her teeth. "We almost got caught. We're lucky we're not on our way to jail right now."

"Eh." Matt shrugged, staring at the apartment. "Grey would've bailed us out."

Jesus! How could he be so flippant about all of this? "Working undercover is one thing. This is a horse of an entirely different color, Matt. This is criminal."

"Sometimes to get to the truth, we have to color outside the horse's lines."

Every step of the way, you've broken protocol on this case... Meredith's words rang in her head. Taylor pushed off the hood and balled her fists. "I can't be this person, Matt. I'm sorry. I want to solve this case, but I can't do it this way."

A humorous frown passed over his features. "Did you not feel that? The rush. The nudge in your gut that you're onto something that'll crack this case wide open?"

It had been a rush all right. That didn't make it okay. "Are you nuts?"

Matt boosted himself off the car and took one of her hands. "Look, we're after a killer here, and maybe a child abductor. With the press shining a light on this case, and the FBI rushing to find someone to prosecute, we may have to bend a few rules to make sure justice is served. I thought you understood that and were on board with it."

Taylor blew out a breath, kicked at a rock. "I thought I was, too, but this is completely new territory for me. I'm one of the good guys, remember? You, Grey, and the others—you're used to doing things more...creatively. I may push a few boundaries here and there, but I don't break laws, Matt."

He released her hand and took a step back. His face was stern. "Do you want to solve this case or not, because the last time I checked, you're suspended from the Bureau, and from what I can see, they don't deserve you?"

He was pissed. Royally.

Didn't he understand?

He stepped toward her again, close enough he had to look down on her. His voice was low when he spoke. "I told you going in how I work. So don't give me this bullshit that I'm corrupting you."

She'd never seen him like this and she didn't like it. "Bullshit? Are you serious right now?" Her voice shook. She couldn't help it. The adrenaline was wearing off and she felt weak from the seriousness in his voice, on his face.

"I promise you, we will solve this case for better or for worse, and I don't go back on my promises. But I need to know. Are you in or out?"

An ultimatum. Lovely.

She paced away, aware of the no-win situation she was in. She'd made sure her whole life, since Isabel's disappearance, that she'd done the right thing, because when she didn't, bad shit happened.

Isabel had been taken because Taylor had shamed her into staying in that goddamn tent. Her parents had become distant and their marriage had fallen apart because Taylor had made the mistake of leaving Izzy out there alone.

Her family had imploded and it was all her fault.

She'd worked her ass off to be the good daughter, the hotshot FBI agent, the perfect citizen, boss, employee.

Was she seriously going to blow all of that to bits over this case? Over this *man*?

A headache pounded in her temples. A throbbing pain pulsed in her chest as well. Her feet moved of their own accord, bringing her back to face Matt. "You really know how to seduce a girl to the dark side, don't you?"

His face was neutral, but curiosity lit his eyes. "Does that mean you're in?"

"Yes. No." She sighed. "Maybe."

He grinned. "You haven't even scratched the surface of the dark side yet, Agent Sinclair, but stick with me and you will." He sat on the hood again and playfully chucked her chin with his knuckles. "And that's a promise."

He grinned and Taylor felt herself melting under those pretty eyes. She took a step closer, her fingers itching to touch him.

What am I doing?

"How did you get the nickname Mad Dog?"

He seemed surprised. "When people push me too far, I tend to get a bit snippy."

Yeah, she'd just seen that. "Good. I was afraid it was because you're insane."

With that, he threw his head back and laughed. "Maybe that too."

She had to admit, she was incredibly relieved that Rosalind hadn't seen him hiding behind her office door. That they wouldn't be spending the night in separate jail cells. "There was a birth certificate and adoption papers in the folder," she told him. "I snapped pictures of all of it and sent them to Grey."

He grabbed her by the hips and pulled her in close between his long legs. "Risky move, sweet cheeks, but I admire your guts, among so many of your other attributes."

He dropped a kiss on her lips and she responded, because, honestly, she couldn't resist him, no matter what.

After a long, deep kiss with lots of tongue, Matt helped her into his car.

"Where are we going?" she asked.

"To talk to my boss. She worked an identity fraud case and is now somewhat of an expert on birth certificates. Let's talk to her and see if she can tell us about the one you snapped a picture of."

16

—————

$\mathcal{A}$t the office, Matt printed the photos and they now stood in front of Charlie's desk as she studied the birth certificate.

"If I had the original," she said, "we'd be able to tell from the intaglio and seal if this was an official document. The watermarks are there though." She looked up at Taylor. "Do you remember what the paper looked like? If they'd used the intaglio technique, there'd be an almost grooved surface. The printing plates have depressions. When the birth certificates are printed, depressions are made and they hold the ink. The grooves are almost unidentifiable unless you know what you're looking for. They could be fractions of a millimeter."

Taylor shook her head. "I didn't touch it, but the surface looked smooth. I remember the seal though. It was flat."

That got Charlie's attention. Her head snapped up from her study of the documents. "It wasn't embossed?"

"No. Should it have been?"

"All states do it differently, but yes, this particular one, if the document was the original and not a copy, should be raised."

"Well, unless it was a color copy, it looked like an original. It had the steel engraved borders and everything."

"Look, guys, without seeing what you saw, it's hard to tell. Complicating this are the adoption papers. Typically, when an adoption is finalized the birth certificate is amended. The biological parents are removed and the adoptive parents are added. Then the records are closed. Now, that's not always the case. In some states, the biological parents can request that the information remain open."

Matt walked around the desk and compared the names on the birth certificate with the adoption papers. "The parents' names are different."

"Which," Taylor said, "indicates this could be the original birth certificate."

"Yes."

Taylor shook her head. "I don't understand what this woman is doing. Even if it were an open adoption, she should have an amended birth certificate."

Matt leaned against the wall and rested his head back. They needed to research the adoptions Rosalind had handled. And that whole comment she'd made about the baby's parents being good stock? What the hell was that about?"

From her spot near the desk, Taylor eyed him. "What are you thinking?"

"I'm thinking Teeg better get moving on intel for Hearts of Love. I don't care how positive the reviews are. Something, somewhere is screwed."

Taylor whipped out her phone. "I'll call him. Besides, he owes us an update on the list of people who own silver trucks."

Ha. Good luck there. Even if nerd boy had that list, there could be thousands of people on it. It would take a small army to check each one. "Don't bet the farm on that list. It'll take us a month to run it down."

"Don't be so negative. Turns out Grey's little wonder kid is developing software that will help."

Now this sounded promising. "What software?"

"I don't know the exact deets, but it's basically an eye in the sky that lets agents zoom in on addresses."

"Like a street view?"

"Yes. Grey mentioned it the other day, then I asked Teeg about it when we were at the armory earlier. The way he explained it, he can upload a giant list of addresses and a street view for each will pop up on the screen. Initially, he was hoping to track specific people. Now, he's testing parameters to figure out if there are things that could be entered and searched for."

"Like stickers on the back of silver trucks?"

She waggled her finger. "Now you're getting it."

"If we could use that software, it'd speed things up. In the meantime, I'm gonna take another run at Walt, see if he remembers this sticker."

"I'll come with you."

Oh, right. That'd be brilliant. The suspended FBI agent sitting in on a meeting with a senator who Matt had signed a confidentiality agreement with. He glanced at Charlie, whose gaze ping-ponged between them.

His boss wasn't stupid. By now, if she hadn't already figured it out, she at least suspected Matt and Taylor were actively swapping bodily fluids. He jerked his head to the door.

"Let's finish this in my office."

Not waiting for a response, he led Taylor down the hall and closed the door behind them.

"Honey," he said, "I'm sorry. You can't come with me."

"Sure I can. I'm acting as a private citizen, consulting with your firm. Remember?"

Did he ever. "Yes, but the last time you met with Walt, it was on behalf of the FBI. We weren't there together. No matter what we think he's hiding, he's still my client and you're an FBI agent. Even on suspension."

"And you signed an NDA."

Non-disclosure agreement. "I did. Plus, Walt isn't exactly your biggest fan."

As irritated as she must have been, she hid it well. No pissy pressed lips or glaring looks.

"I understand," she said. "If the roles were reversed, I'd tell you the same."

"If you want, stay here. Work from my office. I shouldn't be gone long. When I get back, we'll huddle up."

The Schock office was quiet. Too quiet.

Taylor was used to the hustle and bustle of the Bureau with the constantly ringing phones and people rushing to meetings.

Here it was the opposite. Matt was gone, Charlie was busy, and Meg was having coffee with a friend.

Taylor checked her phone for messages. The same as five minutes ago. Beck had texted her five times. Janiece two. No calls from Teeg or Grey.

Beck and Janiece were keeping her abreast of the shitstorm at the Bureau that Grey's highjacking of the Jarvis case had caused. Everyone, from Cunningham down to Leo, was blaming her.

It felt righteously good to be the thorn in their side right now, even though Grey was the one who'd stuck it there.

Beck had brought her up-to-date on the fact that he'd checked all the area hospitals and no one fitting the description of her attacker had turned up with a gunshot wound. No surprise there. Whoever had broken into her condo and evaded the parking garage security in an attempt to mess with her car was no amateur. He wouldn't be dumb enough to go to a public hospital for treatment, and the wound hadn't been life threatening. Anyone with basic medical treatment could probably handle patching him up.

Especially someone who might have medical training and a military background.

She had the list of silver trucks, she just needed access to Teeg's software. Matt's laptop had gone into sleep mode waiting for that access. Until Teeg did his magic, Taylor was stuck twiddling her thumbs.

Rocking back in Matt's office chair, she studied his desk. Solid, honey oak. Very pedestrian for such an energetic guy, but he might not have had any say in it.

Colored files and various folders were stacked all over the top. Amongst them were investigator manuals and a car magazine with a beautiful, very busty gal doing a move on the hood of a car that Taylor was sure only a gymnast could pull off.

Go figure.

Inside the pencil drawer, highlighters and pens fought for space with paper clips and loose change. Dry erase markers tangoed with notecards and a travel-size bottle of hand sanitizer.

Underneath a spiral notebook lay a set of handcuffs.

Taylor fingered the cuffs, wondering how many criminals Matt had arrested over the years.

How many women had he used these on?

Jealousy flitted through her stomach and she shoved the drawer closed. The feeling was a new one. She hadn't felt jealousy over anyone since...

Isabel.

Their parents had never treated Izzy any differently when she'd been around, but after her kidnapping, they'd been all-Isabel, all the time.

She couldn't blame them, but they'd had another daughter still around who felt just as lost and awful as they did. A little attention would have been like an oasis in the desert of her childhood.

Now, here she was, feeling jealousy for the first time in years.

I've totally fallen for Mad Dog.

As in...

Love.

Her phone buzzed, jarring her, and giving her the much-needed excuse to slam the door on that thought. She snatched it up and saw Teeg's text.

She was in.

Waking up Matt's laptop, she followed the instructions Teeg sent and loaded in the address at the top of her list. The software took her to the street view of the first silver truck.

No sticker or emblem of any kind on the back window.

As the next half hour went by, Taylor *click-click-click*ed her way through dozens of addresses and street views, her shoulders getting tight and the quiet of the office closing in on her. She took a break to text Beck and Janiece and tell them to keep their heads down and stay out of Leo's path. As soon as she wrapped up this case, she'd be back and things would once again be normal.

I hope.

Click-click-click, she went to work again.

This could take all day.

This will take all day.

Could the owner of the silver truck be the same person who'd broken into her condo? The same man who'd attacked her?

Of course, the emblem could have peeled off after all these years. Or the truck could have been sold.

And while she'd rather be chasing down Rosalind and the baby adoption ring, Matt wanted this truck thing cleared up first.

Because his job was to find the man who'd taken Felicity, first and foremost.

What seemed like a thousand clicks later, Taylor froze and blinked her tired eyes.

There. A decal in the back window.

She zoomed in, blinked again, and yep. *That's it!* The eagle with 'God Bless America.'

Shazam!

Unlike the current programs available to the general public that blanked out license plates and other personal information from street views, Teeg's software allowed her to get up close and personal to the plate. She was jotting down the number and address when a voice from the doorway startled her.

"You must be Taylor."

Taylor looked up to see who she assumed to be Meg Schock smiling at her.

The woman raised a hand with a purple mug that said, *I brake for unicorns.* "I brought you coffee."

Meg looked like a unicorn kind of gal. The boho artist getup she wore was topped off with a long braid and hemp necklace at her throat.

The smell of a good Colombian roast drifted into the air, teasing Taylor's nose. She returned Meg's friendly smile. "Just what I need. Thank you."

Meg entered and handed Taylor the mug. "I'm Meg, by the way. Charlie told me you and Matt have a couple of fresh leads on the Jarvis case."

The coffee was smooth, dark, and warmed Taylor's throat. She sighed her pleasure and nodded. "Matt is speaking with Senator Jarvis now about the silver truck with the decal. I may have located it, in fact, so I need to call Matt and let him know. We also have our sights on Rosalind Gardener who runs an adoption agency that's somehow linked to the TriCare Birthing Center."

"Hmm." Meg sipped her coffee and sat in the chair across from Taylor, adjusting the folds of her multicolored skirt. "Do you have any pets?"

Taylor stilled with the mug halfway to her lips. "Excuse me?"

"You know, cats, a dog, fish, anything?" At Taylor's look of confusion, Meg went on. "There's a stray cat in our neighborhood. I'm trying to find it a home."

A stray cat. Right. "I work long hours, so no, I don't have pets. Doesn't seem fair to leave one alone all the time."

"What made you want to become an FBI agent?"

Not the first time she'd been asked that question, but it still seemed out of place. "Who wouldn't want a job with long hours, mediocre pay, and bad guys shooting at you?"

They shared a smile. "Must be tough being on suspension."

Ah. The rub. "The Bureau is under a lot of scrutiny and pressure to solve this case. Once I do that, my suspension will be lifted."

Meg's smile turned cool. "You and Matt seem to be working well together. I assume you'll give him credit where it's due."

"Of course. I didn't mean to imply—"

"Your family," Meg interrupted. "Do you see them much?"

Charlie may have been the more assertive sister, but Meg knew her way around an interrogation. A sharp, sarcastic reply burned on Taylor's tongue, and she bit it back. The sisters were Matt's employers and she didn't want to piss them off or offend them. "My mother and father are divorced and living on opposite coasts. I see them when I can."

"Your job gets in the way."

Was this leading somewhere? "Much like you, I love what I do, and I'm devoted to my career. You're lucky to work with your sister. Do you see *your* parents much?"

Charlie swung into the room and stopped at Meg's chair. "No, we don't."

One side of Meg's mouth quirked. "Touché, Agent Sinclair."

Charlie leaned a hand on the back of her sister's chair and put the other on her hip. "I believe what my polite but curious sister here is trying to get around to is that we think of Matt as a little brother and we don't want to see him get hurt."

Taylor jerked back. "Get hurt? By *me*?"

Meg held up a hand as if to reassure her, but Charlie slapped it down. "Professionally, Matt could get a black eye over this case if you screw up. Oh, wait, you already *did*. The potential for us to lose Walt as our client is nearly a certainty if he finds out Matt is working with you, which means, you're jeopardizing our agency, Taylor. Add to that the fact that your recent actions have gotten you shot at and suspended, and I'd say you're definitely putting Matt's career—and possibly his life —on the line along with yours."

Meg scooted forward and set her mug on the desk, giving Taylor a serious look. "It's obvious Matt cares about you. In fact, I've never seen him so...enamored. I'm concerned about his emotional well-being once you go back to being an FBI agent and no longer need him for this case."

Taylor's hackles weren't just up, they were shooting light-ning bolts. "I'm not *using* him for this case. I care about him too. Very much so. And I'm sure you two have done your home-work. You probably ran a background check on me the minute Matt mentioned my name. What is it that you really want to know?"

"As you just stated," Meg said, "you don't have time to visit your parents, or even to keep a pet. Exactly how do you propose you have time for a committed relationship?"

Was she serious?

Charlie cleared her throat. "Matt's relationship with you is none of our business, but we do care about him, and don't want to lose him. He's the best we've had at our agency in a long time, and we only hire topnotch candidates."

Maybe it wasn't just Taylor they were worried about. They were worried about Grey poaching Matt.

For some reason, that made Taylor smile. "Matt is committed to you and this agency, but he's a grown man with a stubborn streak and some pretty lofty goals in life. All of us want what's best for him, but I doubt any of us can keep him from taking risks and doing what he believes is right, fair, and just. I fully support him in that, and you should too."

Charlie winked at her. "I think you just answered our biggest question, Taylor."

Meg smiled, a big, goofy grin. "With flying colors."

It took a second for Taylor to realize she'd just been had. She ran her hands through her hair and chuckled. "Well played, ladies. You had me going there for a moment with the big sister act."

"Oh, we do consider ourselves his big sisters," Charlie said. "If you break his heart, I guarantee your suspension from the FBI will be the least of your problems. But, yeah, we wanted to see what you'd say if we pushed you about him. I think you passed."

"She did." Meg gave a real smile and rose. "I'm glad we're on the same page, Agent Sinclair. We'll let you get back to work now."

Taylor silently shook her head as the sisters left. It was good that Matt had these two looking out for him, and their points were valid. She had no intention of bringing Matt down if she took the fall on this case.

She also wasn't going to break his heart.

She dialed to tell him about the silver truck, and the call went to his voicemail. *God, I love that voice.*

She left a message, then decided to push her luck with the sisters.

Charlie was in her office, typing on her computer. "What's up?" she asked when Taylor stopped in her doorway.

"I need to borrow a car."

"Do I want to know where you're going?"

"I found a silver truck that matches the one we're looking for. Matt's still tied up with Walt and I don't have my car here."

"Matt left orders not to let you go anywhere on your own." Charlie stopped typing and grabbed a set of keys from her desk drawer. She rose and shoved her office chair in. "You can ride shotgun."

The ride to the address wasn't as bad as the interrogation in Matt's office. Charlie had once been FBI. She spoke Taylor's language and drove like a bat out of hell. So mostly, Taylor held on to the door handle and kept her mouth shut.

"This is it," Charlie said, pulling to a stop at the curb.

Taylor looked at the house number, back to her notes, and then to the empty driveway. "Dammit. In the time it took to drive here, he's already gone."

"Do you have a name?"

Taylor dialed Grey. "I will in a moment."

Grey answered on the first ring and she fed him the license plate number and address. "This could be our guy, the one who kidnapped Felicity."

"Give me a sec..." The sound of keystrokes filtered through the phone. "Whatever you do, do not engage the owner of the truck. Let Stephens do it. If this is our kidnapper, he could also be the killer."

"Matt's not here. I can handle it."

"You went by yourself?"

The annoyance in Grey's voice set her nerves on edge. "I'm with Charlie Schock, but seriously, you're all acting like I can't take care of myself. I know how to apprehend a suspect."

"Where is Matt?" Grey ground out.

"He's at Walt's asking about the decal on the truck."

Frustration strained Grey's voice even more. "We're running in too many directions with this case. The silver truck is a solid lead into Felicity's kidnapping, but I'm not sure about this Rosalind or if she has anything to do with Baby Jarvis."

"Charlie clued me in on how the illegal birth certificates and adoption papers work. Teeg could run the names on the birth certificate I sent you and see what pops up."

A long pause. A heavy sigh. "This is spinning out of control. We need to regroup and work up an effective plan. I want everyone in my office in one hour. Including the Schock sisters. *Capisce?*"

"You want me to bring them to your place?" Taylor sat back and glanced at Charlie. "Are you sure?"

"Yes. Get your ass in gear, round up your partner, and let's get this done."

It wasn't everyday Justice Greystone called a meeting that included his team, a suspended FBI agent, a private investigator, a forensic sculptor, and a psychologist.

This was either the A Team or they'd wind up killing each other.

Either way, it'd be interesting.

Matt grabbed one of the beat-up metal-framed chairs stacked in the corner and pulled it in front of the giant whiteboard Grey had wheeled into the center of the Justice Team's command center.

"Okay, people," Grey said, waving a marker at the motley crew sitting in a quasi row/semi-circle in front of him. "We need to divvy up assignments here. I can't have all of you running around half-cocked."

On the whiteboard he made five columns. "The silver truck. Stephens, I want you on that. I've got the owner's name. I need you to run the guy and see if he has a record."

"Fine."

In the first column, Grey wrote *truck* then Matt's name in

the far left side of the board. He placed a checkmark in the column.

"Rosalind Gardener. I'm putting Mitch and Caroline on her."

He wrote the woman's name in the next column, then M/C under Matt's name with another checkmark in that column.

Caroline held her hand up. "What exactly are we doing?"

"The same as the other adoption agencies you've been working on. Pose as a potential client. You're looking to adopt."

"Might I suggest," Taylor said, holding up her pen, "that they pose as an upscale couple. When Matt and I were in her office, we heard Ros say something about parents with good breeding; the child was from good stock."

"I'm not wearing a tie," Mitch said.

"Idiot," Caroline said, "you don't have to. We'll put you in some Yeezy jeans and sneakers and you'll be all set. Just try to control your mouth."

"That'll set Grey's budget back," Taylor said.

Mitch blew Caroline a kiss and Matt snorted.

"Are we done screwing around?" Grey wanted to know.

Caroline jotted a note on her pad. "Sorry, boss."

"Charlie and Meg. Since Walt is your client and I'm sure you're bound by a confidentiality agreement, it's probably best that we leave all things Walt-related to you."

"I agree," Charlie said, "Obviously, I can't share that information with you."

"Yes, but you can share it with Matt."

Matt liked the sound of this so far. Two out of three assignments involved him. Grey wrote Felicity's name in the next column then added Meg/Charlie to the left sidebar along with two more checkmarks.

Taylor held her pen up again. "How about the guy who broke into my place and attacked me in the garage? I believe he's linked to the Jarvis case. My team has had no luck finding him, but maybe if we go back over the evidence?"

"Let me look into it," Charlie said. "I can get a friend in the Bureau to pull camera footage from the garage."

Taylor chewed her pen. "He was wearing a mask, so facial rec won't work."

"We have something better," Teeg called. "It can match a perp's gait and other things. We don't need his face."

Charlie grinned. "I've got to see that."

Grey added the next column and appropriate check marks. "Okay. Let's start breaking all this down. We'll list anything related to your individual assignments to the corresponding column. When we're done, take a picture of this board if you have to because these are the assignments. If there's any cross-over, I need to be notified. At any given time, I want to look at this board and know who is doing what. Got it?"

A series of yes-sirs filled the otherwise quiet room.

"As usual, we'll use Teeg as support. Just don't bombard him. He's working another case for me so we'll all have to cooperate."

"I know I'm a catch, but don't fight over me!" Teeg called, rolling back and forth between three oversized monitors.

Jeez, the kid had a lot of activity happening there.

Grey sighed. "Shut it, Teeg. Where are we on that birth certificate?"

Using one foot, Teeg pushed off and sent his chair backward just enough for him to reach the printer perched on top of a folding table. A practiced move, for sure.

Matt leaned sideways and bumped Taylor. "Wonder how long he's been practicing that move?"

She offered up a winning smile. "I was just thinking that."

"Long time," Mitch said. "He's wrecked three printers. Keeps running into the table and knocking it over. Bye-bye printers."

"Ouch," Matt said.

The printer spit out a sheet of paper and Teeg snatched it up. "You're gonna love this, boss."

"What is it?"

"They're dead."

That statement had everyone spinning to face the computer nerd. "Who?" Matt asked.

"The parents. The ones listed on the birth certificate."

Dead? Now that he hadn't anticipated. "Both of them? What happened? They die in an accident and that's why the baby was up for adoption?"

That sounded harsh, but hell, if both parents had no other family, it could happen.

"Nope," Teeg said. "They've been dead since 1950."

Moving fast, Grey crossed the room and ripped the report from Teeg's hands. "Seriously?"

Taylor hopped up and joined Grey at the printer where he handed the document over. "Are we sure this is the same couple?"

Teeg's computer dinged and he rolled back to it. "Unless there are two other married people with the same exact names who are dead. And, nothing else came up when I ran the search."

"That's a little screwy," Taylor said.

His mind ticking through possibilities, Matt kept his gaze on Taylor as he sorted his thoughts. Mistaken identity, fake names. *Identity theft.* Well, shit.

"Hang on," Matt flicked his hand back and forth. "This could be identity theft. I went to the academy with a guy who later joined the CIA. If he needed an alias, he'd walk through cemeteries to find men about his age. Then he'd lift their identities. This couple? They may not even have any kids. Who knows?"

Taylor screwed up her face. "Rosalind stole the identity of these people to use on a fake birth certificate? That's ballsy."

"It's a theory."

Caroline nodded. "We've seen this before."

"Then where did the baby come from?" Taylor asked.

"Move over, kids," Mitch said, rising from his chair and smacking his hands together. "Make room for Mr. and Mrs. Joshua Hamilton, a couple of rich assholes looking for a spanking new white baby from a good bloodline. Even if it means doing a black market adoption."

Taylor snap, snap, snapped her fingers. "That could be it." She pointed at Matt. "She did say the baby came from good stock."

"Yep. She could also be lying about that. If it's on the black market, the adopting couple wouldn't file a request with the state to unseal records so they can prove the bloodline. They'd have to take old Ros's word for it. And, for insurance, she gives them this bogus birth certificate with the biological parents' names and makes up a story about their good bloodlines."

"Then," Taylor added, "if the adopting couple searches for the biological parents all they'll find is two people with the same names that are dead. No real way to prove anything. They can't go to the authorities. What would they say? Gee, Mr. FBI agent, we did a black market baby adoption and just discovered the original birth certificate is fake. They're not going to turn Rosalind in. Doing so means they go to prison right along with her."

Grey held up his hands. "Everyone take a breath. Let's get all these theories into a report. Then we send Mitch and Caroline in."

"And maybe," Taylor said, "Rosalind will bite and we can figure out where the hell she's getting her babies and if Baby Jarvis was one of them."

17

*T*aylor's stomach rumbled. Dinnertime had long since passed and she was starving. She folded down the shiny silver wrapper of a burger and handed it to Matt. "How are we playing this?" she asked. "Good cop-bad cop?"

"Did you really just ask that?" He took the burger, giving her a chastising glance.

"Hey, I've always wanted to say that." She unwrapped the second burger from the bag and her eyes nearly rolled up in her head when she sank her teeth into it. "Man, oh man. How do you find all of these delicious places to grab food?"

He snickered, already halfway through his. "Beat cops know all the good places. And no, we're not playing good cop-bad cop."

"Oh, come on." She batted her eyes at him. "I've always wanted to be the bad cop."

"You watch too much Law & Order. First, is a drive-by." He turned a corner. "If the guy is home, I'll handle approaching him. You'll sit in the car."

"Oh, hell no. I'm coming in with you. If he's not home, are you doing another B&E? I don't think that's wise."

"I'm not breaking in, just surveilling his place. I want to know what we're up against. And although it totally turns me on that you're willing to accompany me in my life of crime, you are not going anywhere near him. He could be a killer."

"He could be the guy who jumped me in the parking garage, too," she said around a mouthful of fries. "And broke into my condo. I owe him a swift kick to the nuts."

"You shot him, Taylor." Matt balled up his wrapper and tossed it in the back. His grin was pure evil. "Isn't that enough?"

"Hell no." She matched his evil grin and pointed a couple of fries in his direction. "I've got plans for him."

Matt snatched the fries from her and shoved them in his mouth. "Remind me not to get on your bad side."

The truck wasn't at the curb when they arrived at the townhouse. Matt parked down the block under a large oak tree while Taylor polished off her burger and fries.

Pulling out his phone, Matt reviewed the info Teeg had sent on their suspect. "Dwayne Glaw, age 41. A captain in the US Army. Served overseas on multiple tours from 2008-2012." His voice trailed off as he scrolled and read. "Wait a minute. Now this is interesting."

Taylor leaned over to squint at the screen. "What is it?"

"The last year of his tour in Afghanistan, he was a task force flight surgeon."

"He's a doctor?"

"Board certified in osteopathic medicine. Looks like he worked for Walter Reed before joining the army."

"Why would he leave a lucrative job as a doctor to join the army?"

Matt was silent as he continued reading and, eventually, Taylor nudged him. "Matt? What is it?"

"Teeg says the file from his time at the hospital is incomplete, but it looks like he had some complaints issued against him for medical negligence."

"Malpractice?"

"Maybe that's why he joined the army."

"So he knows his way around the body with a scalpel. Maybe enough to perform a C-section."

"Or kill someone."

"And,"—Taylor held up a finger—"to take care of a bullet wound to his shoulder."

They exchanged a look. Headlights cut across the windshield, nearly blinding Taylor. "That's him," she said, sitting up straight and pointing at the silver truck pulling up in front of Glaw's townhouse.

"There's no direct link from him to Rosalind or anyone at the birthing center." Matt tucked his phone away and dropped a kiss on her lips. "Sit tight. I'll go feel him out."

Up ahead, under the soft, yellow glow of a streetlight, Glaw hopped out of his truck, reached back in to grab a bag of groceries, and then locked up the truck.

Taylor's body hummed with nerves and she put a hand on Matt's arm to stop him. "He's only using his right hand, Matt."

Glaw held his left arm close to his body, a definite hump showing under his jacket.

"By golly, you might just be right, Agent Sinclair."

Matt reached under his seat, grabbed a .45 that was tucked into a holster and slipped it on his belt.

"Be careful," she said as he shut the door on her.

The humming in her system ratcheted up a notch. She didn't like sitting in the car. Hated it, in fact. This was no doubt the guy who'd attacked her. What if he had a gun under that jacket?

Glaw was halfway up the stairs to his place when he stopped, set the bag down, and yanked out his cell phone. Matt was just hitting the sidewalk and slowed as the man checked the screen.

Bag forgotten, Glaw turned and went hauling back down

the stairs, pocketing his phone once more. Matt picked up his pace, hailing the man with a wave. "Dwayne Glaw?"

Glaw glanced Matt's way, startled, then jumped into his truck.

Taylor threw her door open and started running as the tail-lights came to life and the truck took off.

Matt gave chase for a second, managing to bang a hand on the tailgate, but there was no way to catch the truck.

"Shoot the tires!" Taylor yelled, going for her personal backup weapon.

Matt turned, giving her a pointed look as he sprinted back toward her and motioned wildly. "Get back in the car."

What? But this was his gig as much as hers, so she did. As they peeled away from the oak tree and started to follow, she asked, "Why didn't you shoot the tires and stop him?"

Her phone was buzzing. It was Grey.

Matt skidded around the corner. "I'm not gonna shoot up this street, Taylor."

She had to hang onto the door handle,. "He's a killer!"

"Yeah, but I'm not a cop anymore and he didn't threaten me. What reason do I have to open fire?"

Another buzz and Taylor answered. "We're in pursuit of Dwayne. What's up?"

His voice was tight. "Mitch and Caroline are in trouble."

"How do you know?"

"They were wired. Their covers are blown. I need you and Matt to get to them asap."

Frustration screamed through Taylor. "But...but..." But nothing. Mitch and Caroline came first, even if it meant losing Glaw. "Yes, sir. We'll divert and get to Rosalind's right now."

"She told them to meet her at a different location. A new construction building outside of town where she supposedly leased office space last week. I'm texting you the address now. I'll meet you there, but it will take me longer to get there than it will for you. You're only a mile from the site. I'm all the way across town."

Matt was giving her a *what the fuck* look. She put Grey on speakerphone and held the phone between them so he could hear. "You think Mitch and Caroline are in danger?"

The text with the address appeared on her screen and Taylor hit the link for Google Maps. Grey was right. They were only blocks away.

"Would I be calling you if I didn't?" Grey asked.

She showed the pulsing red pinpoint on the screen to Matt and he nodded.

"This is Mitch and Caroline," Taylor said to Grey. "They know how to handle themselves. Is there something you're not telling us?"

Grey's car roared to life in the background. "Rosalind knocked Mitch out and has a gun on Caroline. We're code red at this point, people."

"Holy fuck," Matt said.

The funny thing was that the silver truck was still in front of them as they sped toward the address Grey had provided. Taylor squinted at the rear lights of the truck. "Did Rosalind, by any chance, call in backup?"

"She may have. Why?"

Taylor pointed at the truck and Matt gave her another knowing nod. Dwayne Glaw was going to the same address. "We're almost there already, Grey. Don't worry."

"Did you call the cops?" Matt asked.

"Better," Grey said. "I called the Justice Team. Brennan and Gerard will be there shortly."

Matt grinned like this was the best time he'd had in awhile. "Hot damn."

Taylor sank back and gripped the door tighter as Matt floored it.

· · ·

Matt slowed to a crawl and watched the silver truck pull into a parking lot half a block ahead. Glaw thought he'd lost them. Hell, he almost had when they'd gotten stuck at a light with a funeral procession making its way through the intersection. Being familiar with the area from his homicide days, Matt cut down an alley, hooked a left on the next block, shot down two streets and made another left that brought them within a half block of the silver truck.

He glanced at Taylor. "Are you thinking what I'm thinking?"

"That Ros just summoned Glaw to help her? You know it. Why else would he be coming to this address after Grey has just told us Mitch and Caroline are blown?"

He cruised by the front of the building, a spanking new single-story cement structure with large windows and warm beige paint. There were three cars in the lot. Caroline's Toyota, Ros's Escalade and the silver truck.

Matt considered pulling in the lot, but what a way to announce oneself.

"Let's see if there's a back entrance," Taylor said.

A woman after his own heart. "Exactly what I was thinking."

At the corner, Matt made a right and—bingo—directly behind the building was another entrance with vacant parking spaces and a dumpster that still contained construction debris.

"Brand new building, I guess."

"Grey said something about that on the phone."

He bypassed the empty parking spaces and pulled behind the dumpster, out of sight from the building just in case someone happened to look out.

"Um," Taylor said. "Plan?"

He grabbed his lock-picking tools from the glove compartment. "We're going inside."

"That's the plan? I think we're missing a few key elements. Like, oh yeah, is anyone armed besides Roz, will we be seen walking in? Will we be *shot* doing so? I mean, for the love of God, we can't just go in there blind."

"Watch me. However, we will be careful. When we pulled in, I noticed the blind on the side window wasn't all the way down. You check that one. I'll take those on this side. See if we notice anything."

"I'm on it."

He handed her an earbud and plugged one into his own ear. After syncing them, he watched her walk off, her tremendously fantastic ass swinging gently as she made her way toward the window. Jeez, he had no time for this now. He needed his brain to not be focused on the damned pheromones activating it.

Later though, after they bailed Monroe out of this jackpot —*he so owes me for this*—they'd revisit the whole pheromone thing.

At the edge of the building, he stopped and did what one of his SWAT buddies called the very complex quick peek. Pretty much, that's all it was. A look around the edge of the building fast enough to get out of the way of a bullet.

Side of the building clear.

Excellent.

He strode back to the door, listening for any hollering or voices that might drift from inside. Nothing. Maybe they were all at the front of the building?

Taylor swung around the side, moving at a good clip as her heels stabbed into the dirt. She waggled her thumb over her shoulder.

"I saw Glaw. That window is an office. One desk, two chairs. Filing cabinet in the corner to the right of the door. Glaw is in the hallway, leaning on the doorframe. It looked like he was talking to someone."

"Okay. So chances are, this door leads to the hallway."

"Which means if I open it, he'll see us."

"Shit," Matt said.

"What now?"

He blew air through his lips. With only two entrances and one of them out of the running, they had a decision to make. "Well, sweet cheeks. We have one option."

"Oh, my God. Don't say it."

He shrugged. What did she want from him? It was what it was.

"Matt, we are not breaking in via the front door. There's a major street right there. Do you not think someone will see us?"

"I'm guessing they will, but from the street they won't see we don't have a key. And the way the front door is positioned, I'm gonna go out on a limb and say they can't see it from the hallway."

"Holy mother," Taylor said even as she followed him around the side of the building. "I'm going to jail. I know it. Yesterday a rising star at the FBI and today a common low-life criminal. My mother will die of humiliation."

"She'll forgive you. Now pipe down before someone hears you."

"You don't know my mother."

"Not yet. But I hope to."

He marched up to the all-glass door—not a break to be had today—pulling Taylor alongside him. "Block the view from the street."

After sliding his lock-picking tools from his pocket, he went to work, his hands trembling more than he'd like to admit because—hell on earth—they were sitting ducks out here. Freaking glass door. If anyone walked into the reception area, they'd spot them and what a handy target the two of them made.

He hit a snag in the lock. Shit. Lost the pins. He started over, but sensed the tension coming off Taylor like a grizzly on the prowl.

"What's wrong?" she whispered.

"Nothing. Tricky lock. I lost the pins."

And then, have mercy, she got quiet and let him focus. Damn, he was crazy about this woman. Lunatic or not, she understood his moods, knew when to leave him be and not pepper him with five million questions.

The lock clicked.

Done.

He shoved his tools in his back pocket and the two of them drew their weapons. Perfect sync. That was them.

"What if there's a chime on the door?"

Now she thinks of that? "Then sweetheart, we're fucked. Let's do this."

Holding his breath, he eased the door open. No chime. Finally a break.

Taylor slipped inside, ducking alongside the wall. He followed and the two of them took shelter behind a decorative half wall that separated reception from an open area with a table and chairs. To their left was the hallway that Matt assumed led to where Taylor had seen Glaw.

Voices drifted from the rear of the building and Matt cocked his head.

"Don't do this," a woman said, her voice calm but riding the edge of it.

Shit. That was Caroline.

"Caroline?" Taylor mouthed.

Matt nodded.

"Let me check on my husband." Caroline again.

"Pfft," Ros said. "He's not your husband."

"Actually, he is. We did the whole Vegas wedding thing, complete with Elvis. Please, I won't try anything. Just let me check on him."

Silence. Seconds passed. Whatever was going on back

there, they needed to get moving. Taylor, once again in perfect sync, pointed toward the hallway and Matt started moving.

The two of them duck-walked along the half-wall until it connected with a full-sized one. At the mouth of the hallway, Matt held up his hand. Taylor had seen Glaw in that hallway. If they swung around the corner, they'd be the best goddamn targets a shooter had ever seen.

Distraction.

They needed one. Pronto. Matt held up one finger then hustled to the reception desk, a tall L shaped deal that looked like solid teak. Ros sure didn't skimp on the accessories. The top of the desk held only a phone and three metal stacking trays. Below though was a set of drawers. He slid the top one open and his gaze zoomed to the stapler.

He picked it up, tested its weight. Perfect. He glanced at Taylor, made a throwing motion and she nodded, immediately holding her weapon up, readying herself to charge into the hallway.

Matt mouthed a countdown. "One, two, three."

Winding up, he hurled the stapler against the far wall hard enough to knock a chunk of drywall out of it. That would get some attention.

"What was that?" Ros said. "Check it. I'll watch her."

Staying behind the wall, Taylor pivoted, waiting for Glaw to step into the opening. Matt hustled back to where she stood and she snuck a glance at him. He saw it, that glint in her eye, the adrenalin overload that could send the mind to the worst possible places.

"Relax," he mouthed.

She nodded, raised her weapon again and Glaw, idiot that he was, rushed into the opening, a giant .45 in his hands.

"Freeze!" Taylor said.

Glaw stopped, but still held the gun.

Matt drew down on him. "Drop that weapon! Now!"

But Glaw only smiled, a tiny smirk that told Matt all he needed to know about this asshole.

Matt trained his nine-millimeter at center mass and for effect pressed the button on his laser. The red beam dropped a dot on Glaw's chest. "Not to be trite," he said, "but go ahead, make my day."

With two weapons pointed at him, Glaw made the smart move and lowered his. "Put it on the floor and kick it over here."

Glaw complied, putting his hands up as a bonus.

"What's going on?" Ros hollered from the back of the suite.

Matt jerked his chin at Taylor. "I got him. Go."

Taylor angled around Glaw, giving him a slight push as she went by. *My girl.* He always did love a ballsy woman.

"On the floor," he said, grabbing a couple zip ties from his back pocket.

"Stop!"

Caroline's voice.

Shit.

"Matt!" Taylor's voice came through his earbud. "Get down here. Now!"

---

18

*T*aylor peeked around the doorframe again, hoping to catch Caroline's eye. Mitch was lying on the floor, blood seeping from a wound at his temple, but Caroline had Rosalind's full attention.

By way of Ros's gun pointed at her head.

If Caroline had seen Taylor, she didn't let on. "Shooting me isn't going to make this go away," Caroline said. "Your illegal adoption ring is done. If you cooperate and put down that gun, I can get you a deal with the prosecutor."

Ros chuckled. "Do you really think I'm dumb enough to believe that? You're not a cop, so what are you? FBI?"

"Not anymore," Caroline said. "But I'm still going to kick your ass."

Matt sidled up next to Taylor. She put a finger to her lips and signaled him that Ros had a gun. He nodded and they listened, Taylor once more just barely peeking an eye around the edge of the frame.

Rosalind laughed and sat on the edge of a swanky desk with several folders and her cell phone on it. "Is that so? Looks to me like you're about to end up one more missing person for that stupid bitch, Sinclair, to try to find."

Stupid bitch? *Seriously?* Taylor clamped her jaw and felt Matt's hand on her shoulder, a subtle way of keeping her from taking the woman's head off.

Except, Taylor knew there was no way this would end well. Ros was going to kill Caroline. Might have killed Mitch already.

They couldn't wait for Grey or the others. They had to stop this woman. *Now.*

Without taking her eyes or her gun off Caroline, Ros called over her shoulder. "Dwayne? What's going on out there?"

Shrugging off Matt's hand, Taylor swung around the doorframe, gun aimed at Ros. "He's a little tied up right now, thanks to this stupid bitch and her partner."

As expected, Ros jumped up, swinging her gun in Taylor's direction. Caroline, no stranger to hostage situations, took the opening to drop to the floor and sweep Ros's feet out from under her.

Ros's gun went off as she fell, and Taylor suddenly found herself shoved against the opposite side of the frame by two very strong hands.

Mad Dog. The bullet smacked into the wood where her head had been, and Matt rushed past her, yelling at Ros to drop her weapon.

The woman obviously had problems following orders because she scrambled to her feet, waving the gun in the air. God help them if that thing went off again. Matt chased after her, but she leaped behind the desk. Another shot rang out and Matt ducked as Caroline dove on top of Mitch, covering him with her body.

Take her down.

Taylor launched herself across the space. The tackle was clean and she took the woman to the floor behind her desk, knocking the gun from her hand at the same time.

Ros came up swinging, trying to buck Taylor off and Taylor decided she'd had enough of playing nice. Time to go Mad Dog style. She cocked her arm back and—*pow*—punched Ros in the jaw.

The woman's eyes widened, the shock settling in, just before they rolled back in her head. Beneath Taylor, Ros went limp, but she stayed put, waiting to see if the witch might be playing her.

"Nice work," a male voice said above her.

She looked up to see three men staring down at her. Matt, Gerard, and a guy she assumed was Grey's man, Brice Brennan.

Grey rushed in on their heels. "Anyone hurt?"

"Mitch," Caroline said from the other side of the room, her voice carrying a tight anguish Taylor didn't like. All the men's faces disappeared.

As Grey and the others administered to Mitch, Matt handed Taylor a set of zip ties and helped her sit Rosalind up. The woman blinked her eyes open and grimaced. "You broke my jaw."

"Shit happens," Taylor replied with a shrug. "And if it was broken, you wouldn't be able to talk. But you can, so you're going to tell me about your fake birth certificates and where the Jarvis baby is."

Ros sniffed. "I don't know what you're talking about."

"Really? You're going to play dumb now? I should pop you again because you're being a jerk. You know, that gal over there may not be FBI anymore, but I am, and I'm going to send you to prison for the rest of your life unless you start talking."

"I know who you are," Ros said, staring at her desk and the folder lying there. "You're on suspension, Agent Sinclair, so save the threats. I'm friends with plenty of powerful people who can turn your suspension into a permanent firing."

Taylor recognized the colored folders, their Hearts of Love logos shining under the overhead light. "You might want to reconsider who your friends are. I can tie you to the murder of Felicity Jarvis, and that, my dear Rosalind, is just the tip of the iceberg."

A few slaps of his cheeks from Caroline, and Mitch came to. Grey and Caroline helped him into a chair. He reared up, his gaze landing on Rosalind after a moment. "Did she seriously get the jump on me?"

Caroline patted his shoulder. "Relax, killer. Her minion did. He snuck up behind you. You never had a chance."

"Where is he?" Mitch shrugged off Caroline's hands and pushed out of the chair, nearly toppling over with dizziness from his head wound. "Where the fuck is he?"

"You see that?" Taylor said to Ros. "Start talking or I'll turn him and his wife loose on you, and believe me when I say, Caroline there follows through on her promises. Plus, you hurt her husband. That alone warrants an ass-kicking."

Caroline and Mitch advanced on Rosalind, although Mitch continued to be unsteady on his feet and Grey had to grab him before he ran into the other chair. But the fierceness in their faces made Ros press back in her chair.

Taylor wheeled the chair around so the woman faced her. She leaned down in front of her and pointed at the red folder. "Tell me where the baby is that's on that birth certificate."

Matt disappeared out the door.

Ros's cell phone played a melody for an incoming text. "No."

Frustration burned in Taylor's veins. She wanted to hit something. Some*one*. While she was sure no one in this room would blame her if she clocked Rosalind again, it wasn't how she did things.

Taylor glanced at the phone. The caller ID read "BabyDot" and included a message: *Stork run confirmed for 7 pm.*

Stork? Storks delivered babies. "Who's BabyDot?" she asked Ros. "Is she delivering the baby tonight to the new family?"

Matt came back in, hauling Glaw with him. He shoved Glaw into one of the chairs and the man winced. For the first time, Rosalind looked worried. "It's a legitimate adoption."

"Bullshit." Matt flipped open the folder. "The parents listed on the original birth certificate are fake. If this is the kid being delivered to the new parents, it's not a legal adoption. Where's the drop-off?"

"I'm not telling you anything. If you have evidence to charge me of a crime, then haul me to police headquarters and I'll call my lawyer."

Matt wheeled away from Ros and yanked on the back of Glaw's neck. "Tell us where your friend is delivering that baby or you're going down with your boss."

"Don't say anything, Dwayne!" Ros said.

Taylor flicked her gaze from Ros to Glaw. "Fine. Let's discuss Baby Jarvis. Where is he?"

"I don't know what you're talking about," Glaw said, monotone. "The adoption agency is legit."

Right. And she was Taylor Swift.

Playing with Ros's phone, Taylor tried to circumvent the passcode so she could read all the texts, not just the one that had flashed on the lock screen. Looked like old Ros had set up a touch ID. That would make things easy. And she had a sneaking suspicion BabyDot was none other than Dottie Hernandez.

Taylor studied Glaw, took in the stiffness in his body, the tension. The build was about right. Could he be...

"You broke into my home, didn't you?" she said to Glaw as she yanked Ros's tied hands up and placed one of her thumbs on the phone. "You tried to sabotage my car, and you beat me up. Assaulting a federal officer is a felony. Add to it that you caused bodily injury and were carrying a weapon at the time, and you're looking at twenty years, probably more. Oh, and by the way," Taylor turned to Ros. "Since Mitch and Caroline are both former agents, and Matt is a former cop, you're looking at four counts of the same, Rosalind. That's just the beginning of what I can charge you with."

Matt yanked on Glaw again. "We know you killed Felicity Jarvis. She ID'd your truck on the phone to her husband. It's only a matter of time until we prove it."

While Ros was occupied with Matt, Taylor grabbed her hand and shoved her thumb to her phone's screen. Before the woman's brain engaged and she snatched her hand away, the cell phone recognized the thumbprint and—*hello*—opened to the main screen. Taylor hit the button for text messages.

"I want to cut a deal," Glaw said.

Ros swung her head. "What?"

"Got it," Taylor waved the phone. "I've got the address for the baby delivery."

Grey pointed a finger. "Matt and Taylor, go get that baby. Brice and Caroline, take Mitch to the hospital. Gerard and I will handle these two."

"My head's fine," Mitch groaned. "I hate hospitals."

"March," Caroline said, slapping him on the backside.

Matt headed to the door and waved at Taylor to follow. Taylor wanted to do a fist pump. They finally had these scumbags. She leaned down close to Rosalind again, the woman's expensive perfume making her nose twitch. "This stupid bitch is about to take you down, lady."

Matt tore out of the parking lot and hit the gas. "What's the address?"

"It's in Georgetown, but the delivery isn't for another ninety minutes."

"Then we'll try Dottie's house first. Grab her before she goes."

Taylor reached over, squeezed his arm. "I love the way you think. I can't believe we're doing this. We're figuring it out."

A green light turned to amber and Matt hit the gas. Typically, he'd stop. Why take a chance on an accident? Now? Not stopping. Not with a baby on the line.

Late evening traffic was picking up, cars littering the road and slowing their progress, people heading home or to the bars. Frustrated, he turned left, shot down the side street and took an immediate right, screaming down the road that ran parallel to the main street while tension and anticipation had him pressing the gas harder.

He needed to find this baby. And Baby Jarvis. Beat the damned feds to it. Wouldn't that be his own twisted brand of satisfaction? The feds had rejected him and he—along with one of their own—was about to solve one of their biggest cases.

He glanced at Taylor and the amazing rush was better than any drug. The two of them, working together, saving a baby. Hopefully finding another.

That's what mattered. None of the ego bullshit that had driven him all these years since the Bureau had dropkicked him. And, really, after what Taylor had been through, those bastards suspending her, one of their top agents without even a warning? What the hell kind of loyalty was that?

Not the kind he wanted any part of. He'd stick with the sisters.

They appreciated him.

Ten minutes later, he drove onto Dottie's street, slowing their pace in an effort to blend in. Not likely in a vintage Mustang, but at least no one would be calling the cops complaining about the guy blowing a gasket racing down the block.

Taylor poked her finger against the windshield. "There's her car."

"Got it." He parked in front of the neighbor's house, flipped the ignition off and faced her. "How do you want to play this? Back door? Sneak up on her?"

"No. Let's do it right. Chances are she hasn't heard about Ros yet."

"Okay. So, we knock on the front door, tell her we have questions. You know she's not gonna open the door, right? By now, she's figured out we were undercover at the open house."

"But there's no place for her to go. Except out the back."

He pointed to Dottie's yard. "Which is fenced in. Unless there's a rear gate, she'd either have to hop the fence—which I don't see her doing, or come around the front to get out." He pushed open his door. "I'm gonna sneak around the side, see what's what as far as gates. You knock on the front door. Not to be sexist, but she's more likely to open for a woman. I'll meet you there."

The neighbor's house appeared quiet so he walked along their property line to where the two yards met. A quick scan of the four-foot wooden fence indicated no hardware or latches. No rear gate.

Excellent.

He hustled back to the front, found Taylor standing on the porch, to the side of the doorway. Good girl. If Dottie opened that door and started shooting or threw something, Taylor would be out of range.

Matt stuck close to the house, ducking beneath the front windows. He avoided the steps and climbed over the railing, staying mostly out of sight.

"Did you knock?"

"Yep." Taylor murmured. "No answer."

Matt rapped on the door again, waggled a finger at Taylor. They needed to get this show on the road. "Dottie, this is Taylor Sinclair and Matt Stephens. Open up."

No answer.

Now I'm done.

Matt hopped off the porch and peeped through the front window. The blind was down, but the edge left enough of a gap to spot someone moving inside.

"Someone's in there. I can't tell if it's her or not."

"Did you see anything else?"

"No, but let's pretend I saw a weapon on the floor and give ourselves probable cause, shall we? I mean, who knows what's going on in there. Someone could be dead on the floor. It's our duty to check it out."

Taylor rolled her eyes, but she wasn't arguing so he lined up in front of the door, lifted his foot and kicked it right beside the door handle, sending the thing flying open.

Someone—presumably Dottie—yelped from inside and Taylor hustled in, weapon drawn and covering Matt until he got situated with his own.

"Dottie!" she said. "We're here for the baby. Don't do anything stupid."

The house went silent. No shuffling feet or voices, not even a rumbling furnace and the quiet set Matt's nerves on edge. This type of silence was never good. It was dangerous.

They cleared the living room and crossed the hallway to a set of double doors. One sat ajar and a sudden gurgling noise came from the other side.

Baby.

Shit.

Taylor's jaw dropped. Here they were, guns drawn, Dottie somewhere in this house, possibly behind those doors and armed, with a baby.

Visions of them pushing the door open and finding Dottie using an infant as a human shield flooded Matt's vision.

Goddamnit. He hated when children were involved.

Taylor gave him the crazy eyes and mouthed, "Crap."

Using hand signals, he indicated he'd open the door and she should cover him again. She nodded and they lined up on opposites sides, using the wall and closed door as a shield while Matt set his hand on the cracked open door and pushed.

"Stop." Dottie said.

Matt did a quick peek and a shot rang out. A bullet whizzed by just as he snapped his head back and his heart slammed so hard the pounding drowned out any noise.

"Dottie," Matt said. "This is over. There's no place to go. Ros and Glaw are in custody."

"Liars! She texted me a little while ago."

"Right before she and Glaw were apprehended."

Taylor met his gaze. "Dottie, I read your text. The one that confirmed you'd deliver the baby an hour later."

Silence.

"Dottie," Matt said. "let's get the baby out of here and we'll talk. Maybe see if we can help you. Okay?"

When she didn't respond, he slid along the wall, putting one foot into the doorway.

"No!" Dottie said. "Don't come in here."

Another shot went off, the bullet flying through the doorway and Matt's already banged up nerves sent his blood barreling.

He stepped back, rested his head against the wall and drew a few breaths. "Dottie, all I want right now is to get the baby to safety. That's the most important thing. Can we do that?"

On cue, the baby howled.

Jesus. A baby near a gun. He hated crap like this.

"Dottie," Taylor said, adding just enough desperation in her voice to hopefully make a damned difference. "Please. We're adults. We make our own choices. The baby can't do that. He's innocent in this. All of it. If one of us gets hurt, that's on us. But the baby? We can't let that happen. I know you don't want him to get hurt. Please, let one of us come in and get him."

"Her."

Matt exchanged a look with Taylor.

"Pardon?" Taylor said over the screaming.

"Shh, shh," Dottie said to the kid. Then to them, "The baby. She's a girl."

Matt gave Taylor a double thumbs-up. One for distracting Dottie from taking another fucking shot at them, and two, for driving the point home that a baby shouldn't be anywhere near this fucked up mess.

Matt rolled his hand, urging Taylor to keep talking while Dottie went silent. *Don't lose her, Taylor.*

"I know you love kids and would never hurt one of them, no matter what. How about we do this? Matt and I will stay where we are. You put the baby by the door and then step back. One of us will take her outside. To safety. Is she in a seat or something?"

"She's in a baby carrier."

Excellent.

"Good," Taylor said. "Just put her near the door."

"Don't try anything. I swear I'll shoot you."

Taylor raised her eyebrows and met Matt's gaze. They stood there for a solid minute, waiting for Dottie to make a move. He'd give her another three seconds and all bets were off.

Then there was movement from inside the room. Footsteps and then a shuffle.

"Dottie?"

"She's by the door. Take her. Hold your hands out so I can see them."

Taylor pointed at him. At this point, Taylor was making progress and it made zero sense—none—to break that connection. He'd let her keep talking and get the baby out.

And call 911 for some fucking help.

Matt slid his waist holster to his back, draped his shirt over it and put his hands just beyond the cover of the doorway where Dottie could see them. "I'm coming in."

"Don't try anything, you hear me?"

The woman had just fired at them and he was stepping in front of her, a big-ass target that she'd hit with no problem and she wanted to know if he heard? *Oh, I hear you.* "Yes. Everyone stay calm."

He took a breath and stepped into the opening, the barrel of a .38 pointed right at him and another burst of adrenalin flooded his system. But the baby was right there. A foot in front of him.

Baby.

"I lied," she said. "That baby isn't going anywhere."

She pulled the trigger.

19

ottie, you double-crossing...

Bam-bam! Taylor fired in quick succession.

Matt, always quick on his feet, spun, dodging Dottie's bullet. He almost succeeded, but the *oof* he let out told Taylor he hadn't quite been fast enough.

He dropped to the floor at the same moment Taylor's shot hit her mark. A loud squall went up from the baby as the echoes of the gunshots faded away. The wail continued, but Taylor focused on Dottie's body reeling back. Her gun and body fell in a quick 1-2 succession. A blaze of red bloomed square in her chest.

Taylor's gut had warned not to trust the bitch.

Score one for my gut.

"Matt? You okay?" Taylor kept her gun trained on Dottie as she kicked her weapon away, then she checked on the baby to confirm she was okay. The baby didn't have a mark on her. Taylor dug out her cell to dial 911 and glanced over her shoulder. "Matt?"

He didn't move, but she heard a soft groan.

Oh no.

The baby kept screaming, her little face bright red. Dottie was bleeding profusely from her chest. Matt wasn't moving.

Dammit. Taylor recited the info to the 911 operator, and prayed the ambulance wasn't going to be too late.

For Dottie or Matt.

"Hey, hey...*shh*," she soothed the baby, running her hands over the little girl's arms and legs reassuring herself that she wasn't hurt. Nothing seemed amiss, so she scooted the carrier closer to Matt and knelt beside him.

He was on his side, eyes closed, blood spreading in a pool on the floor near his shoulder. Gently, Taylor shifted him onto his back and saw the torn shirt and sizable hole between his clavicle and shoulder bone.

"I'll live," he said between gritted teeth.

"Of course, you will, Mad Dog." She almost laughed from sheer relief. She'd finally found someone to trust with her heart. No way she could stand to lose him now. "You're way too stubborn to die on me."

His blue eyes were cloudy with pain. "How's the kid?"

"Can't you tell?" Taylor practically had to yell over the baby's screams. "She's fine. Ambulance is on the way."

Matt cocked his chin down to eye his busted up shoulder. "And Dottie?"

Taylor had a hard time working up empathy for the woman. "I probably should administer first aid to her, see if I can slow that bleeding."

Pushing himself up with his good hand, he glanced over at Dottie's limp form. "Center mass. Nice shot."

His skin was the color of ashes. Taylor's heart did a little squeeze. "Looks like you could use some first aid, yourself. You're bleeding pretty good. Lay down and I'll find something to stall it."

"Nah." He waved her off, getting to his feet. "Take the baby. I'll put some pressure on Dottie's wound."

This man. What an amazing human being. "She shot you and you're worried about saving her life?" Taylor shook her head as she holstered her gun and reached for the crying baby. "The sisters are definitely lucky to have you."

"And what about you, Agent Sinclair?"

He was grinning as he pulled a sweatshirt off a dining room chair and wadded it up, but his eyes darted away from hers.

Was it the pain straining his voice, his face? *No.* Taylor's pulse did a skip. It was...fear. Fear of rejection.

Taylor tucked the baby into her arms and bounced it gently. The little girl continued to cry but not at decibels that made Taylor's ears bleed. "Hell, yes," she said over the noise. "I couldn't have handled this without you."

The forced grin faded and Taylor knew that wasn't the right answer. Her gut twinged. God, she sucked at this shit.

Tell him.

Even one-handed, he was skilled, using the balled up sweatshirt to put pressure on Dottie's wound while his own ran.

Dottie's taste in furniture revealed her love of doilies and lace window curtains. Jumping up, Taylor carried the baby over to an old wooden dining table covered with a white tablecloth. Using her own single-handed skills, she whipped the tablecloth off, knocking over two silver candlestick holders. The baby picked up her crescendo again and Taylor bounced her on her hip, shushing her.

Which did absolutely no good. Taylor bent down next to Matt. "Let me wrap this around your shoulder. You're losing too much blood."

The blood was everywhere, running down his useless arm, soaking his shirtsleeve, dripping on the floor. "I'm all right, Taylor."

"Look, I get it, you're a macho man, but macho or not, stop being an idiot."

Wrapping Matt's shoulder with one hand wasn't possible.

Using a foot, she snagged her toes around the carrier and drew it close, depositing the infant into her seat, then carefully maneuvering the sheet under Matt's armpit and around his shoulder. "Clean exit wound. Looks like it went straight through."

"Taylor..." His tone was impatient.

The baby quieted into hiccups, her eyes round and brimmed with tears as she watched Taylor work on Matt while he kept pressure on Dottie's chest.

"Shut it," Taylor said, her hands shaking. *Too much blood.*

The tablecloth was thin enough, making it easy to tie. She snugged it down with a knot on top of his shoulder and Matt winced.

In the distance, she heard sirens. Her phone buzzed in her back pocket. Probably Grey. "I hear the ambulance. Hang in there. It's almost here."

"Good," Matt ground out, a muscle in his jaw jumping. He teetered slightly on his knees. "I think I'll take you up on your offer and—"

Boop, over he went, just like that. Lights out, his face smacking the floor next to the carrier.

The baby's face screwed up and froze for half a second, and then, yep, *here we go again.*

Shrieking howls split the air.

"Matt!" Taylor pulled his head into her lap and tapped his cheeks, then checked his pulse. Slow and thready, but solid. The loss of blood had probably shocked his body.

Tell him.

But he couldn't hear her now, even if she did say the words that terrified her as much as seeing this man unconscious.

The baby was swinging her fists, her cries reverberating in Taylor's ears, and for a moment, Taylor felt like having a good old-fashioned cry as well.

Suck it up. Nobody is dying on my watch today.

Reaching over, she extracted the baby from the carrier and held her close. "It's going to be okay," she told the little girl. "I promise, everything is going to be okay."

The baby didn't buy it, smacking Taylor with her fists as she cried into Taylor's shoulder.

Taylor rocked the baby and patted Matt's face. "Thanks a lot, Mad Dog. Leave me with the screaming kid. I'm going to get you for this."

His lips parted on a sigh and he spoke so softly, Taylor could barely hear him. "You'll make a good mom someday, Sinclair."

"Matt?" She patted his face again, but he didn't open his eyes. "Stay with me, Matt."

His face went slack, his head dropping to the side.

Tell him.

Taylor screwed up her courage as she heard the ambulance pulling up outside. "I love you," she whispered, rocking, patting, and praying. "Whatever you do, Matt, please don't leave me."

Matt opened his eyes to a bright light overhead, an annoying beep-beep-beep and his left shoulder hurting like a mother. What in the holy hell?

"Jesus," he muttered.

Taylor's face appeared, her forehead creasing as she studied him. "Hey there. We're still in the ER. How do you feel?"

"Whupped."

"It's the drugs. You woke up in the ambulance and they gave you something for the pain."

No wonder. "They knock me out. For future reference, I don't do pain meds."

"Okay, tough guy, I'll make a note. The good news is the bullet passed straight through and didn't wreck anything important on its journey. The doc said you probably won't need surgery. They might be able to just stitch you up."

"When can I leave?"

"Relax, fella. We didn't get that far. They caught a trauma so you got bumped."

He glanced down, took in his bare chest and the blood-soaked bandage on his left shoulder and wiggled his fingers. Good sign. "Where's my shirt?"

"They cut it off you in the ambulance. Sorry."

His parents. He needed to call them. With all Dad's contacts at the PD, he'd get wind of this.

"I called your father," she said. "I looked in your phone for the number. I hope that's okay."

Was it? Heck yeah. Even if having a woman—or anyone for that matter—handle things for him was...weird, he didn't mind. Appreciated it even.

He lifted his good hand and she grabbed hold. "Thank you."

"You're welcome."

Then she leaned in and kissed him. His impression was the kiss was meant to be quick, but, as always with her, things went to another level and before he knew it his tongue found its way into her mouth. Another thing he could get used to.

At least until her phone rang.

She intensified the kiss, sending the message that whoever it was could wait, but...he knew her. Like him, she operated a certain way and that meant when in the middle of a case, the job came first.

He squeezed her hand and retreated half an inch. "You should take that."

"I don't need to."

"Yeah, you do. We still have a kid to find."

That got her attention and by the third ring she'd checked the screen. "It's Meredith, my boss."

Given the events of the evening, this call would go one of two ways. Either Taylor was getting canned or she was a hero. Time would tell.

She poked the screen, grabbing the call on the fourth ring. "Hi, Mer....Really? When?" She met Matt's gaze and bit her lip. "I'm not sure I can get there right now."

"Whatever it is," he said, "go."

Shaking him off, she continued to listen, her gaze steady on Matt. "All right," she said. "But, I'm at the hospital with Matt. Let me call you back."

After disconnecting, she propped a hip on the bed. "Well, I'm being reinstated."

"You shouldn't have been suspended in the first place, so I'm glad they got their heads out of their asses. Morons."

"Ros isn't talking, but Glaw is a regular chatterbox. Mer has agents standing by at the crime scene. When the techs are done, they're going to tear the place apart and see what they can find. She wants me over at Ros's apartment to help search it. Since I've been on the case, she thinks I might recognize something. More or less, this is her way of apologizing."

"You should go."

"I'm not leaving you."

In short, this sucked. For a solid ten seconds he considered walking out of here. Shirtless or not, they still had a kid to find and the investigator in him, the guy who wanted to solve every case, who'd been rejected by the feds, wanted to show those bastards up.

Except, Taylor had his back. They'd worked this case together. Put aside the competition between them, the booze, and that driving need to one-up each other and formed a partnership. She'd risked everything for this case. Put it all on the line to find Baby Jarvis and her moment, that victory, needed to be hers.

A senator's missing baby.

Jesus, she'd be a hero.

"I'm all set here," he said. "They'll stitch me up, load me full of antibiotics and send me home. Besides, you said my folks are on the way." He gripped her hand, met her gaze. "You need to go. Find Walt's kid, Taylor. Finish what we started. That's what I need from you. Either that or I'll walk out of here myself and do it."

"Not while I'm standing here, you won't."

"Then do it for me."

She set her free hand on his cheek. "Are you sure? I don't want to leave you."

"Let me get this straight, Special Agent Sinclair. There is a little boy out there somewhere. He probably has no idea his biological mother was murdered and that he was ripped away from a father who never got to meet him. That kid is most likely living with people who have no idea who he is. And somehow you think babysitting me is more important than finding that little boy?"

"Well," she said, leaning in and getting close to his lips, "since you put it like that, I'm dumping you for Baby Jarvis." She kissed him hard then straightened up. "I'll call you later. And, in case you didn't hear me before, I'm pretty sure I love you."

Before he could respond, she grabbed her purse and hustled out the door.

"That's good," he said to air, "because I'm pretty sure I love you too."

20

*R*osalind's file cabinet was a treasure chest, full of hundreds of adoption cases.

Thank God she's Type A.

Unfortunately, Taylor still hadn't found the gold she was looking for.

Hours ago, she'd started searching for the file on Baby Jarvis. Hours ago, she'd had hope.

More than hope. She'd been sure she'd find a red folder from all those years ago with a child's stats inside that matched the ones she'd worked up for the Jarvis boy. A folder that held a fake birth certificate.

So far, she'd found plenty of blond-haired, blue-eyed male babies—they were the most popular it seemed. None of them from the correct time frame though. Regardless, Taylor had put Beck to work on a handful of them, running down the information on the natural parents and double-checking birth certificates. Every single one had come up legit.

The file has to be here. He has to be here!

Taylor sat on the floor of Ros's office with folders scattered around her in a circle, the overhead light too bright for her tired eyes.

Meredith's voice came from the doorway, interrupting her. "Glaw finally admitted to the murder."

Taylor did a fist pump. "I knew it. Matt will be so happy. He's the one who uncovered the truck sticker, and that's what led us to Glaw."

Mer folded her arms over her chest and leaned on the frame. "Glaw claims Rosalind and Dottie hired him to kidnap Felicity Jarvis, and later, after the Lamaze gal delivered the baby, they told him to kill her. He got cold feet; it wasn't what he'd signed up for. He claims the only reason he kidnapped her in the first place was because he needed money for his brother, to help him pay for cancer treatments. Ros threatened him, told him she'd ruin him and he'd never work again, legitimately or otherwise and he could kiss his brother goodbye, so he caved and did the deed."

"So Kristina was in on it too." Taylor shook her head and yawned. "How do people with no heart at all end up running an adoption agency?"

"Why do most people go into crime?" Mer shrugged. "It's lucrative. Any luck tracking down the Jarvis boy?"

Taylor closed the folder in her lap. "Ziltch. Honestly, most of the files I've had Beck look into are all legal adoptions. It doesn't fit. Ros and Dottie only did black market ones on occasion, it seems. Why?"

At that moment, Grey walked in. "Because of the buyers."

"Grey? What are you doing here?"

He rocked back on his heels and shot Meredith a steely look. "It's still my case, as I recall, or do I need to call our mutual friend at the Justice Department?"

Meredith paled. "Don't push your weight around with me, Greystone. It's your case for the moment, but my people are currently doing the dirty work of getting confessions and lining up prosecution."

The corner of Grey's lips twitched in his signature non-smile. "Speaking of confessions, I just had a powwow with Dottie. Sounds like Ros occasionally attracted whales—big spenders—who provided incentive pay to find the perfect baby for them. If she couldn't find what they wanted from her normal pool, she forced the issue. Found a set of parents with the right genes, IQ, or talents and did what she had to in order to get the baby she needed."

Taylor's stomach was empty, but it still churned at the injustice these women had perpetrated. Not only on people like Felicity and Walt, but on their children.

Meredith waved a hand. "Aside from the fact you must have booted Leo down the chain of command in order to talk to one of our suspects, did Dottie give up anything about the Jarvis kid?"

"We were interrupted by her lawyer before I got her full confession. And, by the way, Leo wasn't even at the Bureau when I was there. Apparently, he had a dinner date that was more important. Crack team you got there, Meredith. Taylor aside, of course."

Grey crouched near Taylor and eyed the files. "Would you like some help? I have Teeg on standby if we need him to dig deeper than Agent Pearson can for anything on the birth certificates and records."

Maybe that was it. Maybe Teeg could create some Justice Team magic and find Baby Jarvis.

Matt should be here. He'd been the key to solving this. A part of Taylor wished she could turn the birth certificate search over to Grey so she could go back to the hospital.

At least Grey was willing to sit down on the floor with her and get his hands dirty. "I'll take any help I can get. All the dates and stats are starting to blur."

Mer pushed off the frame. "I can help, too. Why didn't you say something?"

Competition—sometimes a healthy thing.

Taylor waited for each of them to settle on the floor, then divided a pile of folders from the last drawer of the cabinet between them. She reminded them of the physical profile she'd built for Baby Jarvis and the date range they were looking for.

She took the final stack and dug in. "Are Mitch and Caroline all right?" she asked Grey as she thumbed through the folder on top. *Girl*. She passed it into the stack of female babies.

"Right as rain. Mitch is already lining up a lawyer to bring a civil suit against Glaw for giving him a head concussion. Caroline, I believe, had my fiancee, Sydney, line up a spa appointment for her at Syd's favorite place."

"Good call," Taylor said, imagining a long spa weekend in her future. Maybe she could talk Matt into going with her.

"I could ask Syd to get you an appointment too," Grey offered, as if reading her mind. Concern touched his eyes.

Damn, how long had it been since she'd pampered herself? Months? Years? She opened the next folder. "Thanks, but I'm guessing Sydney has better things to do than book spa appointments."

"She likes taking care of people."

Taylor was about to respond when her attention landed on the date of the birth certificate in front of her.

Six weeks after Felicity's kidnapping.

Sex: boy.

She flipped to the next page for the child's description. Blond hair, blue eyes, weight, length...the stats were a match.

An *exact* match to what she'd profiled.

Taylor hated to get her hopes up yet again, but *oops*, too late. As she cruised through the remaining paperwork, she found the intake form for the couple wanting to adopt. A power couple from Tampa—billionaires—looking for a son. Was this the whale who'd offered Ros enough money she'd committed murder for it?

In Ros's handwriting, a note listed several things the couple were adamant about, one of them making Taylor's pulse speed up.

Good stock, the note read.

Jesus, she now absolutely hated that phrase.

Apparently from the copied check attached to the folder for the down payment, they were willing to pay big bucks.

A six-figure down payment? Looked like they had a contender. "I have something here," she told Mer and Grey. "A boy named James that fits the parameters."

"Send the info to Agent Pearson," Mer said.

"And Teeg," Grey added.

Ah yes, competition was a good thing. Using her phone, she took a picture of the birth certificate and sent that, along with the info regarding the birth parents to both techies. She'd see which one could confirm or deny the legitimacy of the adoption first.

"You should think about joining my team permanently," Grey said, continuing to look through his stack of folders. "I can use someone like you."

"Are you kidding me?" Mer blustered. "And give up her career at the Bureau? She'll be filling my shoes soon. You can't even offer paid vacation."

Taylor snickered, not because Meredith was correct, but because it felt nice to have people fighting over her.

Grey started to retort and Taylor held up a hand to stop the brewing argument before it gained speed. "I'll think about the offer, Grey, thank you, but at this moment, all I want to focus on is finding this boy and helping Matt get back on his feet."

"He's a good PI." Grey shuffled his stack. "A good man."

Yes, he is. The Bureau had definitely blown that one when they'd denied his application. "Agreed. You might consider using his skills on future cases, but I advise against poaching him from the sisters. They're very protective of him."

Her phone buzzed, two incoming texts in quick succession. One from Beck, the other from Teeg. She read both of them, a grin breaking over her face. "Gotcha."

Mer closed the open folder on her lap. "Is it him? The baby?"

Taylor held up James's folder. "The parents listed on this birth certificate both died in the 40s and are buried in the cemetery right down the street. Ros used their names and social security numbers. What do you want to bet that Baby James is the child of a US Senator and a former world-renowned ballerina?"

Meredith stood and brushed off her slacks. "We'll need more than conjecture. Let me speak to Ros first, see if I can get her to confirm it. If that doesn't work, I'll get a judge to issue a warrant for a DNA test."

Grey stood too. "I can help with Ros. I have a special technique for getting confessions."

Taylor just bet he did.

Mer started to say no, then stopped. "I have your word that you'll get out of my hair after this?"

He shrugged. "Maybe."

She rolled her eyes and waved at him to come along. Taylor smiled, watching the two enemies walk out together as she hopped up and followed. She couldn't wait to get Ros's confession and tell Matt.

Baby Jarvis was alive.

After a restless night spent in the hospital, Matt sat in a wheelchair under the entrance canopy waiting for his ride. A fucking wheelchair. Hospital regulations, the nurse had said. Which he knew, but actually sitting in the chair, being pushed around when he was capable of walking on his own, made him insane.

The familiar knock of the Buick's twenty-year old engine sounded—he'd know that car anywhere—and he levered out of the chair careful not to put any pressure on the arm wrapped in the sling. Somehow he'd managed to get out of that mess with only a hole in his shoulder. As soon as he got in the car he was ditching the sling. That thing bugged him more than the wound.

After coming to a hard stop at the curb, momentum rocked the Buick forward and Matt shook his head. His father needed serious lessons in finessing the brake. Still, he laughed, taking comfort in the brutal fact that some things never changed. Like his father's impatient driving.

"You ready, kid?" Dad asked.

"I am."

Dad hustled around the car and opened the door, a mile-wide grin on his face. "Let me help you, princess."

"If you weren't my father, there's a phrase I'd use. It starts with an F and ends with the word you."

Dad, being the grisly retired cop he was, snorted. "Watch your head getting in."

"Wait!"

Matt swung back and spotted Taylor, dressed in her wrinkled FBI-wear, charging around the side of the building, her blonde hair flying and damn she was a sight for sore-eyes. Watching her run, every curve of that body he now knew so well coming at him, he wanted his hands on her. Immediately. He hadn't spoken to her since he'd kicked her out of the hospital last night. Sitting with him there wouldn't bring Baby Jarvis home.

Besides, he hadn't been up for his family en masse and the questions about the hot blonde at his bedside. Being stoned on painkillers wasn't exactly his idea of a good meet and greet for Taylor and his crazy relations.

"Matt!"

His father cocked his head. "And, *hello*. Who's this?"

"Taylor Sinclair. She's FBI."

Dad let out a low whistle.

"Shut it, Dad."

She halted in front of him, waving her hands and somehow her body, the whole of it, seemed to still be buzzing. As if she couldn't quite control it. She drew a deep breath and her chest heaved, making her tits bounce and yep, he needed hands on her. "What are you doing here?"

"I've been calling you." Still breathing heavy, she held her phone up, then tucked it into her pocket. "Your phone is off."

"The battery died. I don't have the cord with me. You okay?"

"I'm great."

Without warning, she stepped forward, grabbed his cheeks and planted one on him. Right in front of Dad.

She backed away an inch and met his gaze, her green eyes bright. Taylor in a good mood made a cloudy day sunny.

"Um, have I introduced you to my father?"

A gasp exploded. "Are you kidding?"

"Nope. He's standing right next to you, babe."

Her eyes turned into saucers and Matt cracked up. "Special Agent Sinclair, meet Matt Stephens, Sr."

She dropped her hands, made a show of throwing her shoulders back and held her hand out. "Sir, so nice to meet you. I apologize for my rudeness."

"Didn't seem rude to me. Hell, I was hoping I was next."

"Dad," Matt said. "Shut. It."

Taylor ran her hands through her hair, attempting to straighten the windblown tangles. God, he was crazy about her.

"I'm glad I caught you," she said. "You need to come with me."

"Where?"

"Press conference."

"Honey," Dad said, "my son got shot last night. He's going home."

Taylor, being Taylor, ignored him and her face lit up again. "We found him."

"The baby?"

"Yes! Baby Jarvis."

"No way."

What the hell was wrong with him? Could he not manage more than a one or two word sentence?

"Yes way. After I left here, I hightailed it to Ros's apartment. That filing cabinet we saw when we were there? Total treasure trove. I told them not to touch it until I got there and we went through every damned file. She's got stuff in there from ten years ago."

"Taylor?"

"Yes."

"Baby Jarvis?"

"Right. Sorry. By the time I got to the last drawer of files I was losing hope and then—voila—I found a file dated six weeks after Felicity went missing. Inside was a birth certificate. Beck and Teeg ran the names of the biological parents. Guess what?"

Matt rolled his eyes. Seriously? She wanted to play games right now? "What?"

"Dead."

"Just like the other birth certificate."

"Yep. And there's more. The bottom drawer had a binder in it. Each page had photos of couples and all kinds of interesting information. Income, family history, the works. It's a damned catalog of upper crust parents."

In two minutes, she brought him up to speed on what had happened overnight with Rosalind, Dottie, Glaw, and Kristina.

"We even found the scalpel Glaw used on Felicity at his place. They're all going down and we now know who has James—the name Ros gave Walt's son."

"What's this press conference about?"

"The director is going to update the media on the Jarvis case and what we discovered about Ros's illegal adoptions. I told Mer you had to be there."

"She must have loved that."

Taylor waved that off. "Ask me if I care? You worked this case longer and harder than everyone. You deserve the credit."

"Honey," Dad said, "I like you already."

Matt grinned up at his father, enjoying the lightness of the moment. Enjoying Taylor, the ace Special Agent, something he'd never achieved, allowing him to share her spotlight. All these years, he'd allowed the Bureau's rejection to define him. To make him feel inferior.

And, in the end, make him a better investigator.

Damn, he'd been looking at this thing upside down. The Bureau had actually done him a favor.

"Thank you," Taylor said to Dad. "Your son is an amazing man."

Dad set his hand on top of Matt's head and shook it. "That he is. No thanks to his pain in the ass old man."

"So, what do you say, Mad Dog? Want to come to an FBI press conference and have those jerks choke on the fact that you solved their case for them?"

"*We* solved their case."

"Ha! We solved their case. I like it."

"Me too," he said. "I like it a lot."

21

The dog and pony show made Taylor want to barf, but it was necessary for the FBI to alert the media and public at large that a killer had been brought to justice and another cold case solved. Especially since it involved Senator Jarvis. Hence the large press conference currently underway in the first floor conference room of FBI headquarters, Assistant Director Cunningham laying out the details to the standing-room-only crowd.

The only good thing about the press conference was that Taylor was squished in next to Matt. He'd complained all the way to his place, where she'd helped him clean up, and then to the Hoover building, but she'd given him her best puppy dog eyes and he'd finally agreed to stand behind the podium with her. Little did he know her real reason for wanting him front and center with her. When Meredith had balked again at allowing him to stand with the rest of the cold case team, Taylor had simply pulled Matt along with her anyway.

Beck and the others were packed in like sardines with her. Thank goodness Leo was nowhere in sight.

Licking his wounds, no doubt.

Taylor gave herself a mental high-five.

Matt's body heat warmed her left arm and back. He smelled amazing and her fingers itched to touch him. Thanks to a phone call she'd snuck in earlier, his bosses were part of the crowd gathered in the room, so she forced herself to keep her hands to herself.

At the podium, Cunningham droned on, a dozen different local and national news reporters making notes as he informed them about the outstanding work the Bureau had done in uncovering Felicity Jarvis's killer and shutting down Ros's illegal adoption ring.

Taylor couldn't keep from coughing loudly, since it was actually Grey's team, along with her, Matt, and the sisters who'd managed to put the pieces together and shut it down. She could just imagine Mitch watching this on TV and cursing out Cunningham while he nursed the bump on the back of his head.

"You look beautiful," Matt whispered in her ear, his breath sending goosebumps down her neck.

He'd changed into a sharp blue suit that brought out his eyes even more than usual. He'd gone sans tie and left the top button of his steel gray dress shirt undone. He'd refused to wear the sling and she'd given up arguing with him since she'd hate the darned thing too.

Taylor couldn't help it. Her hand went right to Matt's and gave it a squeeze.

Thank God he was here with her. That he was alive.

I'm lucky.

For once, it didn't seem like a sacrilege to think that. For once, she didn't need a scotch to numb her. Her life had been a series of unfortunate events, but there had been good stuff too. Her job, the families she gave closure to, the children she saved. While her own family may have drifted apart after Isabel's disappearance, she'd managed to reunite many families with their missing relatives.

Like Walt and his son.

Taylor had already initiated calls trying to quietly work out an arrangement between Walt and his son's adoptive parents, the Mercers, so that all parties could get to know each other. The boy—James—was an innocent party in all of this. Taylor had insisted that there was no way in hell she was letting Walt or anyone in the Bureau turn this reunion into a circus. His identity had been kept confidential for now, and Walt and the Mercers were working out an arrangement so that Walt could meet the boy.

For now, the Mercers appeared to have been victims as well. All they knew was they'd paid a boatload for a private adoption that appeared legal.

Taylor had to admit she was mildly impressed that Walt hadn't insisted on jerking James out of his stable home, but he'd done the right thing and was taking things slow.

"Where is Senator Jarvis?" a female reporter in the front row asked, drawing Taylor's wandering mind back to the present. "You said his son is alive. Where is he? Who is he living with? Will he be returning to the senator's home?"

Cunningham gave the crowd his fake smile, one that was meant to convey patience but really meant he was annoyed. Taylor had seen it more times than she cared to count. "I'd like to introduce the head of our cold case division," Cunningham said, "Special Agent Taylor Sinclair. She'll be able to answer your questions."

Way to put me in the line of fire.

Taylor felt Matt squeeze her fingers before she released his hand and stepped to the podium.

Flashes went off. The reporters slid forward in their seats, piranhas waiting for their next morsel of juicy meat.

Taylor had been here before in the media spotlight, under

their scrutiny. There really was no need for Cunningham's introduction, since every one of the reporters had been present for Taylor's press conferences in the past. It had always given her a sense of accomplishment to stand before them and announce to the world that she had reunited another family, or at least given them much needed closure.

This press conference made the previous ones pale in comparison. It was career-making, just like the case.

At the end of the year, Meredith would be heading to the New York office to take over a division there. Cunningham had already offered Taylor Mer's position.

"Thank you all for being here today," Taylor said. She was so ready for this. A big smile spread across her face. "To answer your question, Senator Jarvis is requesting privacy at this time. When he is ready, he will make a statement. When that will be, I can't say." She paused a second and looked over at Matt, standing so proudly beside her. Her breath caught and she turned back to the microphone. "You know," she said, "one of the reasons I became an FBI agent is because my younger sister, Isabel, was kidnapped when we were kids. She was never found, and even though I was only nine at the time, I've always felt responsible for not stopping the man who took her."

She had to stop a moment and clear her throat. *Breathe.* "I've never shared this story because it has always been a personal demon for me, driving me to find Isabel and all the children who go missing each and every year. As an agent, I'm expected to keep a professional distance with every case. I've found that difficult to do, because in many ways, every missing child is my sister, every cold case is hers. They are all important, just like she is to me. I take them all very personally."

Now the reporters were hanging on her every word. Some were scribbling notes, others were intently holding their phones and recorders in the air to catch her story.

"For me to have an opportunity to solve an old murder, find

a missing child, and stop the perpetrators from ever doing this to an innocent family again, brings me a great sense of accomplishment. And,"—she chuckled, knowing it was a good time to lighten things up a bit—"a little job security, since I have a dozen more cases to work on now involving the other illegal adoptions by the Hearts of Love Agency."

As expected, the reporters chuckled.

"What Dwayne Glaw and Rosalind Gardener did is deplorable, and it will be my personal mission to make sure every family and child affected by her black market operation receives justice. When Felicity Jarvis was kidnapped, the FBI agents who worked the original case did an outstanding job laying the framework for me and my team"—she waved a hand behind her to include Beck and the others—"to solve the cold case after nearly eight years."

The reporter who'd asked about James started to interject another question. Taylor shut her down. "And when I say my *team*, that includes several people outside the Bureau."

Behind her, Meredith hissed loud enough for her to hear, "What are you doing, Taylor?"

Giving credit where credit is due. "Unfortunately, several of the people who helped with this case cannot be here with us today to receive the recognition they deserve." Nor would Grey allow it. "Their identities must be kept secret. But there *is* someone here today who played a pivotal role in solving the case, and I can honestly say, it has been an honor working with such an amazing professional. Matt?"

She swiveled and saw the look of surprise on his face. He may not have made it through the rigors of the Academy, but he belonged here, especially today, being acknowledged for his talents and skills.

Meredith hissed something else, but Taylor ignored her as she waved Matt forward.

For a second, he didn't move, his blue eyes snapping. Then,

begrudgingly, he stepped to the podium as more flashes went off, giving her a look that told her she was in for a spanking.

Taylor gave him a wink. *Bring it on, Mad Dog.* "Matt Stephens, an elite private investigator with Schock Investigations, uncovered the key to turning this whole case around. Like me, his life was once touched by tragedy, and that has made him the investigator he is today. He, too, has an impressive track record at solving cold cases and finding missing children. I sincerely wish he was on my cold case team here at the Bureau."

Matt lifted a brow. A tiny smile tickled one corner of his mouth. "It was an honor to work with Agent Sinclair," he said, staring at her rather than at the reporters. "One I hope can be repeated."

He nodded at the reporters and stepped back into the lineup behind her. Taylor caught Charlie and Meg's eyes in the audience, and saw they were both smiling. Meg gave Taylor a thumbs-up.

Reporters starting shouting questions and she raised her hands to quiet them. "Because the investigation into the other illegal adoptions is ongoing, I cannot discuss further details of this case, and given the senator has requested his privacy—and that of his son's—be respected, please...leave Walt and his wife, Ann, alone to figure out their family situation. If you don't, and you cross any lines, I'll find a way to prosecute you to the fullest extent of the law."

She said the last threat with a smile worthy of Cunningham. After a slight pause to make sure her words sunk in, she dismissed the crowd.

Cunningham and Meredith left first, followed by the reporters. Charlie and Meg came forward to hug Matt.

"Are you taking the promotion, Tay?" Beck asked her quietly.

Not quietly enough evidently, since Matt gave her a ques-

1ittioningtioning look. She smiled at Beck and the rest of her team. "You're not getting rid of me that easily. I want to stay exactly where I am, with you guys, doing what I do best. Besides, like I told the reporters, our workload just doubled. You guys need me."

Beck laughed. "You just don't want to be Cunningham's bitch 24/7."

"That could be part of it," she agreed.

Matt grabbed her with his good hand and pulled her aside as Beck and the others waved and left. She held up a hand to stop the reprimand she knew was coming. "I know what you're going to say, but you deserved to be up here with me and—"

He kissed her, shutting her up.

When he broke it off and they both came up for air, he said, "You're the most amazing woman I've ever known, Taylor Sinclair."

Inside his pocket, his phone rang—he'd turned off the ringer, but Taylor had heard it buzzing manically during the press conference.

"Matt, I meant every word of what I said. You're as good as any agent I've ever worked with. I really do wish you were on my cold case team."

His phone continued to buzz. "That means a lot to me."

"You better answer that," she said, pointing to his pocket. "It's probably the morning show calling to get an interview for tomorrow. Mad Dog Stephens, ace investigator, does it again!"

"Yeah, right." He pulled her closer. "I have better things to do with my time tomorrow morning."

The buzzing stopped, the call going to voicemail. "Oh, yeah? Like what?" she teased.

"Like making you breakfast."

"I like the sound of that."

Holding hands, they left the conference room and found Beck loitering in the hall.

"LuAnna at the front desk asked me to give you a message to clear out your voicemail," he said. "Apparently, a woman called for you but it's full. She asked specifically for you and said it had to do with one of your cold cases, but wouldn't leave a message with LuAnna. I guess they'll be coming out of the walls now, huh?"

"I better clear out my inbox," she said to Matt, dropping a kiss on him.

He released her hand. "Dinner tonight? I can bring it here if you need to work late."

Yes, indeed, I am so, so lucky. "I'll be at your place by seven."

He grinned. "Deal."

"I'll walk you out."

They started toward the front entrance and Matt checked his own voicemail. He pulled up in mid-stride, his face suddenly going pale.

"What is it?" Taylor asked.

He slowly took the phone away from his ear, incredulousness on his face. "You're not going to believe this, Taylor. I think we just found your sister."

"511!" Heart slamming, Taylor jabbed her finger against the Mustang's passenger side window. "That's the house. The message said 511."

Before Matt could park at the curb, Taylor swung the door open and hopped out, starting to run and then stopping.

What if...?

What if Izzy was actually inside that house?

If the caller was fucking with her, phoning in a bogus tip on Izzy's location—God knew they'd had plenty of those—Taylor might break her FBI oath of office and murder someone.

"Taylor, wait."

Matt grabbed hold of her, spinning her back, but nuh-uh. No way. She whipped her arm free. "No, Matt. I'm going."

"Backup is on the way. You don't know what we're walking into."

True. All the message had said was that the woman was Isabelle Sinclair. Then the line had gone dead, as if the caller had been interrupted. The caller ID was a cell phone. Registered to this address. This rundown, two-story house where the weeds choked out any possibility of vibrant flowers or healthy life.

Tears stung Taylor's eyes. Could her sister be living in this dump? After the safety and comfort of their parents' home? A fresh bout of rage flashed through her and she squeezed her fingers into a tight ball. "Oh, Matt. If it's her..."

The front door of the house flew open and a woman with mousy, long, blond hair—*her*—stood on the inside of a storm door, alternately kicking at the glass and banging on it.

Taylor launched into a dead run.

Her feet pounded the sidewalk, feeling like hundred pound weights. *Get to her!* It felt like one of those dreams where your feet were caught in quicksand.

Her heel—damned shoes—caught in the dirt and Matt overtook her, sailing by and taking the rickety porch steps two at a time.

The woman smacked her hands against the Plexiglass and Matt yanked on the door as Taylor finally got free and sprinted up the steps behind him.

Inside, the woman pointed furiously. "Padlocked!" she cried.

And Taylor stood there, stock still, frozen as she stared into the same big green eyes as her own. As their mother. "Izzy!"

"I can't get out!"

Taylor elbowed in front of Matt and kicked at the glass. "The son of a bitch locked her in."

"Move," Matt said, shoving her sideways. He poked at the door, pointing at Izzy. "Back up. I'm gonna kick it in."

Izzy did as she was told, taking cover beside the door and Matt lifted his foot—*boom!* The full-length glass shattered, sending shards of tiny plastic ice picks flying inward and leaving a giant opening for them to step through.

Or for her sister to step out of.

Izzy, too skinny and dressed in torn jeans and a ratty, stained T-shirt, flew through the opening and drew up short as Taylor stared in disbelief. "TayTay?"

Hearing Isabel's voice, the familiar childhood nickname on her tongue, was bittersweet. Taylor's knees went weak for a second, and then she swept Isabel up in a bear hug.

They'd found her.

Finally!

The relief was almost too much.

Taylor had solved another cold case. The biggest of her career.

As two police cars arrived on the scene, sirens and lights going, Isabel returned the hug with force as the two sisters cried out loud. Then Taylor drew Isabel away, allowing Matt and the police officers to invade the house.

On the sidewalk, Taylor held Isabel at arms' length to look her over. "My God, I can't believe it's you. Are you all right, Iz?"

Isabel's response was to hug her again and Taylor laughed through her tears as her sister said, "Never better."

They stayed like that for a long couple of minutes. As the sounds of Isabel's captor being arrested echoed from the house, Taylor pulled her sister farther from the house.

There was so much to say. Too much. Where should she start?

Mostly, she had to keep staring at Isabel, touching her, afraid she might disappear on her again. Isabel didn't seem to mind, keeping her own hands locked on Taylor's arm as well.

Izzy's captor, Gordon Mullins, was escorted from the house as an ambulance arrived and Izzy huddled behind Taylor. Hiding. "That's him. He was drunk and passed out. I was watching TV. He lets me watch soap operas. That's it. But there was a special news report and they cut to you talking at the microphone."

"The press conference."

Izzy shrugged. "I guess."

Could her fully-grown sister not know what a press conference was? The weight of that, the knowledge that Taylor had gone on with her education, with her life, while her sister... what? She gazed up at the rundown house, imagined the atrocities. Imagined her sister stuck in time and not experiencing school, dating, and falling in love. A wave of guilt cinched Taylor's lungs.

"I snuck his cell phone into a bedroom closet and called the FBI. A woman patched me through to your voicemail, but it wouldn't let me leave a message. I looked up Matt. He has his cell number on his office website."

And thank goodness he did.

"Izzy," she said. "I'm so sorry."

"Ma'am," one of the EMTs said to Izzy, "we need to get a look at you."

"Ma'am?" Izzy repeated. "No one has ever called me that."

Taylor turned Izzy over to the EMTs, watching her until Matt came out and motioned her toward him.

Isabel was hardly a model patient, arguing with the female EMT trying to take her blood pressure and ordering the male paramedic to move out of her line of sight—she didn't want to lose Taylor in the crowd.

Matt told Taylor to stay with her while he answered the lead officer's questions. Isabel sat wrapped in a blue blanket inside an ambulance, the whirling red and blue lights of police cruisers blocking the residential street in front of Mullins' house not more than five miles from their childhood home. A haunted look chased through her eyes as Taylor sat close and Isabel told her what had happened.

"I saw you on the news before today," Izzy said softly, after explaining what her life with Mullins had been like. "I thought it was you, but until today, I just... I didn't have the courage to call. My brain is...a mess. I wasn't sure anymore if the memories I had of us as kids were even real."

Taylor reached across the expanse between them and patted Izzy's hand. Her sister had been held captive for a long time, and according to what she told Taylor, Mullins had brainwashed her into believing she was his child. He'd home-schooled her, moved her to six different places over the course of the past nineteen years, and had never let her out of the house. Even as an adult, she'd been a prisoner in the man's delusional life.

Until today.

Isabel had still clung to the memories of her earlier life with her real family. Hearing Taylor's story at the press conference had been the impetus to break free and reach out.

"You're safe now," Taylor said, one arm around her. "We'll take things slow. I'll call Mom and Dad, and we'll get you settled."

"Where will I stay?"

"You can stay with me. For as long as you want."

A police detective approached. "We're good here, Agent Sinclair. You and your team are welcome to go over the scene, if you like. I'll need a formal statement from your sister as soon as possible."

Izzy's gaze came up. "Can we do it now?"

Taylor recognized the determination burning in Isabel's eyes. "If you want to, absolutely." She turned to the officer. "We'll meet you at the station as soon as I have a doctor look her over."

"I don't need a doctor," Isabel said. "I want to give my statement and then I want to go home. With you."

Matt sauntered up, leaning on the open door. "Is there anything from inside that you want, Isabel? Clothes, shoes, personal stuff?"

"No." Izzy shook her head. "I don't ever want to go inside that house again."

Taylor was so going to enjoy prosecuting Gordon Mullins. "You can borrow some of my clothes, and when you're up for it, we'll go shopping, okay?"

Isabel swallowed hard and nodded. Her gaze bounced to the police officer, then to Matt. "He can't get out of jail and come after me, can he?"

The detective shook his head. "He's never going to bother you again, Isabel. You have my word."

"And mine," Matt said.

Isabel gripped Taylor's hand.

"Ditto," Taylor said. "I'm a badass FBI agent, little sister. Your kidnapper is going to spend the rest of his life in prison."

For the briefest of heartbeats, Isabel's lips trembled before she took a deep breath and let out the sigh of the century. "I've missed you."

Tears burned in Taylor's eyes, and she drew Isabel into a hug. One of many she was going to shower her sister with. "God, I've missed you, too, Iz."

"If you're not going to the hospital," Matt said, "how about we pick up some Thai from my favorite food truck up the road? You look like you could use some decent food, Isabel."

That was an understatement. Food, clothes, her real family...Isabel needed it all.

A tiny smile lighted on Izzy's face. She threw off the blanket and walked to the ambulance doorway. "I've never had Thai food. What's it like?"

Matt helped her down. "Be prepared to be amazed."

"And probably poisoned," Taylor added, allowing Matt to help her down as well. They sandwiched her between them, guiding Isabel to Matt's car.

The detective, following, snorted. "Ain't that the truth." He waved and headed toward his cruiser. "I'll see you folks at the station. Take your time."

"Thank you," Taylor called after him.

Time. All she'd ever wanted was to have more time with Isabel.

Now she did.

Matt tucked Isabel into the backseat, then caught Taylor and drew her to him. "I love a happy ending, don't you?"

Happy endings and Mad Dog Stephens—now there was an anomaly. "Thank you for this," she said.

"For what?"

"Taking care of my little sister like you do me."

He grinned, flashing those pretty eyes at her. "You haven't seen anything yet, Agent Sinclair. This is just the start of all the happy endings we're going to forge with our combined skills."

Taylor's pulse skipped. "I love you, Matt."

"I love you, too." He plunked a kiss on her nose and leaned in close to her ear. "And I still wanna be your stalker."

Taylor laughed and Matt opened the door for her. She slid inside and watched as he went around the front to the driver's side. Thank God he was as nutso as she was.

"He seems nice," Isabel said from the backseat. "Not bad looking either. Those eyes..."

Killer. "Yep, you better get used to seeing him around."

Her sister's voice held a note of teasing. "He's your boyfriend? Are you two serious?"

"Serious?" Matt climbed into his seat, adjusting his injured arm and starting the car. "Who's serious?"

Taylor reached over and pinched his leg. "Yes, it's serious," she said to Isabel. "Matt and I are going to be partners for a long, long time."

Keep the adventure going!

Thank you for reading *Missing Justice*. If you'd like more of the Justice Team Series, check out *Defending Justice*.

Former prosecutor turned hotshot defense attorney, Jackie DelRay, is a star in the shark-infested judicial waters of Washington, DC. Behind her take-no-prisoners façade, she hides a painful secret, and a longing for FBI Special Agent Beckett Pearson— the man who captured her heart during a passion-filled weekend in college. The same man who still holds a grudge over a case Jackie refused to prosecute several years ago. When Beck is arrested for the shocking murder of the FBI director's estranged wife, Jackie breaks every rule about being emotionally involved with her client - knowing the risks to her heart and her career - and rushes to defend him.

Former model and football star, Beck has finally found his home with the Bureau. He wants nothing to do with the sexy lawyer who left him without a goodbye twelve years ago and then destroyed his first, and most important, missing persons investigation. Now, with his freedom on the line, Jackie's brilliant legal mind may be his one hope at staying out of prison.

When their investigation is mired by political alliances and reckless greed, Beck and Jackie battle corruption at the highest levels. That battle includes resisting the long-buried passion they shared twelve years ago, but will a killer bent on stopping their investigation give them a fight they are bound to lose?

READY FOR YOUR NEXT JT ADVENTURE?

o undercover with Beck and Jackie in *Defending Justice*

Chapter 1

The bass of *Hot Child in the City* pounded from giant speakers as Beckett Pearson walked onto the stage and straightened his tie. Bright lights, lots of screaming women—ah, yes, he'd missed the days of walking the runway.

Not.

Being a model in college had given him extra cash. A lot of headaches as well. Beautiful, sexy headaches, but damn, tonight's bachelor auction aside, those days were long over and he was glad.

As Nick Gilder sang about a runaway girl, the room of women watched Beck strut his stuff. The MC—Caroline Foster, a former FBI agent helping out tonight like he was—spoke over the noise, giving the potential donors his curriculum vitae.

Born and raised in Georgia, four brothers and four sisters, helped support himself in college by working as a Vogue model.

A fresh round of cheers erupted. A few catcalls echoed through the room over the heavy bass tempo.

Beck stopped and smiled, giving his fans a wave as he gritted his teeth. Yep, when Taylor got back from her vacation with Matt Stephens, Beck was going to kill her for setting him up like this.

"Hey, Beck," she'd said with that big ol' toothy grin of hers. *"Wanna help a good cause?"*

"Sign me up," he'd replied without asking for the deets, because Taylor, head of the FBI Missing Persons Unit, and his friend, always had his back.

Big mistake. Like Grammie always said, the devil was in those pesky details.

Which was why he was doing a pseudo-Magic Mike impression tonight to raise money for the St. Agnes Women's Shelter and Sydney Banfield. Minus removing his clothes.

Not that he didn't want to support the shelter—he did. One hundred percent. The place offered battered women and their kids sanctuary. Sydney made sure they were safe and helped find them the services they needed. She also lined up educational opportunities and job fairs for them.

Beck just wished Taylor hadn't volunteered him for this particular task. A bachelor auction? Really?

Suck it up. If he was going to strut his stuff and raise money for the shelter, than he was damn well going to give it everything he had.

As he hit the end of the runway and cocked a hip, Caroline mentioned the fact that along with being lead investigator of a missing persons team with the FBI, he had a genius IQ of 144.

And then the real clincher—his former defensive lineman status from his days with the University of Alabama. At her pause, Beck smiled for real at the women cheering for him. "Roll Tide!" he yelled.

His new fans went crazy.

"Bidding starts at three-hundred dollars," Caroline said.

Three hundred? That's it?

He couldn't help it. He gave her a look. Caroline, being Caroline, was totally unfazed. "Did I mention that Agent Pearson is also a talented Reiki masseur?"

He nearly had to slap his hands over his ears as exuberant cheers nearly drowned out good ol' Nick. Technically, he didn't do massages, but whatever. This crowd couldn't have cared less, so he struck his favorite Vogue pose, crossing his arms and placing a finger to his jaw as he made eye contact with the blonde in the first row of tables.

"Three-fifty!" she shouted.

Yep, he was definitely going to get the highest bid and the biggest donation tonight.

And he was just getting started.

Dropping his hand, he rolled his broad shoulders and unbuttoned his suit jacket, using both hands to pull the sides away from his chest. Hands on hips, he gave them a little roll and shot the brunette next to the first bidder a sexy grin.

"Five hundred!" she shouted. The blonde gave her a look, not believing her friend would bid against her.

And so it went. By the time Caroline called *going once, going twice...sold!*, Beck had raised three thousand dollars. The only issue now was the fact that the woman who'd bought a date with him was the estranged wife of Byron Lockhart III.

He was about to escort the wife of the freakin' Director of the FBI to dinner. Oh joy.

Sure they were in the midst of a divorce, but still.

Not much made Beck nervous, but meeting up with Annabelle Lockhart backstage a few minutes later had him sweating like a whore in church.

"Special Agent Beckett Pearson." She extended a well-manicured hand. Thin and model-height in her stilettos, she could nearly look him in the eye. Impressive, since he was 6'4". "I believe you owe me dinner."

He guessed her age around forty, although she might have had some work done. "Yes, ma'am. Thank you for your generous donation to the shelter."

Her red lips parted to show perfect white teeth. Either she had amazing genes or enough caps to cost as much as his townhouse. "I'm sure you're worth every penny," she purred. Slim fingers snaked out and raked across his chest as she leaned closer, putting her mouth close to his ear. "I can't wait to experience your magic hands."

Still smiling like the cat that ate the proverbial canary, she straightened, but left her hand on his shirt, dipping it down to his belt. The way she looked him over from head to toe made him feel like raw meat in front of a starving lion.

Cougar is more like it.

Even if he hadn't been an expert in nonverbal social cues, her bold, suggestive gaze told him everything he needed to know—she expected the night of her life with a side of hot, unabashed sex for dessert. The cherry on top for Annabelle was the fact Byron would find out one of his investigators had played slap and tickle with her. The fact she'd kept the Director's last name so far spoke volumes—she still had a thing for the man.

Can anyone say awkward?

Although Beck found her attractive, he wasn't into casual hookups. He was thirty-two and ready for a meaningful, long-lasting relationship. Marriage, kids. The whole shebang. He wanted magic and love and all that shit. He didn't mind being admired and lusted after—hell, he loved it—but he had no intention of being bought, and he'd hang up his cleats before he let anyone use him to get back at their almost-ex.

Make the best of it. Wining and dining Annabelle might be fun and he'd make it his mission to leave things on a good note. No sex, but she was still going to have the time of her life after shelling out three thousand dollars.

"Let me take care of everything," he said, offering his arm. He liked taking care of people, and outside of Taylor and the other team members, he rarely got to flex his instinct to do so. Now that Taylor had Matt, he had one less person to play big brother around.

At least there's Tink. His cat still needed him, at least as much as any feline ever needed an owner. He winked at Annabelle. "I have the perfect evening planned for us."

The cougar licked her lips. Her arm slid through his. "Let's stop at my place first, okay?"

It wasn't a question. She was going in for the kill, no holds barred.

Good thing he loved a challenge. This one was going to rate right up there with the game of '07 against LSU. Nasty one, that, but the Tide had prevailed, thanks to him.

But damn it, he was definitely going to ring Taylor's neck come Monday.

"It's your night, Annabelle," he said, already strategizing how he was going to get out of sleeping with her.

Under a pitch-black sky, Jackie stood on the steps of the U.S. District Court in DC waiting for the cameramen to assemble themselves for the defense's impromptu press conference. She didn't need a podium for this show, just the hungry batch of reporters awaiting her post-verdict statement. And they'd get it, despite the late hour and her thoroughly trashed mind and body.

Every inch of her ached, but the long days – and nights – had been worth it.

A spotlight flashed and she dropped her gaze from the harsh glare to her previously unwrinkled suit. Damnit. The navy Chanel number her mother bought her for her very first case looked like an army had marched over it. And not because it was nearly ten years old. Fifteen hours she'd been in this suit. Now, after six hours of deliberations in a case that had monopolized not only her time, but just about every emotion she possessed, she was...numb. Completely pulverized by waves of self-doubt regarding her performance.

"Ms. DelRay," the reporter from DC's ABC affiliate called. "What are your thoughts on the verdict?"

Her thoughts? Oh, she had plenty of those. The reporters closed in, shoving microphones at her, intensifying the already thick air of an unusually warm fall evening. She pushed her shoulders back, taking it all in. The five-deep crowd, the cameras, the reporters jockeying for the best vantage point.

Her moment. Right here. Right now. Her mother had better be watching.

"Obviously," she said, "we're pleased. We've said from the beginning the evidence in this case was suspect, at best. Clearly, the jury agreed."

Beside her, Josh, the young lawyer she'd snatched from the D.A.'s office six months earlier, stood a little taller. As hard as he'd worked, he deserved this moment as much as she did.

"What about the DNA evidence?" a blonde from CBS shouted. "How big of a factor do you think that was?"

Um, how about the biggest? "Critical. There was no smoking gun here, people. The entire case was strung together based on detectives' hypothesizing. Yes, they had my client's blood in the bathroom, but – hello – the man lived there. For God's sake, he shaved every morning in that bathroom. Of course his blood would be there. The question to ask is why the criminologist felt it wise to package together and ship multiple pieces of evidence to the lab. They obliterated the control sample. When you co-mingle evidence, it's contaminated. Useless."

If Josh wasn't her employee, she'd have kissed him right on the mouth for discovering the shipping info. Hell, she'd have even slipped him the tongue.

From there, it hadn't taken her long to figure out the evidence could be tainted. In a case involving a United States senator and his murdered wife, the whole thing screamed reasonable doubt.

And they'd gotten a not-guilty verdict on the biggest case DC had seen since that four-star general got busted sharing top-secret intel with his mistress.

We did it.

"Ms. DelRay," a CNN reporter called, "what if the government appeals? Will you stay on?"

Bet your sweet ass.

"We'll decide that later. Right now, we're going to get Senator Watkins settled and give him time to grieve for his wife." Jackie held up her hand. "Thanks, all. That's it for now."

Josh stepped in front, making himself a human bulldozer, shredding the crowd as reporters screamed questions Jackie wouldn't answer.

Now she needed her bed and sleep. Peaceful sleep that wouldn't be interrupted by anxiety and the ever-present mind-racing that came with a case of this magnitude.

At thirty-four years old, she'd just defended a United States senator.

And won.

Go, Jackie.

A black stretch limo pulled to the curb, catching Jackie's attention. The rear window slid open and the glow of the streetlight illuminated a man's face. Familiar craggy lines registered and a burst of energy expanded Jackie's chest. *He came.* He waved her over and the window slid closed.

She clutched the sleeve of Josh's cheap suit, reminding herself to give the kid a raise. After this win, she could afford it.

Yep. DelRay and Associates just catapulted itself to the top of the hot-shot lawyers list.

Josh glanced at the limo, then to Jackie. She jerked her head. "Our ride is here."

The limo door flew open, revealing her father in dark dress pants and a gray blazer. He slid across the seat and Jackie piled in to find her mother and brother on the adjacent seat. Mom wore her usual pantsuit, blue this time, with a white shell under the jacket. Her ash blond hair fell to her chin, the ends curling up a bit from the humidity. Even with the stray curls, her mother pulled off 'poised and polished'. She'd built a career on that look.

And she'd come to celebrate with her daughter.

A huge win and now Jackie had her family. How good was life? She let out a squeal.

Before the mob of reporters could flash photos, Josh shoved her over and slammed the door behind him. Jackie launched herself at her father, squeezing him tight as the limo lurched from the curb leaving the shouting reporters behind.

"I can't believe you came."

Her mother held her arms out. "A little bird told me the verdict was in. We wanted to be here."

"How did you get here so fast?"

Her mother gave her a bored look. "Darling, I'm the Mayor of Philadelphia. I have a helicopter."

"Holy crap," Josh blurted. "That's cool!"

Calvin, her PITA of a brother, held up his hand. "Hey, sis. Don't mind me. I'm just along for the ride."

Always a smartass. That's what coming from a family with three lawyers got her. "Hey, Cal." She plopped on the seat between Cal and Mom, then gave him a squeeze and a smack on the cheek. "I can't believe you guys are here."

"What?" Cal asked, "You think we're gonna let you celebrate the biggest case of your career alone?"

"At ten at night? Yes, besides, if my estimate is right, when you left Philly, you didn't know I'd won."

"True," Mom said. "But I had no doubt. My girl destroyed the prosecution."

Being a career prosecutor, her mother would know. Her family. Unbelievable. A bunch of hard-noses, all of them, but this impromptu visit? Crazy devotion. Jackie tucked her hair behind her ears and let out a breath.

"Lord, I feel ninety years old."

Mom's gaze moved to Jackie's mangled suit. "Sorry, honey, but you look it, too."

Yep, same old Mom. "It's been a long day." She elbowed her brother. "And, silly me, I forgot to check my lipstick before I went into court."

Mom would have. Even as a lowly prosecutor on a tight budget, she'd amped up her beauty queen appearance. Now that she had money and the title of mayor, she didn't leave the house without designer duds and perfect makeup. Elegant and strong. That was her mother.

Jackie may have inherited Mom's legal prowess, but when it came to her appearance, she just hoped her blouse matched her suit. One of the main reasons she stuck to solid, easily matched colors. The family joke had long been Jackie's need for adult Garanimals.

"Jon and Will wanted to be here," Dad said. "They couldn't swing it. Will is on call and Jon has court in the morning."

Will, the next oldest from Jackie – yes, she'd dealt with three older brothers – was a heart surgeon. Mom liked to joke that with three out of her four children being lawyers, she'd somehow gone astray with Will.

"Where to?" Dad asked. "Have you two eaten?"

Jackie pondered the question, then looked at Josh. "Did we eat?"

"Yesterday, I think."

"We'll fix that." Mom hit the button to lower the glass screen separating them from the driver. "Take us to Charlie Palmer's. We have celebrating to do."

Jackie, still wedged between her brother and Mom, gripped both their hands and rested her head back. So much for sleep. Who cared? She had her family and the biggest win of her career. What more did she need?

Grab your copy of *Defending Justice.*

WANT MORE OF SEXY THRILLERS?

The Justice Team Series

Stealing Justice

Cheating Justice

Holiday Justice

Exposing Justice

Undercover Justice

Protecting Justice

Missing Justice

Defending Justice

SCHOCK SISTERS MYSTERY SERIES

1st Shock

2nd Strike

3rd Tango

MORE BY ADRIENNE GIORDANO

DEEP COVER SERIES

Crossing Lines

PRIVATE PROTECTORS SERIES

Risking Trust

Man Law

Negotiating Point

A Just Deception

Relentless Pursuit

Opposing Forces

THE LUCIE RIZZO MYSTERY SERIES

Dog Collar Crime

Knocked Off

Limbo (novella)

Boosted

Whacked

Cooked

Incognito

The Lucie Rizzo Mystery Series Box Set 1

The Lucie Rizzo Mystery Series Box Set 2

The Lucie Rizzo Mystery Series Box Set 3

THE ROSE TRUDEAU MYSTERY SERIES

Into The Fire

HARLEQUIN INTRIGUES

The Prosecutor

The Defender

The Marshal

The Detective

The Rebel

JUSTIFIABLE CAUSE SERIES

The Chase

The Evasion

The Capture

CASINO FORTUNA SERIES

Deadly Odds

JUSTICE SERIES w/MISTY EVANS

Stealing Justice

Cheating Justice

Holiday Justice

Exposing Justice

Undercover Justice

Protecting Justice

Missing Justice

Defending Justice

SCHOCK SISTERS MYSTERY SERIES w/MISTY EVANS

1st Shock

2nd Strike

3rd Tango

STEELE RIDGE SERIES w/KELSEY BROWNING
& TRACEY DEVLYN

Steele Ridge: The Beginning

Going Hard (Kelsey Browning)

Living Fast (Adrienne Giordano)

Loving Deep (Tracey Devlyn)

Breaking Free (Adrienne Giordano)

Roaming Wild (Tracey Devlyn)

Stripping Bare (Kelsey Browning)

Enduring Love (Browning, Devlyn, Giordano)

Vowing Love (Adrienne Giordano)

STEELE RIDGE SERIES: The Kingstons w/KELSEY BROWNING
& TRACEY DEVLYN

Craving HEAT (Adrienne Giordano)

Tasting FIRE (Kelsey Browning)

Searing NEED (Tracey Devlyn)

Striking EDGE (Kelsey Browning)

Burning ACHE (Adrienne Giordano)

MORE BY MISTY EVANS

SEALs of Shadow Force Series

Fatal Truth

Fatal Honor

Fatal Courage

Fatal Love

Fatal Vision

Fatal Thrill

Risk

SEALS of Shadow Force Series: Spy Division

Man Hunt

Man Killer

Man Down

The SCVC Taskforce Series

Deadly Pursuit

Deadly Deception

Deadly Force

Deadly Intent

Deadly Affair, A SCVC Taskforce novella

Deadly Attraction

Deadly Secrets

Deadly Holiday, A SCVC Taskforce novella

Deadly Target

Deadly Rescue

Deadly Bounty

Deadly Betrayal

Deadly Threat

The Super Agent Series

Operation Sheba

Operation Paris

Operation Proof of Life

Operation Lost Princess

Operation Ambush

Operation Christmas Contraband

Operation Sleeping With the Enemy

The Justice Team Series (with Adrienne Giordano)

Stealing Justice

Cheating Justice

Holiday Justice

Exposing Justice

Undercover Justice

Protecting Justice

Missing Justice

Defending Justice

SCHOCK SISTERS MYSTERY SERIES w/Adrienne Giordano

1st Shock

2nd Strike

3rd Tango

The Secret Ingredient Culinary Mystery Series

The Secret Ingredient, A Culinary Romantic Mystery with Bonus Recipes

The Secret Life of Cranberry Sauce, A Secret Ingredient Holiday Novella

ACKNOWLEDGMENTS

Misty and Adrienne would like to thank both of their street teams (the Dangerous Darlings and the Rockin' Readers), early reviewers, and all of our fans for the love you guys always show the Justice Team books. We write these books for you!

And a huge thank you to Isabel Seligstein Hofmann for lending her name to Taylor's sister.

Missing Justice

Copyright © 2017 Misty Evans and Adrienne Giordano

ISBN: 978-1-942504-12-2

Excerpt *Defending Justice* © 2018 Misty Evans and Adrienne Giordano

Cover Art by Fanderclai Design

Formatting by Author E.M.S.

Editing by Gina Bernal, Elizabeth Neal, Marcie Gately

ABOUT ADRIENNE

 Adrienne Giordano is a *USA Today* best-selling author of over forty romantic suspense and mystery novels. She is a Jersey girl at heart, but now lives in the Midwest with her ultimate supporter of a husband, sports-obsessed son and Elliot, a snuggle-happy rescue. Having grown up near the ocean, Adrienne enjoys paddleboarding, a nice float in a kayak and lounging on the beach with a good book.

For more information on Adrienne's books, please visit www.AdrienneGiordano.com. Adrienne can also be found on Facebook at http://www.facebook.com/ AdrienneGiordanoAuthor, Twitter at http://twitter.com/ AdriennGiordano and Goodreads at http://www. goodreads.com/AdrienneGiordano.

Don't miss a new release! Sign up for Adrienne's new release newsletter!

ABOUT MISTY

USA TODAY Bestselling Author Misty Evans has published over seventy-five novels and writes romantic suspense, urban fantasy, and paranormal romance. Under her pen name, Nyx Halliwell, she also writes cozy mysteries.

When not reading or writing, she embraces her inner gypsy and loves music, movies, and hanging out with her husband, twin sons, and three spoiled puppies. She's a crafter at heart and has far too many projects to finish.

Don't want to miss a single adventure? Visit www. mistyevansbooks.com to find out ALL the news!

Check out her humorous pen name Nyx Halliwell for magical mysteries https://www.nyxhalliwell.com .